BOOKS BY KRISTA STREET
SUPERNATURAL WORLD NOVELS

Fae of Snow & Ice
Court of Winter
Thorns of Frost
Wings of Snow
Crowns of Ice

Supernatural Curse
Wolf of Fire
Bound of Blood
Cursed of Moon
Forged of Bone

Supernatural Institute
Fated by Starlight
Born by Moonlight
Hunted by Firelight
Kissed by Shadowlight

Supernatural Community
Magic in Light
Power in Darkness
Dragons in Fire
Angel in Embers

Supernatural Standalone Novels
Beast of Shadows

Links to all of Krista's books may be found on her website.
www.kristastreet.com

FATED
BY
STARLIGHT

paranormal shifter romance

SUPERNATURAL INSTITUTE
BOOK ONE

KRISTA STREET

PREFACE

Fated by Starlight is a paranormal shifter romance and is the first book in the four-book *Supernatural Institute* series. The recommended reading age is 18+.

CHAPTER ONE

AVERY

"Three months. Three months. You can do anything for three months," I whispered.

The brakes squeaked on my black Explorer when I rolled up to the portal leading to the SF's headquarters. A narrow road stretched in front of me. Trees towered alongside it like giant sentries, swaying gently in the summer breeze. Forest filled this part of Idaho, but it was the glimmering red line wavering across my hood that truly captured my attention.

Humans couldn't see the SF's magical barrier or scanning devices. Lucky for me, I was one step more magical than humans.

Well . . . barely . . .

I took a deep breath. *Three months. You have to do this for three months or you'll never become a supernatural ambassador.*

I rolled down my window when a glowing scanner materialized on the other side of it and placed my hand on the pad. Magic enveloped my skin, warming my palm.

"Please state your reasons for requesting access to the Supernatural Forces," a robotic voice said. There wasn't a speaker, so it was as though the voice came from an invisible entity.

"Avery Meyers, reporting for duty."

The magic heated further, then released my palm. "Welcome, Avery Meyers. Please proceed."

Another shimmer of magic erupted, and an opaque garage-door-style opening materialized in front of my car, a billowing fog pouring out. I drove forward, and my Explorer disappeared into the mist.

I swallowed a yelp when a free-falling sensation made my stomach flip, but the portal transfer was over before I knew it. Thankfully, when I emerged on the other side, my swallowed squeal meant nobody had noticed my reaction.

Around me the SF garage loomed. The ceiling soared to at least fifty feet, large enough to comfortably house a 737. Parked cars filled the perimeter of the massive enclosure, and in the center several aircraft had technicians climbing over them like ants surrounding an ant hill. One of the technicians interrupted my ogling and flagged me to an open parking spot.

I snapped my jaw shut and carefully parked within the lines.

The technician opened the door for me, a grin stretching across his face. "Avery Meyers, welcome to the Supernatural Forces."

"Thank you. It's good to be here." I grabbed my bag and threaded my fingers through my long, dark hair, working out the tangles from the drive. I smiled for good measure, too, hoping it hid the butterflies flapping in my stomach.

Banging sounds reverberated throughout the garage as technicians worked, and scents of spicy magic and gasoline accompanied the busy workplace.

"You can wait with the other new recruits until your commander arrives." The technician waved toward two men and a woman standing near the corner. One of the guys kept shifting his weight, and the woman's eyes were as wide as saucers.

I hefted my bag over my shoulder and proceeded to the

group. They all watched me, and despite vowing to keep my chin up, a moment of trepidation filled me. After all, the other new recruits were all future SF members—they weren't at the SF temporarily like I was.

"You're a new recruit too?" one of the guys asked when I reached them. He was of medium height, which meant he wasn't a werewolf. His terra-cotta skin hinted at a Latino background. And since his complexion hadn't been paled by a transformation, he also wasn't a vampire. That meant he was either a glamoured fairy, a sorcerer, a half-demon, or a mixed-blood like me.

I nodded. "Yep, I'm Avery Meyers, although I'm only here for three months, then I start my new ambassador job in Geneva."

"*Ooh*, you're going to be an ambassador?" the woman said, cocking her head. She had purple hair and pointy ears—an unglamoured fairy.

Neither gave off overly strong power surges, so my death grip on my bag eased. Maybe I wouldn't be the only magically inferior after all. "Yeah, I graduated from college last week, so after training here is done I'll be off. What about you guys?"

The medium-height guy replied, "I'll be joining the Magical Forensics squad here at the SF. I'll be permanent staff. Name's Bo Sanchez—sorcerer."

Ah, so that's what he is.

The purple-haired fairy twirled one of her locks around a finger. "And I am Eliza River. I shall be permanent staff as well, except I shall be a Processing Bay technician."

"And you?" I asked the taller guy. He hadn't said anything yet since he was too busy casting anxious glances toward the door behind us.

"Chris Larson. I'm the newest recruit to Squad Six." A buzz of energy surrounded Chris. Now that I stood closer to him, I felt its strength.

I pressed my lips into a smile. "So you'll be in the field?"

"Yep. I've been waiting for this day for years."

In other words, Chris was a *real* supernatural. Given the hum of dominant werewolf energy flowing under his skin, I wasn't surprised. He had to be from one of the high-ranking pureblood families, which explained why he'd been accepted into a numbered SF squad.

A numbered squad was something I would *never* be worthy of since the Supernatural Forces only accepted the strongest supernaturals into that fold, but I did feel thankful for the SF and was grateful supernaturals like Chris existed.

If it weren't for supernaturals like him, the community would no doubt erupt into lawlessness and chaos. Thankfully, that hadn't happened in hundreds of years, not since the organization had first been created.

Nowadays, the SF was like the armed forces and law enforcement combined. The SF regularly dealt with all the dangerous crap most of us never knew existed, and they were the reason relative peace existed among our kind.

A second rush of magic blew behind me as another vehicle entered the SF garage. I averted my attention from my squad mates to see who the newest arrival was.

A guy sat behind the wheel of a sleek white Porsche. It practically reeked of money. He pulled forward without hesitation as a technician directed him to a parking spot.

Before I could scrutinize him further, a single loud bang came from the corner on the far side of the garage, and a group of six men and women strode out. They all wore matching combat suits with weapons strapped to their backs, chests, and legs. None of them gave us a passing glance before they hopped into an infinity craft which the technicians had just finished servicing.

The infinity craft roared to life, then it lifted from the ground, levitating before it shimmered as an invisibility cloaking spell washed over it. I blinked, and the craft had disappeared, but the spell didn't stop the heat from the craft's engine or the rumble when it shot skyward.

Then . . . it was gone.

My eyes popped. *Holy shit. That was a squad that just took off for a mission.*

My heart beat faster when it hit me that I was here, really *here* at the Supernatural Forces headquarters.

Once the magical display of the departing craft was over, Bo muttered, "Wicked."

Eliza merely twirled her purple hair more while Chris continued to watch the portal where the squad had flown out, an envious expression on his face.

"You must be the new recruits?" The man who'd driven the Porsche swaggered toward us.

His pale face split into a smile. Sharp fangs glistened behind his lips. Why his fangs weren't retracted was a mystery, but maybe his maker hadn't taught him that keeping his fangs out was a sign of aggression.

When his gaze swept to me, he didn't hide his appraisal. "Hello, gorgeous. And who might you be?"

Unperturbed by the vampire's blatant sexual interest—after all, vamps were kind of known for that—I replied, "I'm Avery, and this is Bo, Eliza, and Chris. And you are?"

"Zaden Lane."

Bo and Eliza shook his hand, but Chris merely cast Zaden a curious stare. "You must be a *new* vamp, huh?"

If Chris was right, that would explain the fang spectacle.

Zaden's lips thinned. "What gave it away?"

Chris crossed his arms. "For one, your fangs are out. And two, there aren't many vamps working for the SF. Most of the old ones find the modern ways and rules too boring for their tastes, but the new ones . . ."

Zaden quirked an eyebrow but didn't respond, although he did retract his fangs into his gums.

"Who's your maker?" Chris asked, arms still crossed.

"That's a rather personal question, don't you think?" Zaden replied.

"Only if you make it personal."

Zaden's smile broadened, and his fangs lengthened again. "Shall we make it personal?"

Chris snorted. "Is that supposed to intimidate me?"

Bo, Eliza, and I shared a side-eye. I rolled my eyes at Eliza and whispered, "Too much testosterone?"

She giggled quietly.

A wave of dominant werewolf magic shot from Chris, directed entirely at Zaden, but I still got a hint of it. My easy smile vanished.

Whoa. Chris's power made my shoulders fold inward and forced me to submit my neck even though I tried to fight it. I gritted my teeth.

Chris was obviously young if he hadn't learned that werewolves shouldn't assert their dominance every time they got into a verbal dispute. Either that or he had a personal vendetta against vamps.

Clicking footsteps sounded behind us, then a woman called, "Is this where the new recruits wait?"

Chris sucked his magic back inside him, and the heavy feeling in the air dispersed. I glowered at him, but his attention was already focused on the latest arrival.

A woman sauntered our way. She was probably around my age and had wavy auburn hair and chiseled cheekbones. Given that she was damn near six feet tall and was built of sculpted muscle, I strongly suspected that she was a female werewolf.

When she said to Chris—"Didn't your mother teach you better manners? My mom would have killed my brother for using his dominance like that."—I knew for certain that she was a wolf.

She smiled and winked at me.

"Which pack are you from?" Chris asked her.

"Alberta. You?" she replied.

"Idaho."

"Ah," Zaden interjected. "A homeboy. Is this your first time leaving the nest? Or maybe I should say the *den?*"

A low growl rumbled from Chris, and he stepped forward.

I immediately lunged between them and placed my hands on each man's chest. Power vibrated through my palms as their magic registered in my internal radar. Despite Zaden being a new vamp, he wasn't a weakling. "Okay, fellas. Let's try and play nice, hmm? We have three months together. Might as well try to get along."

Eliza laughed, the sound as sweet and high as tinkling bells. "Already the ambassador, I see." She grinned at me, and a lock of purple hair fell over her forehead.

I lowered my hands since both Zaden and Chris had stepped back.

"I grew up with two ambassadors," I told Eliza. "I suppose you could say I've been in training since I was born."

The tall female werewolf eyed me curiously. "And who might you be?"

"Avery Meyers. My parents are Bryce and Danielle Meyers, both ambassadors. And you are?"

"Charlotte Morris."

I nodded knowingly. The Morris line was a well-known family in the pack-run town of Granite Springs, Alberta. They were descendants from the Originals, not like my half-werewolf mother or myself.

"What job are you going through basic training for?" Chris asked Charlotte.

She tossed her thick auburn hair over a shoulder and planted a hand on her hip. "Newest recruit for Squad Three. What about you?"

Chris's grin stretched across his face. "I'll be in Squad Six."

Charlotte inclined her head but didn't seem as impressed with Chris as he was with her. "And the rest of you?" she asked us.

One by one, everyone recounted which position they were here for.

When she got to me, I shrugged. "None. As you might have guessed I'm only here for the three months of training required by the Supernatural Ambassador Institute. I won't be SF staff."

Charlotte arched an eyebrow. "So you've already been accepted into the Institute, obviously, if you're here."

"That's right."

I expected to see a hint of derision flash across her face now that she knew my full history. It certainly wouldn't have been the first time I'd experienced it since everyone knew most ambassadors were either mixed-blood or on the weaker side of their magical species. It was what made ambassadors so good at their jobs since we had to rely on our communication skills to get us through situations as our magic was usually modest at best.

But instead of scorn, Charlotte nudged me. "We should bunk together. It wouldn't hurt to have a friend in the Institute, and I'd love to hear about the places you visited growing up."

"Sure, although I don't know if we get to pick where we live, and Eliza—" I glanced toward the fairy who watched us avidly. "She'll probably want to crash where we do since we're all women, right?"

Eliza grinned, revealing rows of pointy teeth. "I would most love to."

A further rush of magic billowed into my back as another car entered the garage. Before I could talk more with Charlotte or Eliza, a seventh recruit joined us.

He was almost as tall as Chris but not as broad. Little blue sparks emitted from his fingertips, as if he was unaware of it, but those blue sparks gave away his species—sorcerer. And considering his swell of magic that flowed over me, I knew he was full-blooded.

His magic didn't abate either, like it usually did after I detected a supernatural's strength. It clung to him, like a hint of cologne when a man stood near.

Jeepers creepers, he was *powerful*.

"Hey guys, you're all new recruits too? I'm Nick Baker." He grinned, his demeanor friendly, but before I could ask what his position would be, the door inched open behind Chris.

A wave of dominant werewolf energy registered in my senses from whoever had cracked it open. I shivered, and goosebumps broke out across my skin.

Shit. If I thought Nick, the newest sorcerer packed some heat, that was nothing compared to what had just come from behind me. And strangely enough, something about the newcomer's power felt . . . familiar . . . but before I could place it, a man stepped over the threshold.

My jaw dropped.

I blinked, but he still stood there. *No way. No freakin' way.*

Wyatt Jamison stood in the doorway.

The Wyatt Jamison.

Holy shit.

He looked exactly as I remembered him—four inches over six feet, brown hair and moss-green eyes, a square jaw, and a body sculpted from chiseled muscle and smooth flesh.

As the third son of the British Columbia Alpha, Wyatt Jamison was a pure-blooded werewolf, and like he had eight years ago, he still oozed power, but unlike when I'd known him as a teenager, his power now *dominated* the room.

He took a step forward, surveying all of us. Chris stood ramrod straight, his eager smile returning. Everyone else shuffled their feet nervously.

I did my best to calm my breathing, but it grew shallow.

When Wyatt's appraisal passed over my face, he didn't hesitate. Not even a hint of recognition crossed his features.

I let out my breath, and my shoulders drooped, but seriously, what did I expect? I wasn't exactly the memorable type.

After sizing us up, Wyatt placed his hands behind his back. "New recruits, I'm Major Wyatt Jamison, your new squad commander."

Despite trying to stop it, a shiver danced down my spine. His voice was so deep, just like I remembered it.

"You may follow me," he said.

With that, Wyatt did a one-eighty and walked back through the doorway into the SF.

Charlotte leaned down and whispered in my ear, "Damn, he's a hunk."

"Oh?" I picked up my bag. "I didn't notice."

She snorted. "Please, girl. You're as white as a ghost. Anyone with eyes can see you noticed."

Before I could reply, she gave me a sly grin and followed Wyatt into the Supernatural Forces headquarters.

CHAPTER TWO

WYATT

So Avery Meyers was back in my life.

I walked steadily down the stairs to the underground tunnel, the new recruits scurrying behind me as they tried to keep up. I didn't look back at them. I couldn't.

I knew meeting Avery again was going to affect me. I just hadn't anticipated it being so powerful.

But seeing her again had caused a cataclysmic response in my chest that I hadn't felt in . . . well . . . not since the last time I'd seen her eight years ago, which meant I needed to get my shit together.

"This tunnel is what we commonly use to access the garage from the main buildings," I called over my shoulder. "There are walking paths on the grounds, if you prefer to be outside. However, this is the most direct route."

Chris Larson followed hot on my heels. I could scent his eagerness as easily as the cleaning detergent used on the recently scrubbed floors. He was so impatient to prove himself that he reeked of hope.

The corner of my mouth kicked up. I remembered that feeling. I'd felt the same when I'd first joined the Supernatural Forces seven years ago.

"We'll go first to the barracks so you can drop off your bags. Then we'll do a tour."

"A tour of the entire grounds, sir?" Chris asked.

"Yes, Private, of the entire grounds."

I inhaled when I turned the corner down another hallway in the tunnel. The new recruits all had their own scents, and their heightened emotions gave off unique smells, but it was the underlying lilac scent that I focused on.

Avery's flowery fragrance hinted at her witch background, but since she was only half witch, and not a very strong witch at that, it was subtle, but it was enough for me to know she was there.

Eight years had passed since I'd detected that scent. Eight years since she'd left Ridgeback, my pack town in British Columbia.

Even though I'd purposefully breezed over her figure when I entered the garage—not wanting to draw attention to our shared history—I'd still caught the inquisitiveness of her eyes and the thick length of her hair.

She had the same dark lashes and clear apricot skin that she'd had as a teenager. But she'd matured more, her breasts were fuller, her hips more curvaceous. *Damn.* If I'd thought she was hot eight years ago, that was nothing compared to her now.

Even though she was only at the SF temporarily—the gateway to the Supernatural Ambassador Institute—I had a feeling it was going to be a long three months.

I fought the urge to pinch the bridge of my nose.

Shit. I was going to be a goner again if I didn't control this.

I took a deep breath and called over my shoulder, "Living barracks are on the west end of the property. You have to leave the facility to reach them. Does anyone need a refresher on admittance protocol to the buildings?"

A string of, "No, sir"s followed.

I gave a curt nod and resumed my fast pace.

"Penny for your thoughts?" Charlotte Morris whispered.

My ears perked up when I caught her quiet question in the back of the group.

"Huh?" Avery replied.

Charlotte laughed. "I knew you were thinking about him. I'm guessing you've heard of him?"

My brow furrowed as I wondered who Charlotte was referring to.

"Charlotte, they can probably hear you," Avery hissed quietly.

She was right. Any vamp or wolf could easily hear conversations yards away. Chris and Zaden were probably listening too.

But Charlotte just laughed again. "Sorry. It's just so obvious that you already have the hots for him."

My nostrils flared, and my ears really perked up now. *Hots for him? Hots for who? Is Avery already crushing over a new recruit?*

That possibility elicited a surprising twist in my gut.

I filtered through the sounds pummeling my senses—the air from the vents, the beating of everyone's hearts, the tap of footsteps—as I turned the corner to the hallway leading to the elevator. With practiced concentration, my senses tuned into Charlotte and Avery's conversation, and the rest fell to the background.

I knew I should respect their privacy, but I had to know who'd caught Avery's eye.

"I don't have the hots for him, Charlotte. No more than you do, but if you're asking if I know that Wyatt's the third son of Walter Jamison, then yes, I do."

Me? They're talking about me?

"It's nothing to be intimidated by," Charlotte replied. "Just because he's an alpha's son doesn't mean he'll lead a pack one day."

"I know that. My reaction was just from nerves. I mean it's our first day. Aren't you a little nervous too?"

"Well, yeah, a little, but your face actually *paled* when you got a look at Major Jamison."

It was true. I'd noticed Avery's change in complexion as well.

I kept walking, pretending to be oblivious to the conversation that had completely captivated me.

"Are you going to confess to whatever caused that reaction?" Charlotte asked. "I know it wasn't just nerves."

Avery sighed. "Fine. It's because I've met him before. We lived in the same town when we were teenagers. It was only for a couple of years, though, while my parents were on assignment there, but during that time Wyatt and I attended school together. I was surprised that he's our commander. I didn't even know he worked for the Supernatural Forces."

My heart stopped. Avery remembered me.

But Charlotte just carried on, oblivious to how that news affected me. "No shit? You lived in Ridgeback, BC, and knew him?"

"I wouldn't say I *knew* him, but we lived in the same town for a few years—" But Avery abruptly stopped talking when my footsteps slowed.

I internally cursed myself for walking so fast. We'd reached the elevators, which meant I had to address my recruits again, which ultimately meant that Charlotte and Avery's conversation stopped.

Turning around, I kept my voice even when I said, "We'll take these up to the main floor. Do you all have your maps from your acceptance packets?"

Everyone nodded and pulled out their materials that they'd been mailed the previous week.

Avery fumbled with her bag, cursing when she dropped it. It made a big *thump* on the floor. Cheeks flushed, she crouched down and pulled out her packet from the front pocket of her duffel.

I bit my cheek to stop my smile. She looked cute when she was nervous.

Clasping my hands behind my back, I reminded myself that my attention should be on training as we waited for the elevator.

"Private Baker?" I said to Nick. "Can you tell me what areas on the map are strictly forbidden to new recruits?"

Nick cleared his throat. "Yes, sir. The prison cell block is off-limits as are the indoor training rooms unless we're instructed to enter them, sir."

I nodded. "Very good. And Private River, what must all SF members do when entering and exiting buildings?"

Eliza twirled a strand of purple hair around her finger before stopping the nervous movement and standing straighter. "Sir. We must scan ourselves in and out of every door so the tracking system knows our whereabouts at all times, sir."

"Correct." The elevator dinged, and the large doors began to open just as my eyes slid to Avery. "And Private Meyers, at what week are new recruits allowed to leave headquarters without alerting security staff first?"

Her lips parted. She licked them briefly before replying, "Um . . . not until week four. The first month we're required to alert SF security to our plans if we leave the premises."

I raised an eyebrow. "Do you care to try that sentence again, Private Meyers?"

Charlotte kicked her from behind, and mortification filled Avery's scent. "Sir, sorry, sir. *Sir*, it's not until week four that we're allowed to leave headquarters without alerting security beforehand."

"That's correct, *Private* Meyers." I bit back a smile, made a precise turn, and stepped onto the elevator.

Avery's heart rate picked up. It was easy to detect amongst

the other recruits. They started to shuffle into the cramped elevator after me.

Chris snickered in Avery's direction, and she looked like she wanted to sink through the floor.

I knew she was still feeling embarrassed that she'd addressed me incorrectly. I should be more irritated that a new recruit hadn't mastered the most basic form of addressing a superior—it was clearly spelled out in the handbook as being an expectation and requirement from day one—but all I felt was satisfaction that Avery remembered me from Ridgeback and addressed me today as she had then.

Damn.

That wasn't good.

Snap out of it, Jamison. She's your new recruit and nothing more.

Avery was the last to get on the elevator. With everyone's bags, it was a tight squeeze. Charlotte's arm pressed against Avery's side while Chris stood at her back.

I stayed in the corner by the elevator controls next to Eliza. As we ascended, I felt Avery's darting glance a few times, but I kept my attention on the doors.

When the elevator opened on the main floor, we all waited for Avery, since she was front and center, but she didn't move. She looked lost in thought.

"Private Meyers?" I said gently.

Her eyes snapped open, then widened, as if surprised to see a hallway in front of her. A blush flooded her cheeks as everyone waited for her to get out of the elevator. "Sorry! So sorry!" she exclaimed. "Sir!"

The doors began to close again since no one had exited, so Avery rushed forward, but she did it so fast that she tripped over the bag at her feet.

She stumbled over it and started nosediving. Her jaw was about to become very well acquainted with the concrete floor.

I lunged forward, my large hand engulfing her upper arm. I

winced at the sudden stop in her movement. It had to hurt. But at least she hadn't face planted.

Her heart was thundering when I helped her stand upright, and her eyes refused to make contact with mine when she mumbled, "Sorry, sir."

I loosened my grip, but I didn't let go. My nostrils flared when her subtle lilac scent flooded me again. Damn. She smelled *so* good.

A second passed, then she raised mortified-looking eyes to mine. I kept my expression impassive, even though my heart rate had just joined her galloping speed.

Her light-brown eyes, flecked with gold and dark brown, stared at me with an intensity that made my breath seize.

I abruptly released her and took a large step back. My heart was beating rapidly now. Too rapidly. My wolf suddenly whined inside me, his attention focused on Avery.

I cleared my throat and said gruffly, "Recruits, please grab your bags. I'll show you to the barracks before we begin the tour."

A rush of air swirled around me as everyone hurried from the elevator. I turned stiffly, hoping none of my recruits noticed the flaming emotions that had just engulfed me. My wolf was now wagging his tail eagerly.

The guys pushed to the front of the group. Chris's ardent eyes followed my every move. I detected lighter footsteps, letting me know the women had joined together at the back of the group.

Good. I needed some distance from Avery, so I could get my head sorted out.

But it didn't stop my hearing. I still caught Eliza's soft tone when she said, "How are you fairing, Avery? Are you gravely injured?"

"No," Avery mumbled. "I'm fine."

From Eliza's innocent questions, I knew the fairy had no

idea what had just passed between Avery and me, but Charlotte's mirth-filled tone was another story.

"Come on, Meyers," Charlotte said. "We'll help you through the door. I'm sure one blundered response to our new commander and a near face plant are enough excitement for you for one morning."

CHAPTER THREE
AVERY

Wyatt led us outside, and I gulped in lungfuls of fresh air, needing it to clear my head.

I'd embarrassed myself enough in the past thirty minutes to last me three months.

It reminded me of how I'd humiliated myself the very first time I'd met Wyatt Jamison. I'd only been thirteen and was brand new to Ridgeback—his hometown in British Columbia. I'd been sitting at the local diner with my parents, eating a gooey caramel sundae with hazelnuts. Wyatt had entered the establishment with three of his pack mates. I'd gone numb when I'd first laid eyes on him. He was so tall and broad, and absolutely *beautiful*.

Wyatt and his friends had ordered extra-large banana splits to-go. I'd watched him so avidly that I'd completely failed to pay attention to my ice cream. The huge spoonful I'd held aloft had plopped onto my lap.

I'd shrieked, and Wyatt's attention had snapped to me. For the briefest moment, amusement lit his eyes. I'd sworn something else fluttered in them, too, but then I'd become consumed with mopping up the caramel sticking to my shorts while my parents frantically threw napkins my way.

Ugh. That'd been my first introduction to the boy I had a painfully wicked crush on all through adolescence.

But I wasn't at the SF to reminisce over past encounters.

I was here to train.

Yeah, so keep that in mind.

The eight of us walked along the sidewalk. Wyatt's broad shoulders filled the width of his green SF uniform top. The material gripped his body like a glove, and his cargo pants clung to his lean waist and muscled thighs, and his ass—

I abruptly averted my attention and focused on the distant training fields and other SF members we passed on the sidewalk.

The damp scent of earth clung to the summer breeze, and the beautiful forest and rolling hills stretched for miles at the base's perimeter. I concentrated on the scenery, and slowly, my pattering heart calmed.

After a few minutes, my composure returned, and I vowed to keep it together. I was here to train and officially start my ambassador position in three months. I *wasn't* here to rekindle an old teenage crush or act like an idiot around Wyatt Jamison.

I nearly groaned at that thought. *Major* Jamison. That was how I needed to start thinking of him. Here he was *Major Jamison*, not Wyatt.

We rounded a curve in the sidewalk and Major Jamison slowed when we reached a three-story brick building.

"Privates Baker, Lane, Larson, and Sanchez," he called over his shoulder. "Your living accommodations will be in this building. Privates Morris, River, and Meyers, you're farther on ahead."

He strode up to the brick building and was about to pull open the door to the men's barracks when something buzzed in his pocket. Wyatt . . . ugh, *Major Jamison*, pulled out his tablet, a frown turning his lips down before he let go of the door.

"If you'll excuse me, new recruits. I have to attend to something quickly. I won't be gone long. Please wait here for my return."

Without another glance at any of us, our commander strode back the way we'd come.

I sighed and let my bag drop at my feet.

"I could not help but overhear you conversing with Charlotte. Is it accurate that you knew Major Jamison when you were a youngling?" Eliza's doe-like eyes batted prettily.

My lips twitched. Given Eliza's formal speech, I guessed she didn't venture out of the fae lands much. "Yeah, sort of. We lived in the same town for a while when we were teenagers."

"Who lived in the same town?" Nick asked. I could still detect his undercurrent of sorcerer energy, unlike Bo's energy which had long since faded.

"Our new commander and Avery," Charlotte answered for me.

"No shit?" Chris pushed away from the brick building he'd been leaning against.

"No shit," Charlotte replied.

"What was he like when he was younger?" Chris asked eagerly.

Zaden rolled his eyes. "Got a crush on the big bad wolf, Private Larson?"

Chris scowled. "Fuck off."

Zaden laughed. "Ooh, I hit a sore spot. Good to know."

"I'd be curious to know too," Nick said, ignoring the growing tension between the vamp and wolf, as did Bo. At least the two sorcerers seemed a bit more even tempered.

"Um, I don't know," I replied evasively. "We had mutual friends so hung out sometimes, but that was a long time ago, and I didn't *really* know him." Which was true. Wyatt and I were never close friends. We'd just hung out on occasion while I'd admired him from afar, him none the wiser of my wickedly painful crush.

But one thing that hadn't changed in the past eight years? My crazy attraction to him, which was apparently hell bent on flaring back to life. *Crap.* That was all I needed.

Chris's hopeful look faded making Zaden laugh harder.

"Got a hero complex for alpha wolves, eh?" Zaden flashed his fangs at Chris.

The werewolf growled at him, then turned away, just as a spark of distant energy filled the air.

I straightened. *What was that?* My internal radar spiked when another magical flare shifted in the air around us.

I whipped my head around, but none of my new squad mates seemed fazed. Charlotte and Eliza were talking quietly. Chris was glaring at Zaden, and Nick and Bo stood casually beside one another.

Yet . . .

Something wasn't right.

"Maybe someday you'll be as strong as our commander, although I doubt it," Zaden added when Chris didn't react to his first jab.

Chris lunged for him.

"Guys!" I said just as a wave of power blanketed the field around us. It tingled on my skin, making my hair stand on end. *What the hell's going on?* It felt as if a storm was about to unleash, yet the sky was blue and the air calm.

"You guys!" I yelled again when Chris tried to tackle Zaden in a headlock, but the vampire twisted at the last moment and broke free.

"What, Meyers?" Chris's concentration finally left the vamp.

I shook my head. "Something's not right. I can feel—"

An explosion rocked the ground, shaking the earth beneath my feet.

I screamed and pitched forward, nearly falling on Eliza, but Charlotte caught me just in time. Her grip tightened on my arm as dark clouds formed above, swirling in a tight circular pattern.

Lightning cracked, flashing in hellacious zigzags across the sky, as the wind whistled through the trees while another great rumble shook the ground.

Holy shit.

"What is happening?" Eliza's eyes grew wide.

"Is it an earthquake?" Bo asked as he placed a hand on the brick building to steady himself.

Nick shook his head, his gaze skyward. "No. This isn't Mother Nature. Magic is causing this."

Chris and Zaden now stood on high alert, their earlier tackling forgotten just as a red mist formed from mid-air only thirty yards away.

Eliza took a step closer to me. "Does everyone else see that peculiar formation?"

"Yep." I gulped.

The mist turned into a swirling fog, covering the ground and slithering toward us as it rose up to create a shifting crimson wall of magic and crackling energy.

"What the fuck," Bo whispered.

I scrambled back, pulling Eliza with me.

Charlotte, Chris, and Nick sprang in front of us, their stances wide while Zaden hissed, his fangs descending.

"Does anyone know what that is?" I asked warily.

"No," Nick replied. "But it doesn't look good."

The blood-red fog crept across the grass, inching malevolently toward us. It was only twenty yards away now.

"Where did everyone else go?" Charlotte squinted, trying to see through the mist.

I tried to look through the red wall of magic, to see the SF members that had been training on the distant field, but I couldn't see anything through the opaque fog.

"I don't know," Chris replied, his skin shimmering as his magic swelled. "Maybe it's advancing on them on the other side."

Bo looked frantically around the grounds. "Should we sound an alarm? Or run for help?"

"I don't think we'll have time," Charlotte replied. "It's coming too fast."

She was right. The fog was advancing rapidly. It would reach us in seconds.

"We should take cover in the building." I pulled on the door handle, but it didn't budge. "Shit, it's locked."

"And we don't have our passcodes yet to get in," Bo said.

"So we fight this if it tries to hurt us?" Nick held up his hands. A blue ball of crackling magic appeared between his palms. "Whatever *this* is."

Charlotte crouched lower, her muscles tensed as the fog swirled only ten yards away. "Agreed, but only if it's intending to do harm."

Hairs sprouted on the backs of Chris's hand as magic danced around him. "How can we know if it's—"

A zap of lightning shot from the cloud.

Nick jumped out of the way just in time. The lightning scorched the earth, leaving a sizzling crater where Nick had been standing only seconds ago.

"I think that answers that question," I replied, my chest heaving.

The sinister fog was only five yards away now, and sparks of magic crackled in it.

Another rumble shook the earth, nearly knocking Eliza and me over as my mind raced.

"But how did it get in here?" I couldn't comprehend how malevolent magic had permeated the SF's protective wards, but it had. I could feel the evil energy slithering from the advancing mist. As for why there weren't other SF members out here helping us fight it . . .

My mouth went dry. The possible reasons behind that made me feel sick.

But I didn't have time to ponder it further. My lips parted just as another flash of lightning shot from the fog and struck the earth only feet from Nick, Chris, and Charlotte.

Eliza screamed, and everyone jumped back as a burst of magic rushed from Nick's hands. His blazing blue ball hurtled from his palms into the scarlet fog just as a figure in the mist began to take shape.

My eyes popped. It looked like a man. *Holy shit.* Someone was coming through the fog.

But Nick's spell just bounced off the red cloud, shattering into sparks as the hooded figure emerged from the magic.

"Who are you?" Charlotte called just as Chris leaped into the air and shifted instantaneously.

Chris's clothes shredded when his wolf erupted from beneath his skin. A huge, snarling beast landed where Chris had been standing only seconds ago, but the hooded figure kept walking our way, unperturbed by the offensive spells Nick continually shot at it.

"Who are you?" Charlotte yelled again. "What do you want?"

But the figure remained silent, his hood hiding his face as the large robe he wore covered his tall body.

I frantically searched the grounds that I could see, but they were silent and still.

"No one's coming to help us, and we need to stay away from whoever that is." I squeezed Eliza's hand and pulled her back closer to the building.

We huddled near the wall, Bo sinking down beside us. Zaden still stood off to the side, hissing and fangs extended, but he didn't join Nick, Chris, and Charlotte who had formed a protective wall in front of me, Bo, and Eliza.

"Fuck this," Charlotte whispered. She abruptly lunged for her duffel bag and wrenched it open before yanking out a bow and arrow. Each arrow glistened, and my eyes widened when I recognized the magical substance. *Kuraia* coated each arrow's tip.

Whoa. Charlotte didn't mess around. One drop of that in any supernatural's bloodstream guaranteed death. She stayed in her human form, though. As a female werewolf, she only carried the werewolf gene and couldn't shift, but her werewolf origins gave her superior strength and speed as was apparent with how quickly she nocked an arrow.

Chris snarled again, his hackles raised as Nick launched another spell at the steadily approaching figure.

Charlotte pulled her bowstring, aimed, and let an arrow fly.

But just when the arrow should have pierced the robed figure, he shifted to the side, the arrow missing his arm by inches.

It sailed into the fog and exploded into splinters.

"Shit," Charlotte muttered.

Another crack of lightning flashed in the sky. Eliza whimpered, and I covered her with my arm and moved more in front of her.

"Try again!" Nick called to Charlotte.

Charlotte readied her bow, her movements so fast they turned into a blur, and let a second arrow fly.

But just when the arrow should have pierced the intruder's heart, the fog abruptly disappeared. Her arrow sailed right through where the figure had stood only a second ago only to lodge in a tree thirty yards away.

I breathed heavily. Confusion filled me as the swirling magic and energy in the air dispersed. The distant training field became visible again. The sky cleared, and the earth stopped rumbling.

Eliza made a small mewling sound as the wind calmed.

Bo let out a relieved sigh, but his breathing was still ragged, and Zaden stood up straighter, his hands fisted, while Nick, Chris, and Charlotte stayed in a protective half circle in front of us.

"Did that really just disappear?" I asked incredulously.

"It appears so." Blue sparks still crackled at Nick's fingertips.

Blood thundered through my ears. I was shaking too badly to stand, but the clenching in my stomach loosened when I saw the training team in the distant field doing their drills, as if the malevolent force we'd just experienced had never entered the SF.

"They're acting like nothing happened." Charlotte lowered her bow.

Regardless, Chris's hackles remained raised. He prowled back and forth in front of us, low rumbles coming from his chest.

"What. The. Fuck." Zaden's skin looked even paler than before.

"Are you okay?" I asked Eliza.

She nodded shakily.

"And you?" I asked Bo.

Bo looked as white as a ghost despite his caramel complexion. He nodded and ran a hand through his black hair. "Yeah, I'm fine. Damn. What the hell was that? And why is nobody else concerned about it? Didn't anyone else see it?"

Zaden hissed but pulled his fangs back into his gums. "If that was someone's idea of a joke, it wasn't funny."

"A joke?" Eliza said uneasily. "Could a troublemaker really accomplish that here?"

I still hovered on the balls of my feet, only then realizing I was shielding both Eliza and Bo with my body.

"Do you think it's over?" Bo asked.

Charlotte spun around, her jaw tight. "It's hard to say. Who knows what just happened, but we *all* saw it. We didn't imagine it." She gritted her teeth. "We need to find Major Jamison and report this. I don't know how the SF *can't* be aware of what just happened, but nobody's—"

The sound of someone clapping cut her off. My attention whipped to the sidewalk that curled around the barracks just as Wyatt and an older man with short graying hair strolled around the corner. Both were *clapping*.

My stomach flipped at the sight of our commander. Gods, he looked so hot and strangely calm.

"Very nice response to your first training test, new recruits." The older man let his hands fall to his side.

And then it hit me—that horrifying event had been a *test*. It hadn't been real.

I gaped when I recognized the older man. Wes McCloy, the man in charge of the *entire* Supernatural Forces, was walking beside our commander.

CHAPTER FOUR
WYATT

N ick let out a shuddering breath, and the small sparks from his fingertips lessened. "That was a test, sir? That wasn't real?"

"That's right," I replied. "What you just experienced was a mock training session our witches and sorcerers created. That figure you saw emerge from the fog was a hologram, and the lightning was a magical trick. We use this training session for all new recruits on their first day."

"But it almost hit me, sir," Nick exclaimed.

"It was designed to miss you, Private, and make you think it would have killed you." I waved to where the fictional sizzling crater had been. It'd disappeared now that the magical display was over. "I know it took you all by surprise, which was our intention. I'm sorry for the genuine fear it caused, but it's something we do to all new recruits so we can gauge your strengths and weaknesses when a crisis arises. It helps us train you better."

Nick ran his hands through his brown hair. Stress lines marred his features.

I forced myself to keep my attention on the tall, powerful

sorcerer, even though I really wanted to look at Avery. She'd done wonderfully on the first test, asking sharp and succinct questions, pulling those at risk closer to the building, and even shielding them with her own body.

Her response was admirable, especially considering she had little to no magic to speak of. My wolf rumbled with approval too.

I frowned. It was the second time he'd shown a reaction to Avery since seeing her in the garage.

Despite my best intentions, my gaze inadvertently drifted to her. She still shielded Bo and Eliza. A flare of pride surged through me, but I was careful to keep my expression neutral.

"You all did well," I continued. "None of you ran, which is always our biggest concern, because we work as a team here."

Wes stepped forward. Since he was also a werewolf, he was of similar height to me, but since he was a hundred years my senior he had graying hair. His age hadn't diminished his strength or mental sharpness, however. Most wolves lived active lives until at least two hundred years of age.

"Privates Baker, Larson, and Morris you showed true bravery." Wes nodded at Nick, Chris, and Charlotte. "And Privates Lane, Sanchez, River, and Meyers—while you didn't go on the offense, you also didn't abandon your squad. You all stayed together, the stronger on the outside protecting the weaker on the inside. Like Major Jamison said, you all did very well."

Zaden flinched. I knew the vamp didn't like being pegged as a *weaker* one, but he would learn. Vampires had a natural tendency to stay alone or in a coven with other vamps. To work closely with other supernaturals, especially here, often proved difficult for them. But the fact that Zaden hadn't run boded well.

Chris chuffed in his wolf form. I had no doubt if he was in his human form he would have given Zaden a satisfied smirk.

The animosity that had quickly erupted between the two could pose troublesome.

I made a mental note to pair them together when group training started next week. One way or another, they would learn to work together, and given my experience with new recruits, I wasn't overly worried. Most likely, by the time their three months of training finished, they would be teammates who trusted one another. Maybe even liked one another.

They just didn't know it yet.

"Do tests such as this occur often, sir?" Eliza asked.

I dipped my chin to address her. "No, they don't. Rest easy."

She gave a relieved smile.

Bo shuffled his feet from behind Avery, his cheeks pink. He hadn't shown much courage during his first test, but that could change. I'd have to monitor him over the coming weeks to see if that improved, although given his future position was in Magical Forensics, bravery in the field wasn't as needed.

I stepped forward since I knew Wes needed to get back to the command center. "Now that your first test is done, the men can follow me. Your new uniforms are in your living quarters. I'll show you inside and then lead the women to their barracks."

Chris, Bo, Zaden, and Nick followed—Chris still a wolf. If he shifted now, he would be naked.

Wes nodded a farewell before heading back to the main building, which left Charlotte, Eliza, and Avery waiting outside for me to return.

I made quick work of it, leading the men to their second floor apartment, pointing out the uniforms in their rooms that they should change into, and then issuing an order to be outside again in fifteen minutes. From there, I silently retreated back downstairs. When I reached the front door, the women's soft voices floated into the barracks' entryway.

I paused. I knew I should join them, but Avery's profile was visible through the door's window. Her dark hair tumbled down her back, and her lips had lifted in a smile. The vision literally seized me in my tracks.

Gods, she's beautiful.

"Shit, that was intense," Charlotte muttered.

Her comment snapped me back to reality just as Eliza replied, "But you did most spectacularly! Do you always travel with your bow and arrows?"

Charlotte laughed. "Not usually, but my skill with the bow is how I got in here." She bit her lip. "It's a good thing my arrow hit that tree. What if it had sailed through the fake mist and hit an SF member?"

"I'm sure if anyone has the antidote for *kuraia* readily on hand, it's the SF," Avery replied.

She was right. If anybody *had* been hit by Charlotte's arrow, we would have raced them to the healing center.

I finally pushed through the door and stepped into the morning sunlight. "The men are getting changed. You may follow me."

Avery startled, her rich golden-brown irises fluttering to mine. She turned toward her bag. The movement made her lilac scent drift my way. That aroma was more enticing and appealing than any witch fragrance I'd ever encountered.

Damn.

Inside me, my wolf again rumbled his pleasure. I curled my hands into fists, trying to stop the physical reaction Avery was having on me. Correction: *us*.

I paused to let the women collect their things. Avery made a move to lift her bag but abruptly dropped it, her gaze skittering nervously my way. She reached for it again, but I beat her to it, instincts roaring in me to help her.

My hand brushed hers before she lurched back. It was enough contact to send a ripple of pleasure shooting through me.

I tensed and straightened, then easily lifted her bag over my shoulder. "Follow me," I said gruffly.

She opened her mouth to reply, but I was already striding down the sidewalk with her bag in tow. *Fuck.* I'd just reacted to her on instinct.

Not good.

Behind me, Charlotte murmured something to Avery, but I didn't catch it since she spoke quietly and the wind carried it in the opposite direction.

Two buildings down, I stopped at the women's barracks. "Women live here."

I proceeded to show them the passcode to enter the building along with the holographic lock that hovered near the keypad. It registered SF members' fingerprints when we rested our hand near it.

"There's an elevator down the hall or stairs to the right." I headed toward the stairs since it was faster and meant I wouldn't be in a confined space with Avery again. Her scent and presence were doing my head in. Better to avoid that situation until I figured out a better way to handle my responses to her.

The women trudged up the stairs behind me, Avery at the rear.

"Your apartment's on the second floor. Keys are inside, one for each of you. The holographic locks are also available should you decide to leave your keys at home."

When I reached their door, I swung it open, revealing the small three-bedroom apartment with a compact living room and a kitchen.

I waited outside while the women proceeded to enter. When Avery passed me, she darted by, not looking in my direction.

My wolf rumbled. He didn't like her skittishness and was upset that I'd made her nervous. And even though I didn't want to admit it, I felt the same.

Grinding my teeth, I continued, "Meals are served three times a day in the cafeteria, however, you're also allowed to cook in your living quarters if you prefer. Essentials are already stocked in the shelves. Now, I'll leave you so you can get changed into your uniforms, which are in the dressers in your rooms. Report to the front of the men's barracks in ten minutes."

I stepped into the living room only enough to hand Avery her bag. She grabbed the strap on the far side, as if keeping as much distance between our fingers as possible. "Thank you, sir."

I nodded but trained my eyes over the top of her head. Already her scent was distracting me.

Once the women were situated, I left silently and prowled back to where the men waited. Chris straightened like an eager puppy when he saw me, but images of Avery kept flashing through my mind.

It didn't help when the women returned in their uniforms. The cargos clung to Avery's soft curves, accentuating her flaring hips and round ass. And the T-shirt. Hot damn. With it tucked in, her full breasts were prominently displayed.

A growl threatened to erupt from my chest when both Zaden and Chris took notice. Arousal wafted up from both of them, making my nostrils flare, but Avery remained oblivious as she stood beside Charlotte and Eliza, her gaze darting about, seeming to fall anywhere but me.

Taking a deep breath, I did my best to squelch my territorial reaction, but my voice was still rough when I said, "New recruits, let's finish the tour. Follow me."

CHAPTER FIVE
AVERY

After a long first day, I went to bed early only to have a shrill alarm wake me up just before six.

I was never what one would call a *morning person*, so naturally I swatted at the annoying sound. Unfortunately, the alarm was a pre-programmed magical device that only blared louder and louder until its target stood and registered actively *awake* brainwaves. It also steadily pulsed a bright light like some drunk disco ball.

Most annoying.

"Fine," I grumbled once standing. "See? You can shut up now. I'm awake."

The alarm ceased, and the magical orb disappeared from the corner of my room along with its irritating strobe light.

I was tempted to see what it would do if I collapsed back onto bed but knew that being late to my first day of physical training wouldn't bode well.

Yawning, I stretched my arms overhead. Dim sunlight penetrated my bedroom's simple yet practical and thick polyester curtains, highlighting my rumpled sheets. I straightened my bed, dressed, then surveyed my room.

Pale cream walls, a single overhead light, and no closet showcased the bare living arrangements. The bedroom was small and only contained a twin bed and a four-drawer dresser filled with the standard pre-stocked SF uniform, already washed and laundered in my size.

I'd packed my street clothes into the two bottom empty drawers. Who knew when I'd have an opportunity to wear those during the next three months.

I couldn't fault the SF for the rather lackluster accommodation, though. We weren't here to sleep, lounge on the couch, or go out partying every night in halter tops. We were here to train.

Still, I hadn't slept in a twin-sized bed since high school and wasn't sure I liked the change. Granted, it would only be for three months, and once I arrived in Geneva at the Supernatural Ambassador Institute, I would buy myself a queen again.

"Good morning!" Eliza called in a chipper voice when I entered the kitchen. The fairy twirled around on the linoleum floor like an effervescent ballerina, her purple hair bright and shiny in the overhead fluorescent light.

I finished tucking my T-shirt into my cargo pants and sniffed appreciatively. "Is that coffee I smell?"

"Oh yes, would you like a cup of this sustenance?" She opened the cupboard to get another mug.

"Definitely." I was about to drop onto the barstool at the small counter overlooking the kitchen when Charlotte breezed into the room.

"No time, ladies," the tall female werewolf said. "We have to report in ten minutes. Come on, let's get moving."

OUR COMMANDER MET our entire squad in the cafeteria for a quick breakfast. As soon as I saw him, my heart thumped like an excited rabbit. I tried to concentrate on dishing food onto my tray, but Wyatt looked as deliciously appealing today as he did yesterday, making my gaze continually snag his way.

It didn't help that the man's body was built like a god—wide shoulders, chiseled abs, strong and heavily muscled legs. If that wasn't enough to make my heart trip, his attractive face only added to my schoolgirl reaction. His piercing emerald eyes, dark hair, and square jaw made my stomach curl in an entirely too familiar pattern.

Gods. It was like high school all over again. *So pathetic!*

Of course, Wyatt's expression remained cool and calm throughout the meal. I could have sworn he didn't remember me. I mean, I didn't expect him to greet me like an old friend, but I thought by now I would have seen *some* flicker of recognition in him.

But so far—nothing.

After a rushed breakfast, during which Zaden constantly baited Chris, Wyatt stood and grabbed his tray. "Let's get a move on."

Outside, I shielded my eyes from the bright morning sun. Scents of freshly cut grass wafted in the air reminding me of a summer I'd spent in Iowa when my parents had been working with a witch coven based in Des Moines. It was the first time I'd ever had to learn how to run a lawn mower since we lived in a human residential neighborhood during my parents' ambassador stint in the Midwest.

Wyatt led us across a freshly cut field to a ropes course I'd noticed on the tour yesterday. The wooden beams, bridges, and ropes towered into the air.

Our commander planted his hands on his hips. The stance enhanced his muscular torso and round shoulders.

Avery, focus! I mentally slapped myself.

"We're starting at this course today. I want to see how physically fit all of you are. Each of you will be timed. Do the best you can, and remember, this isn't a contest. You all have jobs waiting for you at the end of training, and it's understood that not all of you are going into physically demanding positions, so your final tests will be tailored accordingly. However, you're all still required to pass training, which means a certain level of fitness is expected of you."

The ropes structure loomed above and around us. I tilted my head back, my heart beating faster, and for once that rapid heart rate had nothing to do with my commander.

The course started with a thirty-foot-tall net that climbed to a narrow platform attached to a wobbly-looking bridge. From there, a single rope descended at an angle to the ground. At the bottom were pits, trenches, more nets, and wooden hurdles. After that, it was another vertical climb and more dangerous-looking ropes to descend from.

I took a deep breath. I knew this kind of stuff would be required of me during my SF training, but to actually see it and know it was coming . . .

That was another story.

I nibbled my lip. I wasn't in horrible shape, but I wasn't a fitness nut either, and I'd certainly never done an extreme ropes course before. I just hoped I didn't fall.

"Remember, this is merely a course to test your current fitness." Wyatt's deep-set green eyes slid my way. I somehow managed to muster a smile before he addressed the group again. "Who would like to start?"

Chris's hand shot into the air. "Sir, I would be honored, sir."

Zaden rolled his eyes.

Wyatt gave a curt nod. "Very well, Private Larson."

The rest of the group stepped back as Chris grinned. He rolled his shoulders a few times and danced on his toes, doing a good rendition of Muhammad Ali. The early morning summer air swirled around us. It was already getting warm even though it was only seven. A few mourning doves trilled from the trees as Wyatt held up a timer.

"When you're ready."

"Ready, sir."

"Go."

Chris took off and scaled the thirty-foot netting like he was climbing a flight of stairs. At the top, he swung his legs onto the platform before running across the wobbly bridge with his sure footsteps.

On the other side, he looped his hands and ankles around the angled thick rope, shimmying easily down it like a super-charged monkey until he reached the ground, and then—

He turned into a blur.

Now that he was on the flat ground with the nets, trenches, and hurdles, he was in his element. Werewolves had natural physical prowess and it showed. When he looped around the course and appeared again just at the end, Wyatt hit his timer.

"Not bad."

Zaden's nose scrunched up. "Sir, how fast was he?"

"Two minutes, fourteen seconds."

Charlotte crossed her arms. "May I ask what the record is, sir?"

"One minute, fifty-three seconds."

Zaden grumbled just as Chris returned to our sides.

"Sir?" Chris asked eagerly.

Wyatt reiterated his time, telling him he did well. Chris's chest puffed up like a turkey's on Thanksgiving.

"Any volunteers for who goes second?" Wyatt asked.

Naturally, Charlotte volunteered. Similar to Chris, she flew through the course. While she wasn't as fast as the male were-wolf, she was still much faster than a normal human, and she swung and dove as aptly as an Olympic gymnast.

When she finished, Wyatt nodded with satisfaction. "Very good. Four minutes, twenty seconds."

Charlotte grinned, a light sheen of sweat on her forehead, while my stomach twisted even more.

One by one, each of my squad mates went through the course. Zaden was almost as fast as Chris, given his vampire speed, and while Nick didn't have the physical advantage that wolves and vamps had, he did have magic on his side.

Several times, he muttered spells which created magical gusts of wind propelling him along, and twice he used levitation spells to bypass the ropes completely.

When he did that, Chris growled. "Sir, is that cheating?"

But Wyatt merely crossed his arms. "No more than you cheated. Each supernatural is born with their own gifts. It's best to hone them and use them. Now, who's next?"

Unlike my squad mates, I never volunteered. As each of them did the course, I began to dread it more and more, especially when Bo and Eliza did it without any problems. Of the seven of us, I'd considered them about on par with my magical abilities, but after seeing Eliza's catlike prowess that any fairy would be proud of, and Bo's ability to use basic levitation spells as well, I knew that even the two of them were stronger than me.

"Private Meyers?" Wyatt said softly after Bo finished. "It's your turn."

Around me, my squad mates talked and laughed, their adrenaline-infused high making them excitable. But instead of being eager to share in what they'd experienced, I wanted to sink right through the ground.

"Come on, Meyers," Chris said. "You can do it."

I gave him a tight smile and looked up at the thirty-foot-tall net. I rubbed my hands on my thighs and took a deep breath.

Wyatt stepped closer to me until he was only inches away. "Remember," he said quietly. "This isn't a contest. Just do your best."

While I knew that his soft words of encouragement were

meant to put me at ease, they only made my cheeks burn hotter. Nobody else had hesitated when it was their turn.

"You can do this, Avery," he added. "It's just like gym class back in Ridgeback. Remember the ropes in high school? Not much different."

My gaze whipped to his.

His expression didn't change, but his irises burned like smoldering emeralds.

A deep warmth seeped through my limbs, and a tentative smile followed. So he *did* remember me.

I made myself look away and squash my grin, but a thrill tingled down my spine. Maybe I wasn't as forgettable as I'd always thought.

With a swell of confidence, I squared my shoulders, and a rush of determination filled me. I may not have been strong or magically superior, or have the strength of full and half-blooded female werewolves, but I wasn't a complete weakling.

I was going to do this.

A small smile curved Wyatt's lips. "Ready?"

"Yes."

He held up the timer. "On my count, three . . . two . . . one!"

I lunged forward and grabbed the net. It shifted under my palm, trying to escape backward, but I held it firm. I slipped my feet into the slots and began to climb.

"You can do it, Meyers!" Charlotte called from below.

Zaden whooped, and Eliza cheered. Hearing them all rooting for me made my confidence grow. I clung to the net, slotting my feet into each square, as I clawed my way to the top and the ground fell beneath me.

I knew I wasn't the fastest, not by a long shot, but I managed to get to the top.

Breathing hard, I swung my legs onto the platform, my heart beating painfully fast. My muscles burned, and my arms felt weak, but I managed to stand.

Even though I was out of breath and my limbs shook, I determinedly stared at the bridge in front of me. Tentatively, I reached for the ropes on each side, coarse twine grazing my palms. Holding them firm, I took a step out, my eyes widening when the bridge swung violently.

Below me, Wyatt watched my every move. He'd shifted from the net to stand in the pit below me. He hadn't done that with any of the other recruits.

Gritting my teeth, I put all of my weight on the first wooden plank. The bridge swung again, but I held on.

Little by little, I made my way across it, the bridge swinging with my every step. By the time I neared the other side, my breathing was shallow, since each step had felt insecure and precarious.

When I finally stepped onto the solid platform with the single rope descending at an angle down to the ground, I breathed a sigh of relief.

Until I looked at what waited for me.

A long, thick rope was connected to the thirty-foot platform I stood on. It arced to the ground like a curved blade, and with a sharp swallow, I wondered how I'd descend it. I wasn't as strong as the others.

"You can do it!" one of my squad mates yelled.

I dared a look down at my commander. Wyatt's jaw was locked, his entire attention on me.

"Grab the rope with both hands," he said calmly, "then swing your legs up and hook your ankles around it. You'll shimmy down from there."

My heart beat harder as I tried to imagine doing what he said. The others had made this look so easy.

"Take your time, Avery."

Hearing him use my first name again made my stomach flip despite the adrenaline coursing through me. *He remembers me.*

Standing on my tiptoes, I reached for the rope. It was so thick that I could barely get my hands around it.

"That's it, now swing your legs up and loop your ankles together."

I did as he said, or tried to. I swung from my hands, trying to get my legs vertical, but my stomach burned from lactic acid. Still, I wasn't going to give up.

On my third try, I managed to lock my ankles around the rope, then worked it up so my knees held me more securely.

"That's it!" Wyatt yelled.

I breathed harder and started descending. The rough rope cut into my palms, but I ignored the pain and kept shimmying.

When I was fully away from the ledge, a moment of panic seized me.

I was dangling twenty-five feet above the ground, and my arms and legs burned. No safety net waited below me. If I fell, I'd hit the ground and probably break bones. Unless Wyatt caught me. Maybe that was why he was following me through the course.

Blood thundered through my ears as the rope swung, and my hands began to slip.

"Keep moving, Avery!" Wyatt called. "Don't stop!"

His comments jolted me into action. I squeezed my eyes shut and let gravity help me. I began sliding down the rope, going faster and faster. The rope burned my palms, and I swallowed a yelp of pain, but I didn't let go.

When I dangled eight feet from the ground, I couldn't hold on any longer.

I fell from the rope, and my legs buckled beneath me, but I straightened and ran for the next obstacle.

Off to the side, Wyatt watched, a smile stretching across his face.

I slid, climbed, crawled, and fought my way through the rest of the course. Rope burn made my palms sting, and my muscles screamed in protest, but I didn't stop.

By the time I looped back around to the beginning of the course, my squad mates were cheering wildly.

"Go, Meyers! Go, Meyers! Go, Meyers!" they chanted over and over.

My chest heaved when I reached them. Wyatt had rejoined them, his eyes sparkling as a smile curved his lips.

I couldn't help but grin in return.

I knew that I was the slowest.

I knew that in a crisis situation, I would hold the team up.

But dammit, I did it, and it felt really freakin' good that for once in my life, I was able to do what other supernaturals were capable of.

CHAPTER SIX
AVERY

We spent the rest of the day training and working out. After the ropes course, we ran, did sit-ups and push-ups, and hiked a long trail in the woods. My body ached by the time Wyatt called it quits in the early evening.

The only ones who didn't seem fazed by the physical exertion were Chris, Charlotte, and Zaden, which wasn't surprising. Vamps and wolves gave *super*natural its meaning.

"You all did well today," Wyatt said as we stood around him on one of the large training fields. The sun had begun its western descent, the temp finally cooling. "Tomorrow we'll continue training, much as we did today. Expect to be sore and tired every morning when you wake up. Know that I won't go easy on you. This is why you're here, and physical fitness is expected from all of you."

I made my shoulders stay back and kept my head high even though all I wanted to do was crumble to the ground and go to sleep. Fire burned in my muscles, and my legs felt about to collapse.

Wyatt's attention shifted to me. "I know this isn't easy for a lot of you, but you've made me proud." He placed his hands behind his back. "Now, grab some dinner and enjoy the evening. We reconvene at 0630 tomorrow morning in front of the women's barracks."

Everybody started heading toward the cafeteria, but Wyatt stepped in front of me before I could join them. Scents of oak and pine, his natural woodsy fragrance, wafted toward me. My head spun. I hadn't scented that in eight years, and it brought back a firework of emotions.

Despite reminding myself to act professional, my stomach dipped. It didn't help that I had to arch my neck back to make eye contact. My gaze crawled up his chiseled chest, strong jaw, and aquiline nose.

But his face remained expressionless. "Private Meyers, I noticed that your hands are bleeding."

I curled my fingers into my palms, embarrassed that I was the only one that hadn't properly figured out how to slide down the ropes without hurting myself. "It's okay, sir. It'll heal."

"You should head to the healing center. The witches can help with that."

"Oh, of course, sir. I'll go there now." I bit my lip, trying to remember which building and door would lead me to the healing center.

His lips quirked up. "Do you know where it is?"

I shook my head.

"I'll take you. Follow me."

The rest of my squad mates were already a fair distance away, but Charlotte looked over her shoulder and arched an eyebrow in my direction. I firmly ignored her. The last thing I needed was her making a sly comment about Wyatt and me again. A comment that my commander would undoubtedly hear.

Wyatt led me in the opposite direction of my squad. I hurried behind him, not sure if I should stay following or walk at his side, but he slowed his pace and inched over until we strode alongside one another.

Around us, other SF members walked on the various pathways in the early evening sunshine. Some marched in groups, others practiced shooting in the distant fields, and some just sat on benches chatting with one another. It was easy to forget that this facility wasn't just for training. Hundreds of SF members also called this place home since they lived permanently in the barracks.

"You did well today." Wyatt's chin dipped my way. "I know it wasn't easy for you."

I grimaced in humiliation because even walking at the moment hurt like a bitch, never mind how I would feel tomorrow. "Thank you, sir, but I think we both know that I'm the slowest and weakest in the group. If the Institute and SF didn't have a training agreement, I wouldn't be here. I never would have qualified."

He shrugged. "Maybe not, but you didn't give up today. That's admirable."

I laughed softly. "To be honest, giving up was tempting."

A crack of a smile parted his lips. "Was it the rope burn that made you think twice?"

I studied my palms again. Dried blood caked the cracks. "No. I won't lie, the rope was a bit painful, but it wasn't the ropes course that made me cringe. I think it was the running. In general, I don't really run. Well, not unless it's away from something, like my neighbor at my flat back in London. That woman could talk to you all day about the lotto tickets she'd purchased and how each one was going to be the *big one*. It was amazing how she could spend twenty minutes telling you how accurate her predictions were, only to lose and return to the corner shop the next day to purchase more tickets. I always wished her the best for winning, but when she cornered me it was hard to find an escape, so I generally ran the other way when I saw her coming, but that's probably the extent of my running experience."

Wyatt gave a choked laugh but then smoothed his expression. "So, no gambling either for you then?"

"No." My lips curved up, and despite knowing better, I felt myself slipping back in time, feeling and acting like I had in high school. "I've been a poor college student for the past few years. I prefer to keep my meager savings in my pocket . . . sir." Damn, it was so weird to call him *sir* and not Wyatt.

"So, you're saying to motivate you, I should begin discussing the SF's weekly gambling pot about who's going to return from an assignment with the most scars?"

My eyes widened. "The SF has that?"

His lips tugged up, his eyes sparkling. "No, but if it helps to motivate you, I'm fine with spinning a few tales."

I laughed, the sound bubbling out of me before I could stop it.

Another smile graced his lips just as a fellow commanding officer passed us on the sidewalk. "Major Jamison," he said, nodding his head in greeting.

The smile on Wyatt's face disappeared. "Major Carlisle."

I sobered when I remembered we weren't alone, and we *weren't* back in high school. We were at the SF. And he was my commander.

I garnered Wyatt felt the same since a veil descended over his features, his sparkling eyes dimming.

We walked a bit farther but then curiosity got the better of me. "Sir, gambling and running aside, has there ever been an ambassador recruit who didn't pass training?"

"A few."

I nearly tripped on the sidewalk. Righting myself, I stopped to face him since the healing center waited ahead with its glowing green medical sign hanging above the door.

"So there's still a good chance that I won't pass training?"

His eyes softened. "Given how hard you worked today, I don't think that's likely."

"But will I be able to do it tomorrow?" My muscles were already killing me. A sense of sudden doom came over me. Yes, I'd worked hard today, but could I keep it up? Could I do this day in and day out?

I didn't know.

And if I couldn't, I wouldn't be allowed to begin my ambassador position at the Institute. My heart withered.

All I'd dreamed about during my years at university was becoming an ambassador, but training at the SF was mandatory for acceptance into the Supernatural Ambassador Institute. I'd already finished the other requirement—my degree in paranormal politics—but without passing SF training, that degree would be useless.

Wyatt placed his hands on his hips, his expression fierce. In the early evening sun, his brown hair glinted with chestnut streaks, and his deep-set grassy-colored eyes were so vibrant that for a moment, I completely forgot what I was stressing about.

"I know that you're worried, Avery, but remember that a lot of what we ask of you, what *I'll* be asking of you, is mental." He relaxed his stance, and a slight twinkle lit his eyes again. "And while physically, yes, it can hurt—as you may have experienced with running today—you need to remember that our bodies can withstand so much more than what we ask of them. Every time it hurts, every time you want to give up, remember why you're here. Use that to focus, and it will help you push through the pain to persevere."

I nodded and let his words sink in. "So focus on my goal and remember that it's all mental."

"Exactly. The first few weeks are the hardest. Get through those, and you'll make it."

I took a deep breath, my anxiety subsiding. "Okay. I think I can do that."

His lips kicked up before he said slyly, "Or if all else fails, remember your neighbor in London and pretend that she's chasing you."

I laughed, again unable to stop it. "Of course, sir. I'm sure my imagination could do that."

The corners of his mouth twitched before he nodded ahead. "The healing center is on the second floor. The witches will see to your wounds. I'll see you at 0630 tomorrow morning."

"Yes, sir. Thank you."

He nodded curtly, although I could have sworn merriment still glittered in his gaze, but then he did a one-eighty and strode away.

My heart beat harder as I watched him. I'd seen parts of him during the ropes course that reminded me of the boy I once knew. And just now, while walking here, I'd seen actual sides of him that I remembered from high school—the laughing, light-hearted Wyatt who all the girls wanted to be with and all the guys wanted to be.

But he was different now too. Harder. More serious when his job called for it. More mature. He'd pushed me relentlessly today, but he'd also encouraged me and made me believe in myself.

My heart fluttered when I crossed the sidewalk to the healing center's main doors as his advice filled my mind.

It's all mental.

I chewed on my lip. If I wanted to succeed and become an ambassador, I needed to do this. I had to push past the pain and keep going day in and day out.

Remember why you're here.

I took a deep breath and reached for the door.

Or if all else fails, remember your neighbor in London and pretend that she's chasing you.

I laughed and pushed through the door.

THIRTY MINUTES LATER, I hopped off a bed in the healing center with healed palms and a small vial containing a potion to relieve my sore muscles.

"Now, remember," Rosalie said as she swirled about the room in her long robe, "take that potion tonight, soak for thirty minutes in a hot bath, then head straight to bed. If you follow those instructions, you'll wake up able to train again tomorrow. You won't be pain free, but it will be drastically less. Okay, dear?"

"Yes, thank you. Take the potion, then a hot bath, then go to bed. Got it."

Rosalie smiled sweetly. "Lovely. Now be on your way, dear. It's getting late and you'll want to eat before heading to your barracks."

I thanked her again before leaving the ward. Despite my cuts and rope burn being healed, my legs were another story. Going down the stairwell was quite possibly worse than going up it. My thighs screamed in agony with each step, so I breathed a sigh of relief when I finally made it to the main floor.

From there, I headed out of the building to the cafeteria, knowing that my squad mates had probably already eaten and left.

Sure enough, when I arrived, I didn't spot any of them. With a frown, I grabbed a tray before getting in the food service line.

My stomach growled when I caught the scent of roast beef. Letting my nose lead me, I ended up in the line where they were serving smoked beef brisket. A light reduction sauce was drizzled over the meat before the kitchen server added a hefty portion of mashed potatoes and grilled kale on the side.

It was a simple meal but looked so damned good that my mouth was watering as I grabbed a fizzy soda.

Once back in the large cafeteria that was nearly full with SF members, I searched for a free spot. On the far wall, a small table was empty, so I nabbed it before anyone else could and began digging into my food.

On my second bite, a man said, "Do you mind if I join you? Seats are a bit limited right now."

I looked up to see a tall vampire wearing normal street clothes, which was definitely odd in a facility where everyone wore matching uniforms. He looked to be in his early thirties, and his hair was longer than most SF members. Dark blond strands brushed the tips of his shoulders, and an air of confidence surrounded him that made me wonder if he was a superior who didn't have to follow protocol.

"Of course, sir," I replied, waving to the seat across from me.

He pulled out the chair and smiled before nodding at my tray. "I was tempted by that brisket when I saw it, but I couldn't say no to the burger. It's been a while since I've had American food and it's impossible to find a decently cooked cheeseburger in Eastern Europe." His words lilted with an accent from long ago.

I swallowed the bite of kale I'd been munching. "Oh? Have you been traveling?"

"I have." He squirted ketchup next to his plate of fries. A small dollop landed on his glass of blood, which he wiped off with his fingertip. "I've been working in eastern Europe for several hundred years."

I perked up, a smile lighting my face. "Where in Eastern Europe, sir? I lived in Poland for a while as a child."

"Is that right? Mówisz po polsku?"

"I'm afraid not. I didn't live there long enough to learn the language, sir."

"Neither did I." He lowered his voice to a conspiratorial tone.

"And just so you know, you don't need to call me *sir*. I'm not an SF superior, but merely an SF consultant."

I blushed. Well, that explained the casual clothes.

His gaze swept over my ruddy cheeks, his pupils dilating in desire or hunger—I couldn't be sure—but he had good enough manners to look away and pretend he hadn't noticed the rush of blood to my cheeks.

After picking up his burger, he sank his teeth into it, then moaned in delight. "Delicious. Even though I don't need this food to sustain me, it certainly tastes *sinful*."

A flutter ran through my stomach. Between his moan and the way he appraised me while he chewed his food, I felt like *I* was on the dinner menu.

I sighed internally. Vampires were always so sexual. Everything about them oozed sex appeal and their carnal appetites were legendary. I'd lost my virginity to a vamp when I was nineteen. It'd been a memorable encounter.

I briefly fingered my neck, remembering how my ex had bitten me quite enthusiastically on occasion during sex.

I glanced up to find the vamp watching me, a curious glint in his eyes.

I cleared my throat and forked another bite of meat. "So where in Eastern Europe do you work?"

"Bulgaria," he replied. "And forgive me for being so forward, but I'm quite curious how you came to live in Poland at one point in your life?"

"My parents are ambassadors. I spent my childhood traveling and living in various countries. I lived in Poland when I was eleven."

He cocked his head, a new interest lighting his eyes. "You're not Avery Meyers, are you?"

I paused, my fork halfway to my mouth. "I am. How did you know?"

He grinned, which transformed his face from being merely

attractive to unsettlingly arresting. "I heard an ambassador student started at the SF this week. I contract to the Institute when matters arise in which utilizing the international libraries are needed."

My jaw dropped. Eastern Europe held the largest supernatural libraries in the world. Inside that secretive monolith, hundreds of gargoyles worked, since the little stone creatures were well renowned for their academic achievements. However, gargoyles didn't *live* like other supernaturals. Like leeches, they only came alive after feeding off of a supernatural's life source. Supernaturals condemned in the courts were their unfortunate victims, and the longer a criminal's sentence leeching was, the longer the gargoyle was able to come alive and work in the library. But they only came alive during the day. Each night, they returned to stone.

"So, you're a gargoyle representative?" I said, putting the puzzle pieces together. "Of course, that would explain why you're working in Eastern Europe and why you're a consultant to the SF."

"Indeed. I'm Nicholas Fitzpatrick, at your service." He gave a mock bow, which made me laugh. His satisfied smile followed. "Well, what luck this evening has turned out to be. I thought I was merely asking a young, attractive woman to have dinner with me, and it turns out she's also the sole ambassador recruit at the SF this quarter."

My core tightened, and I wanted to smack myself, but I knew there was no use. Quite simply, vampires and I didn't mix. I had next to no defenses against their sexual pull since my magic was so weak. It didn't help that Nicholas's pull was stronger than most. The strength of his allure hinted at his age. He had to be at least five hundred years old.

Damn. My goal tonight had just changed to not only taking my potion and going to sleep, but to avoid ending up in bed with a vampire fucking me senseless.

CHAPTER SEVEN

AVERY

Nicholas raised an eyebrow, obviously enjoying the effect he was having on me.

My cheeks flushed, but then I reminded myself that he was a vampire so his flirtation didn't necessarily mean anything.

"I suppose it was good luck, or coincidence," I replied, "considering I'm one of the only people here who doesn't have anyone to sit with." I swept my hand toward the hundred SF members currently enjoying their dinner—none of whom I knew.

As I turned my head back to Nicholas, still smiling, an intense emerald glare from across the room caught my attention. Wyatt sat with two other superiors at a table eating dinner. I couldn't be sure, but I thought a faint glow rimmed his irises.

The second we made eye contact, Wyatt dipped his head back to his companions, but his attention made me shift self-consciously on my seat.

"Are your parents the reason you aspired to join the Institute?" Nicholas asked before taking a drink of his blood. He didn't try to hide the crimson drops that lined his upper lip.

Instead, he ran his tongue over them suggestively, his gaze never leaving mine.

Another flutter ran through me. *Ugh.* I seriously needed to get my vagina under control.

"Avery?" Nicholas said, his voice as smooth as velvet.

Flustered, I grabbed my napkin to dab at my mouth. "Um, yes, that's one of the reasons. What I love about being an ambassador is traveling, meeting new supernaturals, and learning about new cultures—obviously, I got that from my parents and their lifestyle. But, if I'm being completely honest, my mixed blood is also why I chose this profession."

His eyes dimmed sympathetically. "Meaning your powers are limited because of your mixed blood? And being an ambassador doesn't require strong magic?"

"Yeah, exactly. I mean, don't get me wrong. I know some mixed-bloods are incredibly powerful, but I'm not one of them." I shrugged. "I suppose you could say I lost the game of genetic roulette when I was conceived."

"And what mixed blood do you possess? If you don't mind my asking."

Since he seemed genuinely curious versus scornful, I replied, "I'm half witch and a quarter werewolf. My father's a low-level sorcerer, and my mother's half werewolf. As I'm sure you know, quarter werewolf females have almost no wolf abilities. And considering my witch magic comes from a sorcerer father it's been effectively diluted since males passing magic to female children usually results in weak magic." I raised my shoulders. "So, there you have it. I'm rather unimpressive."

His attention dipped down, taking in my full breasts in my form-fitting uniform top. "I wouldn't say you're unimpressive."

My cheeks heated and my core clenched again, making an ache form low in my belly. I wanted to sink through the floor. While Nicholas was certainly attractive, I didn't actually want to sleep with him, but there was something about vamps who were at least a few hundred years old. It was as if they pulled at one's sexual appetite whether you wanted them to or not.

Nicholas leaned forward until his elbows rested on the table. Some of his sexual energy dampened when he schooled his features into a serious expression. "So essentially what you're saying is that as an ambassador, you'll use your mind instead of your magic to fulfill a role that serves our community."

"My mind is all I have."

His attention flicked to my boobs again. "We can agree to disagree on that." He grinned wickedly, then gave me another thoughtful look. "On a serious note, there's pride to be taken in that role, Avery. You shouldn't sell yourself short simply because your magic isn't powerful. Remember that some of our best treaties and international dealings have come from magically inferior supernaturals. Remember the war of 1739, in which the Russian sorcerers declared themselves rulers of all of Europe? I still remember that event. There was concern the Russian sorcerers would take over the world. But ultimately, it was Matilda Schlouster who brokered the treaty that ultimately led to the sorcerers backing down. To this day, that treaty is referenced when tensions in that region rise. And Ms. Schlouster was only a low-level psychic whose predictions were often wrong instead of right, yet she thrived in the role of a supernatural ambassador. So keep your chin up, Ms. Meyers. You could be the next Matilda."

He sounded so sincere. And that combined with his sexual tension dissipating . . .

I blinked and realized that I was looking at the man behind the vampire as we stared at one another from across the table. In that moment, I saw a glimpse of who Nicholas Fitzpatrick really was—a decent man who had been turned into a vamp and now suffered from sexual urges that he could no more control than I could control my lack of magic.

I smiled genuinely and shook my head. "Yes, you're very

right. I shouldn't sell myself short. Perhaps I will be the next Matilda."

He laughed and picked up his burger again. Sexual energy pulsed from him once more when he bit into the meat, and I knew the man behind the vamp had just disappeared.

"You know," he said, cocking his head. "I've never fully understood why the Supernatural Ambassador Institute requires SF training for three months before allowing new ambassadors to be admitted."

I took a drink of my soda. "You're not the only one. Most don't. The reason it's required is because of a number of past incidences where ambassadors found themselves in crisis situations in which they didn't know how to react."

Understanding lit his eyes. "Ah, of course. Now that you mention it, I remember an incident about fifteen years ago. An Irish ambassador was taken hostage while trying to solidify trade policies with a vampire coven in Venezuela."

I nodded sadly. "His death is what initiated the change in the Institute's admittance requirement. So I'm here to learn how to fight better, but more importantly, how to escape in one piece if I'm ever in that situation."

Nicholas grinned devilishly. "And we certainly wouldn't want a young woman as lovely as you not escaping in one piece."

I laughed even though another rush of blood filled my clit. It didn't help that Nicholas's eyes dilated, and his nostrils flared. He could no doubt scent the effect he was having on me. But he had good enough manners to raise his glass and pretend that he didn't notice my arousal.

"I wish you nothing but the best, Ms. Meyers, as you learn to fight, slay, and survive during your time here."

Another chuckle escaped me as Nicholas's eyes danced with mirth. When I clinked my glass to his, a sharp shift in energy vibrated in the air. Goosebumps sprouted across my arms, and when I sought the source of the rippling energy, I once again found Wyatt staring at us from across the room.

Mortification filled me when I realized my commander had probably scented my arousal too. My hand shook as I hastily set my glass down, but then I realized I hadn't taken a sip after the toast. I swallowed a mouthful of soda and stood to leave.

"Have I scared you away?" Nicholas asked, his eyebrows rising as his lips curved suggestively. "I was hoping to spend more time with you this evening." His tone dropped, letting me know *exactly* how he wanted to spend that time.

My lady bits throbbed again under his carnal stare. It was embarrassing how easily he was eliciting a reaction from me. "No, of course not, but it's been a long first day of training, and I really need to get back to my apartment. Are you going to be here long?"

He shook his head. "Sadly, no. I leave in the morning since the trial I was called in for ended today, but I'm delighted that I was able to make your acquaintance. Perhaps I'll see you again once you've begun your work." His gaze dipped to my breasts for the third time, his tongue darting out to lick his lips.

Another rush of lust shot to my core as my breasts tingled under his heady stare. *So embarrassing!*

He finally lifted his eyes. "Will you be traveling to Geneva after you finish your time here?"

"I will. And are you returning to Eastern Europe tomorrow?"

"Indeed I am." He pushed to a stand, his movements graceful. He didn't seem the least bit perturbed by his erection tenting his trousers. "Are you sure you wouldn't like an escort to your apartment?" His voiced dipped again.

"No," I squeaked, my cheeks heating as I fought to keep my attention north. "I'm good."

"Oh, I'm sure you are." Nicholas chuckled and extended his hand toward mine.

I automatically accepted his handshake.

His fingers encircled my palm, his skin cool and smooth. He lifted my hand to his mouth, then flipped it over and kissed my palm, his tongue darting out briefly to taste my skin.

I shivered at the feel of his cool lips.

"It was a pleasure, Ms. Meyers. Until we meet again." He let go, a knowing glint in his eyes, before he swept our trays off the table and glided toward the kitchen to drop them off.

For a moment, I couldn't move. My heart stuttered, my breaths shallow. One would think after traveling the world and meeting as many supernatural species as I had that I wouldn't be so affected by older vamps, but such wasn't the case.

I was no different than a human in that aspect.

Embarrassment stained my cheeks red, especially since those seated nearby cast knowing glances my way.

I scurried toward the cafeteria's exit even though my muscles protested at the quick movements.

But with every step I took, angry energy pulsed into me more and more, and it again came from Wyatt.

Shit. Had I done something wrong? Was I not supposed to talk to consultants? I made a mental note to review the SF handbook later tonight.

I had to pass the commanders' table to leave. Wyatt dipped his chin when I skirted by, so I couldn't see his face, but my internal radar spiked at the rolling power pulsing off him.

I picked up my speed and fled the cafeteria as fast as I could, my heart pumping as rapidly as a jackhammer.

CHAPTER EIGHT
WYATT

I threw my napkin on the table after Avery departed. Her scent still drifted around me. The lilac aroma was tinted with heady musk. She was more than turned on, and it made me livid that she'd had such a strong sexual reaction to the vamp.

Never mind that it shouldn't bother me. Never mind that even having these irrational feelings could get me questioned by Wes—my *boss*—since relationships between a superior and subordinate were expressly forbidden.

Bottom line, she was free to fuck who she wanted.

But the thought of her with someone in *that* way, especially Nicholas Fitzpatrick . . .

I leaned back in my chair, my teeth grinding together. At least she hadn't left with the vamp.

A bitter taste filled my mouth when I thought of Nicholas Fitzpatrick. Given what he'd done a few years ago, he was one of the supernaturals that I could honestly say I *hated*.

But I couldn't fault my new recruit for her reaction to him. Especially since she had no idea what a scumbag Nicholas was.

I sighed bitterly. As much as I hated it, I wasn't surprised they'd hit it off. Similar to Avery, Nicholas was educated and well-traveled, yet the scent of Avery's arousal had made me see red.

She'd practically been panting under the vamp's stare. I knew that vampires had that reaction on a lot of women—especially humans—but to see him weave his spell over Avery and elicit that response from *her* . . .

I scowled, my mood blackening even more. Closing my eyes, I took a deep breath. *Keep your shit together, Jamison. You're not in high school anymore. She's a new recruit. You're her commander. Your reaction about this is not only unprofessional, it's against protocol.*

But my pep talk didn't help. My wolf still growled in agitation.

Which didn't bode well given how much my wolf had matured since we'd last seen Avery.

This wasn't like before. When Avery and I had attended high school together, my wolf had still been young since the first shift didn't happen until puberty. He'd shown interest in Avery at that time as well but not to this extent. And worse, now he was an alpha male who was used to getting his way, and one thing he'd made very apparent tonight—he didn't like seeing Avery cozying up to the vampire.

Just cool it, I said internally to him. *She's not our mate. We have no claim to her. Besides, if you keep this up and I do something stupid, I could get fired, and I* can't *get fired. Remember that promise we made to Marcus?*

His response was only to growl louder and raise his hackles.

I rolled my eyes. Typical irrational wolf.

"You finished, Jamison? I can take your tray if you want."

Houston's question startled me from my inner warring. My friend, and fellow commander, who'd I'd had dinner with held out her hand for my tray, her rings flashing on her hand.

"You don't need to take mine. I got it. Thanks." I stood and dropped my tray off at the kitchen's cleaning station, trying to let the magical apparatus that sprayed the dishes distract me.

But the scent of lilacs still permeated the air. My wolf rumbled in appreciation, and then in anger when he caught Avery's arousal again. He wanted that arousal to have been caused by *us*, not the vamp.

"You up for a drink?" Houston asked from behind me. "Jasher and I are heading to the bar."

I raked a hand through my hair and turned to face my friends. "Nah, not for me. I'm gonna turn in since I've got another early morning with my new recruits tomorrow."

"Don't go too hard on 'em," Jasher joked.

"When have I ever done that?"

Houston laughed before she and Jasher walked away. I went in the opposite direction toward the cafeteria's south exit door.

I strode down the hall and was just about to leave the building when Nicholas rounded the corner. We nearly collided.

As soon as he realized it was me, his eyes widened, but then he smoothed his expression and stood immobile in that deathly still way only vampires could manage.

I ground my teeth together. I was tempted to punch him in the face and lay him flat, but that wouldn't be appropriate given where we were, but if I happened to see him again in a bar or outside of the SF . . .

My fingers curled into fists.

"Major Jamison," Nicholas said coolly. "It's been a while."

"Not long enough."

He lifted his hand and inspected his fingernails. "I was lucky enough to have dinner with that delicious new recruit of yours."

Blood roared in my ears, and I took a menacing step forward. Before I could remind myself that Avery's sex life was none of my business, the words tore from my mouth, "You stay away from her."

He dropped his hand and rolled his eyes. "Really, Wyatt. How long has it been? Are you still harboring distaste for me?"

I took another step forward, until we stood toe to toe. His vampire stench flooded my senses, and my nostrils flared. My wolf urged me on until I found myself saying, "She's not for you to play with."

Something flashed in his eyes—almost like . . . regret—but he quickly veiled it. "Well, lucky for you, I'm leaving the SF tomorrow morning, so I won't be playing with her anytime soon."

"It better stay that way."

He opened his mouth, as if about to say something, but then he closed it, his lips thinning. "Good night, Major Jamison."

With that, the vampire stepped gracefully around me and sauntered off, which left me seething in the hall.

My wolf snarled within me, his lips curling back to reveal his sharp canines. He wanted to follow the vamp, tear his throat out, and make him suffer for setting his sights on Avery.

Even though I was no fan of Nicholas Fitzpatrick, my jaw dropped at my wolf's heightened reaction.

What the fuck is the matter with you?

But as before, he only growled more.

After Nicholas had fully disappeared around the corner, I took a deep breath but still found myself heading toward the exterior door that led to the barracks. I knew I should go to the gym to work off some steam, but a part of me had to know if Avery was going to hook up with Nicholas tonight, even though it was none of my damned business.

I sniffed, picking up Avery's trail. I kept my pace swift and silent until I spotted her ahead of me on the sidewalk. She was still alone.

Thank the Gods.

My jaw locked at my reaction, but I kept following her.

Since it was getting late, twilight had emerged. Her footsteps were quiet, and she wasn't walking fast. I knew she was sore and hurting, which made my wolf grumble.

What did I say earlier? You seriously need to get your balls under control. She's not our mate. Easing her pain isn't our concern.

But as he'd been since this morning, he didn't care and just snarled more.

I knew my human side was going to have to talk some sense into him. Since a werewolf's inner wolf ran purely on instinct, it wasn't unheard of for one's wolf to find a female attractive who was entirely wrong for him.

However, I did agree with him about the attraction. Sexually, Avery was exactly what I found appealing in a woman. It didn't help that the grit and determination I'd seen in her today were admirable. And I would be lying to myself if I said I didn't respect how hard she'd worked to be admitted into the Institute.

But practically, we were all wrong for each other.

I sighed in frustration. Avery Meyers and I could never be anything. For one, she was my new recruit. As per SF policy, I was forbidden to become romantically involved with any subordinate. If I broke that rule, I would be fired.

And two, just as she'd been in high school, she was still completely out of my league.

Even though she was two years younger than me, she had traveled to more countries than many elders in my pack in her first thirteen years of life. And since then, her cultural education had only broadened.

Unbeknownst to Avery, I'd kept track of her after she'd left Ridgeback, even though I knew I would probably never see her again. She and her parents had first moved to France for a one-year assignment, and following that they'd lived in Zimbabwe for six months, and then Japan.

By the time Avery went to university in the UK, I was no doubt a distant speck in her memory, yet . . . she remembered me.

I thought of the comment I'd made during the ropes course, when I'd tried to reassure her that it was like the ropes in our high school gym. Her eyes had lit up. Did that mean she was happy that I remembered her too?

I sighed, but the sound came out as a low groan. I was putting way too much thought into this.

Avery continued walking ahead of me, oblivious to my stalking and obsessive thoughts.

I shoved my hands into my pockets, remembering how she'd affected me when I'd first met her in my pack town eight years ago.

My entire life, I'd lived in one place—Ridgeback, British Columbia. Since most wolves lived within their pack, that wasn't unusual, and we had to live with other werewolves, or at least have regular interaction with them. Living amongst our kind was needed in order to live a healthy life. Without that connection, we ran the risk of turning rogue and becoming a bloodthirsty psychotic wolf who preyed on everyone.

But unbeknownst to Avery Meyers, meeting her had inspired me to look at life beyond my pack.

Because of her, I'd joined the SF. It was the only option I had to travel since I needed to live with other wolves close by, and there was a plethora of werewolves in the Supernatural Forces. And since the SF required its members to travel for jobs, it was the perfect fit.

Since being admitted to the SF seven years ago, I'd traveled to dozens of countries, which wasn't the same as what Avery had done, but each time I went somewhere new, I still thought of her.

To my teenage self, Avery Meyers had been an enigma—a beautiful enigma who blossomed from an awkward teenager into an alluring young adult while she'd lived in Ridgeback.

And now, she'd only become more breathtaking.

I smiled, thinking again about her courage and tenacity

during the ropes course today. I'd smelled the blood on her palms when the ropes burned through her skin, but she hadn't complained. Not once.

"Fucking hell," I muttered under my breath. My feelings for her were growing again, and it hadn't been much more than a day.

How can I already be feeling this infatuation again?

I continued to trail silently behind her until she reached her barracks. Thankfully, Nicholas never showed up, and I didn't scent his stench on the breeze, which meant he wasn't hiding nearby either.

Avery was now home safe and there was no vamp dick in sight, yet agitation still oozed through my veins, but . . . why?

I rammed a hand through my hair before doing a one-eighty and heading toward the gym. I knew why. Because once again, I wanted her, but she was *off* limits.

Seriously, I needed to get my head back in the game.

But it didn't help that my wolf had become so demanding and eager in Avery's presence, because *nothing* could come from this even if my old high school feelings were resurfacing again.

In a few months, Avery would once again breeze out of my life as quietly as she'd slipped back into it.

And that was something not only my wolf needed to remember, but *I* needed to remember too.

CHAPTER NINE
AVERY

My first week of training was brutal.

True to his word, Wyatt didn't go easy on us. He pushed us hard, demanding more and more from us physically. The bath and potion had helped me that second morning, but since then I'd woken up each day moaning in pain with limbs that nearly refused to move.

So every morning, I used Wyatt's advice to get out of bed and keep going.

It's all mental.

The first few weeks are the hardest.

Remember why you're here.

Only one week in and already I was giving myself pep talks. Yep. Rather pathetic, but at least it worked.

"How's it going, Meyers?" Chris asked as he ran by me on the track on Friday morning. It was the third time he'd lapped me. He would be done with his mile in less than a minute if he kept his pace up.

"Just peachy, wolf. You better watch out. One of these days I'll catch you!"

He laughed and began sprinting again. Twenty seconds later, he was on the opposite side of the track crossing the finish line.

The morning sun shone down on us, and my ponytail whipped around my face. Eliza breathed heavily at my side. Unlike the other days this week, she wasn't running faster than me.

"Is it horrible that I'm so glad our first week is almost done?" I asked her breathlessly.

She laughed, then coughed. "I am in agreeance. This seems particularly challenging today."

Across the field, Charlotte crossed the finish line, just behind Zaden. She gave Zaden a high five, then Chris. The three strongest among us were like a little club or secret society—admission granted only if you had naturally enhanced strength and speed.

Pretty sure I would never get an invite.

Ahead of us, Nick was almost done with only one lap to go, while Bo trailed slightly behind him. Eliza and I were only at the halfway mark of our mile run test, but at least it was Friday, which meant our weekend off was just around the corner.

Eliza coughed again, falling behind me for a moment.

I slowed my pace, letting her catch up as she tucked a strand of purple hair behind her ear. Her cheeks were beet-red.

"Are you okay?" I asked her.

She nodded. "Yes, I'm absolutely fine. Just a little tired I think."

She didn't cough again. Instead, she put her head down and ran harder.

Wyatt stood on the side of the quarter-mile track, stopwatch in hand.

His sparkling green eyes followed us as we ran. A side of my mouth angled up, and I remembered his teasing at the beginning of the week.

Or if all else fails, remember your neighbor in London and pretend that she's chasing you.

I smothered a laugh and ran harder. When we passed him, I swore his eyes followed me and only me. My inner laugh died as my belly somersaulted in awareness.

It wasn't the first time I'd had that feeling this week.

During the last three days, I'd caught Wyatt watching me on more occasions than I could count, but I kept reminding myself that his watchful stares were only because he wanted to make sure I kept up.

I was the weakest after all.

But despite that stigma, it was hard for me not to admire his teaching style. He pushed all of us, but he wasn't cruel and he never belittled anyone. Instead, he was encouraging but firm when we needed a kick in the rear.

My stomach did a little flip again when Eliza and I passed him on our final lap.

The sun sparkled on his dark hair like dancing stars, and the T-shirt he wore showed off his strong shoulders. Gods help me, but the man lit my blood on fire.

I tried again to concentrate on running, but as had been happening all week, my attraction to him was growing. I was reminded again of why I fell so hard for him in high school. He wasn't as quick to laugh now, but I figured that could be because his job required him to be serious, but he was still kind.

Kind yet tough, which essentially was the Wyatt I remembered.

It was impossible to guard my heart against that, but I had to. I truly didn't have a choice.

In three months, I would be gone, and Wyatt Jamison would be another distant memory. It would be the same as it'd been eight years ago when my parents and I packed our belongings and said goodbye to Ridgeback, British Columbia, and all of the wolves who'd welcomed us and wormed their way into our hearts. After my dad's two-year assignment was up, we were off to France, and Wyatt Jamison was just another supernatural I'd met and left behind.

And now, it would be the same all over again. In three months, I would leave for Geneva and Wyatt would stay here in Idaho. Our lives would once again bisect on different paths.

Exactly, you need to remember that, Avery, and stop this ridiculous crush from forming again.

"Almost done," Eliza said, puffing when we neared the finish line.

"Yeah, almost there."

We crossed the finish line together. Eliza's cheeks were now scarlet. I breathed heavily as sweat dripped down my temples.

"Not bad," Wyatt said. "Eight minutes, ten seconds. In three months, I imagine you'll be down to six minutes or less."

I balked. It felt as though I would pass out, so I wasn't sure how I was going to get down to six minutes.

Eliza merely fanned herself.

I eyed her again. Under her ruddy cheeks, her complexion looked slightly sallow.

"Hey," I said, still breathing heavily from the run. "Are you sure you're okay?"

She smiled tightly, revealing her pointy teeth. "I am most fine. Please don't be concerned."

Wyatt checked his watch again, then gazed at the forest. "Since it's Friday, and you've all done so well this week, I'm going to give you a choice for how we spend our afternoon. We can either break for an early lunch now, or push for another two hours and be done for the day. I'll leave the decision up to all of you."

Charlotte stood straighter and eyed the group. "Should we vote?"

Everyone nodded.

"All in favor of eating lunch now?" she said.

Chris raised his hand, which didn't surprise me since he was always hungry, but Eliza did too. I eyed her chalky complexion under her crimson cheeks, then raised my hand. She clearly needed a break.

Charlotte appraised the rest of us. "And all in favor of another two hours then done for the day?"

Charlotte, Zaden, Bo, and Nick all raised their hands.

Four to three. Onward we went.

Chris scowled, which got a smirk from Zaden, but at least they hadn't physically fought today. That was an improvement.

"Then it's decided. Follow me." Wyatt grabbed the large bag of water bottles that he always hauled around for us. "We have a six-mile course through the forest. It's strenuous and requires scaling a few short cliffs and crossing one river, but once you're done, you have off until Monday."

Zaden grinned, his fangs absent. "Are we to stay in a group, sir, or are we allowed to move at our own speed?"

"Your own speed is fine. Next week, we'll focus on working together as a group."

"Yusss," Zaden said under his breath.

The blond vamp's pale skin looked snowy-white in the sunlight. I still remembered the first time I'd learned about vampires. I'd been around seven years old, and my father had worked with a vamp at the Ministry of Paranormal Affairs in Scotland. I'd been speechless the first time I'd seen one in daylight. According to my children books from the human library, vampires could only come out at night.

My parents had laughed when I asked them about it, saying that was an exaggerated myth found only in human stories. While there was some truth to it—most vampires were sensitive to sunlight, and as they aged, that sensitivity increased—the reality was that the sun didn't burn them or turn them to ash. Well, not unless they were ancient.

The ancient vampires were the only ones who truly couldn't

tolerate sunlight. They *would* burn to death in the sun, but so few ancients existed anymore that I had yet to meet any vampire who didn't enjoy being out during the day at least to some extent.

And considering Zaden was a brand-new vamp, he didn't mind the sun's rays at all. Although in a hundred years, he'd probably be less enthusiastic.

I paused and wondered how much the sun affected Nicholas Fitzpatrick. Since he remembered things from hundreds of years ago, and made my vagina very eager, he was probably pretty old. I imagined the sun had to affect him at least a little bit.

Wyatt led us away from the track toward the trees, and I shook off my thoughts of the vamp I'd had dinner with the other night.

We passed several squads along the way. Those not on assignments were all actively training. In the distance, shouts, drills, and stomping boots could be heard.

Charlotte fell back from the front of the group to join Eliza and me.

"An entire weekend off, ladies. Whatever will we do?" She grinned, which made me laugh. Charlotte had been making comments all week about hitting up the bars this weekend.

"Girls' night out?" I replied.

"I'm counting on it."

When Eliza didn't join in the conversation, Charlotte cocked her head. "Eliza?"

Eliza startled, then gave a wan smile. "Oh, right. Yes, girls' night out would be very enjoyable."

Charlotte frowned, glancing back at me.

"She's tired," I said, "As *most* of us are."

Charlotte laughed since I'd grumbled each morning about getting up early.

We soon entered the trees, the dry earth kicking up small

plumes of dust by our feet. Narrow hemlocks and fragrant fir trees rose up around us, their tips swaying in the breeze.

Wyatt led us to the start of a trailhead. The plaque staked into the ground beside it had the ominous title of *Dead Man's Slayer.*

I wasn't sure if I wanted to know what inspired that name.

"This is the start of the trail," he explained. "The course is clearly marked. Remember, you're allowed to go at your own speed, but wait for the group at the end." Wyatt handed out the water bottles. "Drink up and carry what you don't finish. I'll bring up the rear and will help if anyone gets stuck along the way. Otherwise, do your best and see you at the end."

Chris was already jumping on the balls of his feet. He reminded me of the rabbit in that cartoon about the tortoise and hare. "Sir, when can we go?"

Wyatt checked his watch again. "Whenever you're ready."

Chris took off and disappeared into the forest. Zaden scowled and followed, turning into a blur. As usual, I had a feeling those two were going to make this a competition.

Charlotte took off next, followed quickly by Nick and Bo.

Eliza and I were the last to leave.

"Want to stick together?" I asked her.

"Yes, that would be lovely."

I let Eliza lead the way so she could set the pace. Within minutes, it became obvious that Wyatt hadn't been joking when he said it was a strenuous course. As soon as we disappeared into the trees, the trail began climbing steeply upward, reminding me of urban hiking in San Francisco and the unforgiving hills sprinkled throughout that city that did a number on one's calves.

Eliza trudged steadily up the trail, her breathing audible even though I was a yard behind her. My worry grew the more distance we put behind us.

"Hey, Eliza?" I called, panting. "Maybe we should tell Major Jamison that you're not feeling well."

Her feet slipped on the dry ground. "I do not need special treatment," she gasped. "I'm just tired. Besides, nobody else is struggling, so I *will* do this."

"You know I've been struggling all week, and—"

She gave me a sharp look and resumed walking.

I clamped my mouth shut. *Point taken.*

The trail switched back and forth up the steep mountain. A few miles later, we reached an opening in the trees. A granite cliff loomed in front of us.

Both of us were breathing heavily when we finally reached the vertical rock portion. I glanced behind us into the trees. I didn't see Wyatt. The few times I'd caught sight of him, he'd looked like he was out for a leisurely stroll, not laboring along as Eliza and I were.

Most of the time, though, I hadn't spotted him. I figured he was keeping his distance so he didn't interfere with our pace, but I knew he was there. I took some comfort in that, especially if Eliza truly fell ill.

"How about I go first?" I said as we stood in front of the rock face.

She merely nodded.

Breathing steadily, I concentrated on my hand and footholds, refusing to look down. Thankfully, a few steps later, I heaved myself over the top of the cliff and peered down to where Eliza waited.

My elation at making the climb faltered. Even from the distance, I noted her pallid complexion. My concern grew when she swayed slightly before reaching for the rock.

"Eliza?" I called worriedly.

She abruptly snapped upright. "Coming!"

A flash of clothing in the trees appeared in the distance. Wyatt emerged from the forest at the bottom of the rocky incline. When he spotted us, he placed his hands on his hips and stopped. I tried to ignore the fluttering in my stomach that always began when he was around and instead concentrated on Eliza.

Eliza tensed and darted a glance over her shoulder at our commander. Her brow furrowed and she began climbing, her movements quick and efficient. Some of my worry abated. Maybe she truly was just tired and not sick.

"Almost there." I reached down so my arm was dangling over the edge.

She ignored my outstretched hand despite her ragged breaths and heaved herself over the top. She lay flat, panting, and was effectively hidden from our commander's appraising eyes.

Wyatt continued to watch us from the ground, nodding in satisfaction that we'd done the climb. He had no idea that Eliza looked as white as snow.

I jerked my chin toward the boulder field we now had to scramble over. "Once we're across that, we're back on even ground."

She sat upright, grimacing. "Let's go."

I stayed at her side as we traversed the rough terrain, but as before, with Wyatt watching, Eliza seemed determined.

Once back in the woods, the trail climbed steeply upward again, but at least we reached the top not long later. However, it soon became apparent that going down wasn't much easier than going up. The terrain was so steep that several times we had to get down on our butts to shimmy off rock ledges or grab onto trees to stop ourselves from going too fast.

I helped Eliza when I could, and now that Wyatt was out of sight again, she let me.

"We must almost be to the river," I told Eliza when the sound of rushing water reached us. "Do you hear that? We're almost done."

Her head dipped, letting me know she'd heard me, but she didn't respond.

The *whooshing* sound of the fast-moving river grew louder the more we descended.

"We're almost there," I said.

A few minutes later, we emerged from the trees.

"It's moving really fast." Eliza scanned the broad band of river.

She was right. The water raged here. Frothy white caps and swirling eddies filled my view.

"We can start to cross using those large boulders." I pointed to the rocks jutting out of the water. "And then we can finish crossing on that felled tree."

Eliza leaned against a smooth boulder, her eyes closing. I wasn't even sure if she'd heard me.

I cast an anxious glance over my shoulder to see if Wyatt was near, but he was nowhere to be found, obviously giving us room since he thought we were doing fine.

I stepped closer to her. "If you're not feeling good, Eliza, we should wait here for—"

"I'm fine!" she snapped and abruptly straightened. "Let's go."

But when she tried to pass me, I stopped her and laid a palm against her forehead. I gasped. "You're burning up!"

She took an unsteady step away, and another ragged breath escaped her. "I shall be fine. I can get to the end. I am just a bit unwell today."

"Eliza, you're *sick*. We should tell Major—"

She grabbed my hand, her grip surprisingly strong. "No! I have to get through this, Avery. I *cannot* get kicked out of training!"

I softened my tone. "They won't kick you out of training for being sick one day."

"But I've been sick all week," she whispered, her eyelids dipping down. "I've been trying to hide it, but it's been getting worse, and if I miss too many days, they'll kick me out for sure. Please, Avery. *Please* don't tell him. I just need to get through this and then I shall have the weekend to recover."

The desperation in her tone silenced me. I knew she was in no shape to be out here, but who was I to tell her what to do, especially when I felt the same about being at the SF. Failing training wasn't an option. Period.

"Okay, then how about I go first, and I'll let you know the best place to put your feet. Deal?"

She nodded. "Deal."

I squeezed her hand again before stepping onto a large rock sticking up from the river. Frothy water gushed around it, and when I put all of my weight on my foot, I nearly slipped. Holding my arms out for balance, I called to Eliza, "Be careful. Don't jump too fast, or you might slip."

I waited on each rock until she was safely on the one behind me. We made our way slowly across the river as the deafening roar of the constant rushing water swirled around us. A few times, I reached a hand out to her, helping to keep her steady.

At the center of the river, the felled tree waited. While the rotting wood had a pungent scent, it looked much easier to traverse than the slick rocks behind us.

"We're almost there." I squeezed Eliza's hand again. "This looks more secure than the rocks, so just take your time and we'll get to the other side."

Eliza nodded grimly before we started crossing it. Beneath our feet the river churned, reminding me of whirlpools made in a bathtub. I had no idea how deep the river was, but I couldn't see the bottom.

"Almost there."

When I didn't hear her reply, I peeked over my shoulder.

Eliza stood immobile on the tree, a hand on her forehead. Alarmed, I shuffled my feet, turning to face her as she swayed slightly to the left.

"Eliza!" I lunged for her, but she tipped to the side.

Her eyes opened in awareness just as she plunged into the river.

The second she broke through the water, she shrieked and gasped. "Avery!"

I grabbed for her but already the river was pulling her away.

"Eliza!"

"Help!"

I dove in.

The moment I hit the water, my breath caught. Its icy temperature seized my lungs, but I managed to gulp in a shallow breath before kicking toward Eliza.

She clung to a protruding branch from the fallen tree, but she was a few yards downstream. Cold water pushed into me, trying to force me under, but I kicked as hard as I could until I reached her.

"Keep pulling along the branch until you can grab the tree!" I yelled to her over the deafening river.

Fear filled her eyes as she struggled to move against the current.

I managed to keep my hold on a soggy branch as I reached around her with my other arm. "Pull yourself up!" I scanned the trees for Wyatt, hoping he'd appear, but I still didn't see him. "Come on, Eliza! Pull!" I pushed her butt as hard as I could while the water barreled into my face.

I coughed and sputtered. Icy water rushed into my mouth and matted my hair to my eyes. Kicking harder, I pushed closer to the surface and shoved Eliza with everything I had.

She lurched toward the tree, coughing uncontrollably, but managed to grab onto it and pull herself back up.

I kicked again and tried to follow her, but the water shoved against me. "I can't reach it!" I yelled to her.

"Grab a hold of me!" She lay down on the tree and extended her arm.

I kicked furiously and reached toward her outstretched hand. Her fingers were only inches away.

"Just a little farther, Avery!"

My fingers brushed hers, then the branch I was holding snapped.

I screamed just as water rushed over my face. The white-water sucked me down, blinding me and shoving me into its frigid depths. I thrashed and kicked, trying to break through the surface, but its overpowering current only pulled me farther and deeper downstream.

Several times, I knocked against the bottom of the riverbed. Smooth rocks and coarse sand grazed my skin. I tried to turn, to push off from the bottom, but the harder I kicked, the more my lungs burned.

You have to get to the surface!

I kicked harder, my arms clawing, but just as my hand broke through the water, my body collided with a rock, and I was sucked back down again.

No!

The violent force of the water swirled me down in its unyielding icy realm. My lungs burned, panic seizing me.

I'm going to die.

My limbs grew sluggish. The dark, cold water wrapped around me, welcoming me to its unforgiving depths.

I sank again, blackness beginning to descend over my vision, when a strong arm suddenly encircled my waist.

A rush of magical power barreled around me, and then I shot through the surface.

The second my face broke free, I gasped for breath while sputtering and clawing.

"Avery, it's me! I got you! Don't fight me!"

It took a second before I recognized Wyatt's voice. Water still rushed over my head and threatened to pull me down again, but Wyatt swam toward the shore, cutting through the water despite the powerful current.

I clung to him while I coughed and struggled to breathe.

The bottom of the riverbed suddenly brushed against my soaked hiking shoes, and then Wyatt was carrying me in his arms up the bank.

I shivered and shook. Terror still coiled within me.

I'd almost drowned.

I'd been *seconds* away from death.

If Wyatt hadn't jumped in after me, I'd be dead.

Wyatt laid me against the river bank, his eyes burning like molten emeralds as he looked me over. "Are you hurt? Is anything broken?"

I shook my head, my teeth chattering uncontrollably. "No. I'm . . . I'm okay. But Eliza? Is she—"

"She's fine. I got her off that felled tree before I dove in after you." Wyatt breathed heavily. His T-shirt was soaked and clinging to his strong frame.

I glanced down, my jaw dropping when I saw that I was in a similar state. My shirt stuck to my skin, my breasts clearly visible through the fabric. My cargo pants felt like they weighed twenty pounds, and my shoes felt like concrete blocks.

Wyatt took in my soaked clothes, but his chin abruptly jutted up when he saw my breasts.

"I . . . I . . . don't know how to thank you," I stammered. My teeth wouldn't stop chattering, so I gritted them together to stop my shivering.

Wyatt shook his head, his brow furrowing. "What the hell happened?" he growled. "I came out of the forest to see Eliza reaching for you as she lay on that log and then you went under."

My teeth snapped again. "She fell off the log, and I went in after her, but after I got her up, the branch I'd been holding snapped—"

"You jumped in after her?"

"She fell, and I didn't—"

"You never go in after someone unless you're also secure. Otherwise you both could have drowned!"

A flush crept up my neck. "I'm sorry. I didn't know—" I snapped my mouth shut when another shiver hit me.

A low growl emitted from him before he snarled, "You're freezing." He pulled me against him, and his warm body covered mine. His calloused hands ran roughly up and down my limbs, as he used his large body and the friction from his palms to warm me.

For a moment, I closed my eyes, letting myself revel in the feel of him pushed against me and his blissful heat permeating my limbs.

After a few minutes, his hands slowed. "You're sure you're not hurt?"

I shook my head. "No. I don't think so. Just . . . uh . . . shaken up. I didn't think I was going to survive that."

His arms tightened. "I didn't know if I would get to you in time."

"But you did." I gave him what I hoped was a reassuring smile.

He pulled back, just enough to see my face better. Light rimmed his irises, the same light that I'd seen when he'd been watching me have dinner with Nicholas in the cafeteria.

He lifted a finger, his expression impossible to read, as he brushed a wet strand of hair from my face.

I closed my eyes, relishing his touch, as an entirely new feeling made me shiver.

But as soon as that electric tingle shot to my toes, Wyatt lunged off me.

Gasping, I opened my eyes to see him standing two yards up the bank. His jaw worked, his face dark. "We should head back. Eliza's not well."

My lips parted, as shame flowed over me. *Did I really just bask in my commander's arms while my friend is sick, feverish, and alone on the riverbank?*

"You're right. Of course." I pushed against the bank, my limbs still shaky, but when he reached out to steady me, I shook my head. "I'm fine. I'll follow you."

His hand hovered in mid-air for a moment before he lowered it. "Stay close. You drifted pretty far downstream, so we'll have to hack our way through the brush to get back to the trail."

I nodded.

Wyatt forged our way through the tangled bushes and trees along the river's edge, while I followed closely behind him. Exhaustion made the trek difficult, and I couldn't get images of the icy river and Wyatt's strong arms out of my mind.

One thing I knew? If he hadn't found me when he did, I would be dead.

CHAPTER TEN

WYATT

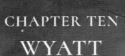

Eliza was lying on the riverbank, burning up with fever by the time we reached her. She was shivering, soaking wet, and mumbling incoherent sentences.

Shit. She was worse than I'd originally thought. I kneeled on the muddy bank and felt her pulse. "Eliza? Can you hear me?"

She only mumbled more.

Avery crouched on Eliza's other side, picking up her friend's limp hand. Tense lines formed around her mouth. "She's *really* sick, isn't she?"

"Yes." Cursing, I pulled out my tablet. Thankfully, it was waterproof. I placed a call to the command center and barked out orders.

Minutes later, a helicopter hovered above us and an SF squad was helping us climb aboard. Nobody said a thing when they appraised our wet clothes and Eliza's fever-glazed eyes. She was so weak she couldn't stand. Two SF members had to carry her into the bird.

The worry on Avery's face increased. She kept her knees locked together and her attention on her squad mate when the helicopter took off. Minutes later, we were back at headquarters.

The second we touched the ground, the team rushed Eliza out, which left Avery and me in the helicopter as the pilot shut it down.

"Bad day?" the pilot flashed me a grin before unbuckling his seatbelt.

I sighed heavily. "Suppose you could say that, although it didn't start out that way."

The pilot chuckled. "Your new recruit should be in the healing center by now. I'm sure she'll be fine. Anything in particular you want me to put in my report?"

"Just the facts."

The pilot nodded before glancing at Avery, his gaze dipping to her breasts. In her wet T-shirt, Avery's tits were on full display, the round globes clearly outlined while her nipples peaked.

Avery's focus was still out the window, to where Eliza had gone, but when she turned her attention back to us, her cheeks flushed.

She hastily crossed her arms, and my wolf snarled inside me, a low warning growl erupting from my chest before I could stop it.

The pilot whipped his attention to his report. "Anyway, take care, friend," he said before disembarking.

I didn't reply. Rage still simmered beneath my skin that he'd been checking out Avery, that he'd seen what was *mine*.

The second that thought registered, I jolted. *Mine?* Avery wasn't mine.

I rammed a hand through my wet hair, my pulse quickening at my instinctual reaction.

Avery cleared her throat, then said hesitantly, "Do you mind if I check on Eliza?"

The part of my brain that functioned on autopilot noted that she didn't say *sir* at the end of her question, but I didn't correct her. I was still reeling from what had just happened. And it seemed hypocritical to demand that she follow protocol when I clearly hadn't—she was a new recruit, off limits, not *mine*.

Concentrate, Jamison. You're the commander here.

"That's fine," I replied in a sterner tone than I intended. "I'd like to check on her, too, but first I need to make sure the other recruits know they're off duty until Monday."

"Oh, right." Avery shook her head. "I completely forgot the others are waiting for us at the end of the trail."

"Exactly." They'd probably been waiting for some time.

I pulled out my tablet again and posted my request on the SF commanders' forum, alerting my fellow Majors that I was in need of help. Within ten seconds, a reply came through. Major Patrichy offered to collect them.

I shoved my tablet back into my pocket. "Okay, let's go." I unbuckled my belt and looked at Avery expectantly.

She floundered with her seatbelt. Not surprising since the buckle had two complicated latches. For someone not used to them, they could be tricky. She also kept eyeing my chest.

I looked down and realized my shirt was sticking to me too. A low hum of satisfaction filled me.

She'd just checked me out.

Her fingers slipped on the latches again.

Before I could stop myself, I reached forward. "Let me help you."

My fingers brushed hers. Her fingertips felt like ice. I scowled. She was cold, and I didn't like that even though it shouldn't bother me. New recruits had to grow used to hardship. It was part of training.

Yet . . . I didn't like it.

A second later, the seatbelt slid off, and she gave me a shaky smile. "Thanks."

I grunted, not able to manage more.

Water droplets fell off our clothes when we jumped out of the helicopter. We began walking to the healing center, Avery at my side. Several SF members marching in the field and training nearby gave us double takes. Our wet clothes were definitely attracting attention.

"Was Eliza sick the entire hike today?" I asked, anything to distract myself from Avery's wet T-shirt.

"I think so, but she was trying to hide it."

"Is that why you stayed at her side, because she wasn't feeling well?"

"For the most part, yes."

My brow furrowed. "That was rather noble of you."

She shrugged, but her cheeks heated. "She would have done the same for me."

"Maybe, but regardless, you shouldn't have been put in that position. I should have noticed she wasn't well. This is my fault."

Her mouth fell open. "No, it's not." She shook her head, and then a thoughtful expression formed on her face.

"What?"

She shook her head sheepishly. "Nothing, I mean, it's just that you still blame yourself for everything when a situation goes bad, like you did in high school, even when you're not the only party at fault."

I grunted again, not sure what to make of that comment, but damn, she remembered those kind of details about me? "It's the alpha in me," I finally said. "It's my instinct to take responsibility and take the blame if someone under my command is hurt."

She sighed. "Even so, you couldn't have known Eliza was sick. She was purposefully hiding it from you and trying to from me. I was right beside her all day, and it wasn't until the river that I truly saw how bad she was, so it's really not your fault."

I made a discontented sound but didn't comment further,

although inside my wolf was preening. He liked that Avery sought to comfort us and make us see reason.

It was exactly what one's mate would do.

My stomach bottomed out, my breath snagging in my chest. *WTF. Seriously.* That was one word that should not be floating around in my vocabulary.

Thankfully, the healing center came into view with its green medical sign hanging above the door.

"I wonder what's wrong with her," Avery said, oblivious to my ridiculous thoughts. "She said she's been feeling sick all week, and it's been getting worse."

I thought about Eliza being a fairy and what it'd said in her file. I had my suspicions about what ailed her, but I wouldn't know for sure until the witches confirmed it.

I pulled the door open for Avery. She slipped past me, our chests nearly brushing as a few SF members strolled behind us on the sidewalk.

"You two go for a swim?" one of them called good-naturedly.

I forced a chuckle, but it was hard to feign lightheartedness considering all that had happened.

The door closed behind us, but instead of heading toward the stairs, I found myself going to the elevators, unable to help it since I knew it was the best option for Avery. "I'm guessing after your first full week of training that the stairs sound rather painful right now?"

She breathed a sigh of relief. "Yes, they do. My calves are already cramping."

I frowned, eyeing her wet clothes again. I had a feeling the healing center's cool air conditioning wasn't helping. Dammit but that bothered me too.

The elevator doors dinged open, and we stepped on board. As we glided up, Avery massaged her neck.

My eyebrows drew together. *Don't ask it. Don't* ask *it!* "Sore?" I asked.

She let her arm fall, her expression sheepish. "A little."

I once again told myself it wasn't my concern, but then I found myself saying, "I'll ask the witches to make you a potion."

The doors slid open, and the healing center waited ahead of us. For once, it was busy. Healing witches hurried down the hallways while a few moans and painful calls came from several patient rooms.

"Is everything okay?" Avery asked in alarm when a particularly loud wail reached us.

I strode forward, my long strides eating up the floor. "It will be. I got an alert that a squad came back this afternoon. A few were beat-up, but they'll be fine."

I thought about the team that flew off on Avery's first day. They'd had a nasty run-in with a group of formidable half-demons and an ancient vamp during their assignment. We were lucky we hadn't lost anyone.

"Major Jamison!" Sally said from the central healing station. The red-headed witch looked at me expectantly, her eyes brightening. "Your recruit is in room 239. Cora's attending to her." Her attention shifted to our clothes, her brow furrowing.

Water dripped onto the floor around us.

Her lips pursed. "Hmm, that will not do. Let me help with that." She came around the station and lifted her hands, her fingers waving elegantly in the air as she whispered a spell.

Warm air blew around us, our hair and clothes lifting from our bodies. Magic shimmered over my skin, and when our clothes settled, they were dry again.

I gave her a crooked smile. "Thanks, Sally."

Pink tinted her cheeks, and a shrill giggle escaped her before she clamped her mouth shut. "Of course, Major Jamison," she said from beneath her lashes. "Always happy to help."

Avery also murmured her thanks as her gaze traveled between me and Sally. I felt the immediate need to reassure her that Sally meant nothing to me and the interest was entirely one-sided, but then I mentally slapped myself.

Just because Avery caught onto Sally's flirtation didn't mean that Avery cared if the witch was flirting with me.

Gritting my teeth, I set off down the hall.

Avery followed behind me, peeking into the rooms we passed. In one room, three witches hovered over an SF member lying on the bed. He writhed in pain, one leg coated in blood. Two of the witches held him down while the third mumbled an incantation under her breath.

When a fourth witch saw Avery watching, she gave her a heated glare before snapping the privacy curtain closed.

Avery's eyes widened, and she jerked her attention away.

When we reached room 239, I knocked on the closed door. "Private River? May we come in?"

The door opened with a flourish, revealing Cora—a stout witch with graying hair. "Major Jamison, your recruit is doing much better." She stepped to the side, allowing us to enter.

The room was small with a single bed and a lone window. Eliza lay on the bed, propped up on pillows, looking the picture of perfect health.

Avery blinked. "Eliza? What the heck, are you okay now?"

"I most certainly am!" She grinned, revealing her pointy teeth. "I feel so much better. Cora's potion helped immensely."

The older witch's jowls jiggled when she shook her head sternly at Eliza. "This young lady was suffering from a severe case of fae lands withdrawal. She should have come to me immediately when she began feeling unwell this week."

So it was fae lands withdrawal, exactly what I'd suspected.

"You mean this week is your first time leaving the fae lands?" Avery asked Eliza incredulously. "Ever?"

Eliza shrugged sheepishly. "I grew up in Elsfairdasvee. Most from my village never come to earth. We're too remote, and the portal is too far."

Avery frowned. "I'm trying to remember where Elsfair-dasvee is. It's in the far north, right?"

"That's correct." Eliza beamed. "My village is small and still follows the old ways. Most never leave."

My brow furrowed as Avery and Eliza continued talking. Even though Eliza had grown up in a small village, it was still unusual for fairies to suffer from withdrawal symptoms upon entering the earthly realm. The only time that typically occurred was when a fairy child visited earth for the first time.

But most fae children had made the realm crossing enough times by the time they reached adulthood that their bodies had adjusted to the lesser magical environment of earth. And most adults never experienced withdrawals even if it was their first crossing. Most. But not all.

I inhaled, taking in the strong magical scent that coated Eliza. She was definitely from the old ways. She had an ancient magical tang to her—it possibly also made her more prone to withdrawals.

But whatever the case for her physiological condition, her sickness was an oversight I shouldn't have missed. I should have been monitoring her better this week, even if withdrawals in an adult were rare. I paused, thinking again of what Avery had said. About how I blamed myself when things went wrong. Another twinge of satisfaction rolled through me that she'd remembered that detail about my personality.

I raked a hand through my hair. *Not important, Jamison!*

"Excuse me, girls, but I have a few more things to chart." Cora brushed to the side of Eliza's bed and held a magical assessment device over the fairy's head.

Avery backed up, giving the witch room.

While Cora was scanning Eliza, I stood at the end of the bed and crossed my arms. "Private River, I owe you an apology. I should have been monitoring you better this week, and for that I am sorry, but I also need you to tell me when you're unwell.

Pretending you're not sick when you are, not only puts you at risk but your squad too." My chest tightened when an image of Avery in the river shot to the front of my mind. "Private Meyers almost died in that river today. You're never to jeopardize your squad mate like that again. Understood?"

Eliza lowered her chin. "Yes, sir. I am very sorry." She raised wide eyes filled with guilt to Avery. "And I am very sorry to you as well, Avery. I very nearly cost you your life. That is a most egregious error in judgment. Please forgive me."

Avery shook her head, looking embarrassed under Eliza's plea-filled apology. "It's fine, really. Don't worry about it, but I appreciate that, thank you."

Eliza dipped her head again, and I grunted, satisfied that the recruit had learned her lesson.

Cora finished with her device and pocketed it. "She'll be spending the night here, Major. Just to make sure that the dose I gave her is strong enough to cure her."

I nodded curtly. "Could you also provide a potion for Private Meyers? She's an ambassador recruit and just finished her first week of training. She's feeling sore."

"Ah, of course." Sympathy dripped from Cora's words, as if Avery's low-magic profession explained her fatigue.

Cora shuffled to the cabinets and extracted a small vial.

"Thank you," Avery said, pocketing it.

We said our goodbyes and left the healing center.

Back outside, the mid-afternoon sun shone brightly above. Avery's stomach gave a loud grumble, and she slapped a hand over her abdomen, her cheeks flushing.

I quirked an eyebrow up. "Hungry?"

"Yes. I mean, we *did* miss lunch, because you know, a certain someone had his recruits run a mile this morning and then hike six this afternoon." The second the words left her lips, she clamped her mouth shut.

It took all of my control not to laugh at her smart comment.

It was so easy to fall back into how we'd been in high school. Even though we hadn't been close friends, we'd had many mutual friends which meant we sometimes hung out. I'd loved every second of those nights.

Still, I smoothed my expression. That was then. This was now. I couldn't joke around like a sixteen-year-old kid anymore. "The cafeteria should still be serving lunch. I imagine the other recruits are there too."

Her smile faltered, and her cheeks flushed. "Of course, sir. I'll go find them."

She scurried away, and against my better judgment, I watched.

Her T-shirt and cargos still clung to her curves even though she wasn't wet anymore. And when she walked, her hips swayed, as if she were a belly dancer entrancing a man with her round ass and narrow waist.

Damn. She was *so* beautiful.

My cock throbbed, stiffening in my pants. I growled in irritation and shoved my hands into my pockets to hide the bulge.

When she reached the door, she glanced back to where I was standing. With a start, I realized she knew I'd been watching her the entire time she'd walked away.

AFTER MY EMBARRASSING display of acting like a besotted teenager, I retreated to my apartment to fix myself lunch in the privacy of my kitchen. I could have followed Avery into the cafeteria, even shared a meal with her, but that wasn't wise.

Not only was her scent still clinging to me, but my thoughts kept clouding with images of her walking away. Seeing her ass move so provocatively . . .

I was permanently tenting.

But more than that, I kept getting flashbacks of her falling in the river.

I stood at my counter, making a sandwich, but the distraction didn't stop the tension that had been building steadily within me.

Now that the excitement of the river was over and I knew Eliza was okay, I allowed myself time to process it all, and one realization kept barreling into me.

I'd almost lost Avery.

Only a few hours ago, she'd nearly drowned. If I'd emerged even twenty seconds later from the forest . . .

Fear ran through me again, and the knife I'd been holding clattered to the plate.

I placed my hands on the counter, leaning into them. Seeing Eliza soaking wet, splayed out on the tree, screaming for Avery, had made panic consume me.

I'd never felt anything like that.

Straightening, I picked up the knife again and finished smearing mayonnaise on the bread. I then loaded it with beef and cheese.

But my wolf still snarled inside me, not caring that our stomach growled.

Agitation oozed from him that Avery had been put in danger. Our protective instincts raged so strongly with her, more so than I'd ever felt for a new recruit . . . or anyone.

A memory of blurring into action, grabbing Eliza off the tree, then diving into the river filled my mind. Class four rapids raged in that part of the river. I hadn't known how long Avery had been under. Terror had ripped through me when I'd swum beneath the surface, searching for her, because even with my wolf's superior strength and speed, navigating the river hadn't been easy.

But then her hand had broken through the surface, allowing me to locate her. I'd turned into a torpedo, shooting straight for her. Even with that clue, though, it was truly a miracle I'd located her and pulled her to the surface in time.

Because if I hadn't . . .

My breath stopped, and I leaned against the counter again, my heart beating hard.

No, I can't think that way. She's okay. She's safe. No harm came to her.

Yet blood still pounded through my veins. I hated that she'd been put in harm's way. *Hated* it.

My wolf snarled. An image of our teeth elongating and biting into the fragile flesh at the base of Avery's neck filled my mind.

I jolted upright, my spine cracking into place at how quickly I'd moved. I pushed away from the counter, my sandwich entirely forgotten.

Claim her? You want to claim her?

He whined.

We can't do that. She's not ours.

He snarled then whined again, his agitation rising.

I stabbed a hand through my hair. *We can't!*

But Avery's near death had propelled my wolf's feelings for her to an entirely new level. He wanted her safe at all costs, and claiming her was the only way to ensure that.

I paced the length of my kitchen, raking my hand through my hair again and again.

I would be lying to myself if I tried to pretend that I didn't feel the same as him. More than anything I wanted to wrap Avery in my arms, shield her from the world, and protect her from any danger. I knew that she wasn't incapable and that she was stronger than she gave herself credit for, but she was still weaker than most supernaturals.

Which made my protective instincts roar with a vengeance.

But . . . she wasn't mine.

She was a new recruit who I had to train even if that occasionally put her in harm's way. That was how training went.

My wolf snarled, enraged that I was fighting what he wanted.

I stalked out of the kitchen, leaving my sandwich uneaten on the counter.

I needed to run.

This was absolute madness. Avery Meyers was my *recruit*. She wasn't mine to claim and protect.

I yanked open my door and bolted down the hallway, but try as I might to run from what I was feeling, I couldn't.

With every fiber of my being, I wanted to take her for my own.

And that wasn't possible.

CHAPTER ELEVEN

AVERY

T wenty-four hours later, Eliza was back in our apartment, chipper, and healthy again—as if the river incident had never happened—which meant Charlotte insisted we finally head out for a celebratory girls' night, even if we were running a day late.

"Which should I wear?" Eliza asked. She held up two outfits from the fae lands. One was a frilly skirt that looked like puffy cotton candy. The other was a neon-green jumpsuit with glittering silver stripes running up the legs and arms.

"Um . . . neither of those." Charlotte snatched them from her, then shoved a pair of skintight black pants and a sleeveless white silk halter top into her hands. "You've got the arms for this, but you gotta keep yourself glamoured. Can you do that for eight hours?"

My eyebrows shot up. "Eight hours? How long do you plan to be drinking?"

Charlotte waggled her eyebrows. "All night, but we'll be dancing too. What fun would it be to drink and not dance?"

Eliza cocked her head and slipped into the black pants. "I've never been to an earthly bar before. Are they like *salopas* in the fae lands?"

I shook my head. "No, there's no *leminai*. Our alcohol is much less potent, and since there's no magic, we have actual servers called waitresses or waiters." In the fae lands, *salopas*—the fae version of a bar—had bartenders but no servers. Magically enchanted glasses and trays served the patrons.

Eliza grinned. "It still sounds most wonderful."

"Most wonderful indeed," Charlotte replied before digging in her drawers again. "Now, as for you . . ." She eyed me. "How about this?" She held up a black miniskirt and a long-sleeved sky-blue off-the-shoulder crop top. "You've got the body to pull this off."

I eyed the miniscule material. "Will anything be covered?"

She laughed. "Come on, girl. Put it on."

I did as she said but couldn't stop from tugging on the skirt. It barely came to mid-thigh, and the shirt left a good two inches of my abdomen showing. Not to mention the low-cut off-the-shoulder top left an abundance of my cleavage on display. Like half of my boobs. I surveyed my appearance in the full-length mirror as Charlotte let out a wolf whistle.

"Holy shit, girl. You're gonna have every hottie in Boise panting after you when they see you in that."

My eyes widened. I wasn't a prude, but I also preferred being dressed in public.

I started taking the top off. "How about I wear that—"

"No way." Charlotte grabbed my hand before I pulled the shirt over my head. "Wear it. Trust me. We won't have to buy any drinks all night."

"That's what I'm afraid of."

She laughed. "You *want* us to buy our own drinks?"

"Well, no, but I'm more afraid of what the guys buying us drinks will expect in return."

Charlotte made a disgusted sound and slipped into a sleeveless button-up dress that she left half undone in the front. At least I wasn't the only one showing off boobage.

Turning to the mirror, she twirled her hair up into a messy bun on top of her head. "If some dude thinks that buying a woman drinks means he's automatically getting laid, then he needs to join the twenty-first century."

Eliza giggled. "I'm quite excited to see what humans are like at drinking establishments. I haven't met many."

I laughed. "They're not much different than fairies. Just no magical tricks up their sleeves."

Eliza smiled at me serenely. "In that case, don't worry about the clothes, Avery. If any humans get too demanding, I'll give them a friendly shove, or if that doesn't deter them, I can always bite." Her lips pulled back, giving Charlotte and me a full view of her wicked teeth.

Charlotte burst out laughing, and I soon joined in. As innocent and naïve as Eliza seemed, she was also a full-blooded fairy, which meant she was significantly stronger than any human male, and one bite from her could tear out a person's artery.

"If only I had enough magic to defend myself," I muttered as I tugged at my shirt again.

Charlotte slung her arm around my shoulders. "No matter. That's why you're here, right? To learn how to get out of tough situations if they arise?"

"True, but other than being so sore I can barely walk up a flight of stairs, I haven't learned shit about escaping a crisis."

AN HOUR LATER, we slipped into my Explorer in the SF garage, and after passing the security checks, we were out of the Supernatural Forces headquarters and cruising down the foothills. The setting sun set the landscape aglow. Fresh summer air flowed in through our open windows, and excitement coursed through me.

It had been so long since I'd gone out for a night with girl-friends. During my last year at university, I'd been so immersed in my studies, that I'd neglected my social life. Thanks to Charlotte, that appeared to now be remedied.

"Where is that bar you heard about, Charlotte?" I asked her as we drove into Boise.

Since it was Saturday evening, the sidewalks were full of people strolling between the restaurants, bars, and entertainment venues.

"Just at the corner up there. We better look for a place to park."

I found a spot on the street two blocks past the bar. When we stepped onto the sidewalk, a few heads turned in our direction.

Charlotte held her chin high, looking the picture of complete confidence, while Eliza looked around with wide-eyed delight. I, on the other hand, managed to plaster on a smile and feign indifference to the attention we were creating. Even though I felt half naked, I wasn't going to let that ruin my evening.

Our heels clicked on the wood floor when we stepped into the bar. Although it was only early evening, it was already packed and *Blinding Lights* was blaring from the speakers.

"I love this song!" Charlotte exclaimed as she began moving to the beat. She propelled us to the bar and slid onto one of the barstools. Eliza and I propped ourselves on the stools at her side.

The bartender came over—a big, burly man with a full beard and paunch stomach—and gave us a once-over. "You ladies have ID?"

We all pulled out our drivers licenses. One of the first things the SF provided for new recruits was in-state identification for instances such as this.

After inspecting our IDs, the bartender's shoulders relaxed. "What can I get you?"

I opened my mouth to order a mojito, but Charlotte placed her hand over mine. "Nothing just yet, thanks."

The bartender shrugged and moved to other patrons farther down the bar.

I raised an eyebrow at Charlotte, and she rolled her eyes. "We're not paying for our drinks, remember?"

"But what if nobody offers to buy us any?"

"Trust me. That's not gonna happen."

Sure enough, not even two minutes passed before a group of college-aged guys made their way toward us. Since my internal radar didn't even vibrate, I knew they were all humans.

Eliza swiveled on her seat and flashed them an innocent smile. Her white teeth were square, her glamour job utter perfection. "Good evening, gentlemen," she said. "What a fine evening to be in this drinking establishment, don't you agree?"

Charlotte muffled a laugh as the guys paused.

"What she means is what are you boys up to?" Charlotte asked coquettishly, leaning back against her stool to prop an elbow on the smooth bar top. The tallest one's gaze dipped to her boobs on display.

The stiffness in the guys' shoulders eased as Charlotte charmed them to our sides. Within minutes, the three of us held free shots as our new acquaintances circled us like vultures.

We talked and laughed, and while the conversation was trivial, it was fun. I didn't catch half of their names, but the guy standing closest to me, Tim, seemed intent on keeping my attention. He was probably around six feet with khakis and a collared shirt. He had preppy frat boy written all over him.

"Have you lived here long?" he asked and gave me a lazy smile.

"No, actually, we all just moved here. We're roommates and new to the area."

His eyebrows rose, his smile broadening. "Is that right? You should let me show you around then. What part of town do you live in?"

"Oh, just north of here." I kept my answer vague and wanted to kick myself for not thinking of a better cover.

But he didn't seem perturbed. "What are you doin' tomorrow?"

I was about to answer when a change of energy shifted the air. A wave of alpha werewolf power wafted toward me, eliciting goosebumps on my arms. The long-sleeved low-cut top did little to alleviate the chill from whoever had entered the bar.

"Shit," Charlotte muttered under her breath. "Our commander just arrived. I wonder if he was sent to keep an eye on us."

I shifted uncomfortably on my stool as Tim tried to engage me in conversation again, but I tracked Wyatt's movements like a hawk.

He scanned the room until he spotted us. Nostrils flaring, he stalked to the other side of the bar. Since he was so tall, he rose over most of the humans, his large build making him look intimidating and lethal. My stomach curled as a burst of lust shot through me. *Damn, he's hot as sin.*

Wyatt took a seat on the opposite side of the room, never bothering to acknowledge us. I had a feeling Charlotte was right about him being here to monitor us. While we were all grown women, we were also new to the Supernatural Forces. No doubt a babysitter had been sent to make sure we didn't do anything against protocol.

"Should we go say hello to him?" Eliza asked innocently.

Charlotte shook her head. "Definitely not. In fact, I think it's time we danced." She hopped off her stool, and the tall blond who'd been doing his best to enamor her grinned devilishly.

"You lookin' for someone to dance with?" he asked.

"Thought you'd never ask." She twisted her finger around his shirt before tugging him toward the dance floor.

The second they hit it, Charlotte swayed her hips and lifted her arms.

Tim looked at me expectantly. "What about you? You wanna dance?"

Another shift in energy peaked my internal radar. Across the room, a waitress set a tall beer in front of Wyatt, which he picked up and half downed in one swallow, but his glower didn't abate.

He still hadn't looked our way, and from the irritated expression he wore, I guessed babysitting was the last place he wanted to be. A moment of guilt stole over me.

We'd essentially stolen his Saturday night. Still, babysitter or not, we were here, so we might as well enjoy ourselves.

"Why not." I hopped off my barstool and followed Tim to the dance floor.

Eliza squealed in glee and joined us as the third guy pulled her into his arms.

The dim atmosphere, flashing strobe lights, and steady beat soon distracted all of my attention from our commander.

I closed my eyes and let myself enjoy the moment. Alcohol swam through my veins, making me lose my inhibitions. I swayed on the dance floor with my girlfriends around me, getting lost in the music, until two male hands gripped my waist.

My eyes popped open to see Tim staring down at me hungrily. He pulled me tighter against him, my hips flush against his. His pupils dilated, and the telltale sign gave away his arousal.

I inched back. I didn't mind dancing with him, but I wasn't a humping pole. More and more humans joined us, and by the end of the song, the dance floor was packed.

I closed my eyes again since Tim had backed off, but then stiffened when his hot breath wafted against my ear. "You wanna come home with me?"

I opened my eyes to see Tim staring at my cleavage. I'd always been well endowed, and the top Charlotte had forced on me left little to the imagination.

"What do you say?" he asked, and pressed against me more. His erection rubbed against my stomach but did nothing to excite me.

I ground my teeth, then opened my mouth to tell him off for rubbing on me like a sex mannequin, when another rush of power flowed over my skin like prickly needles.

I stiffened and swept my attention to the other side of the room.

Wyatt still sat on his dining chair. An empty glass of beer sat in front of him, and his second was already half consumed. A terrifying scowl filled his face, and it was directed entirely at Tim.

"So? What do you say?" Tim pushed, rubbing himself on me again.

I shoved him back. "How about we just dance?"

His jaw tightened, but he nodded. "Sure, we can dance."

I moved to the beat again and inched closer to Charlotte and Eliza. Charlotte's hands were still in the air as she waved her arms in tune to the music. She was a natural on the dance floor, which wasn't surprising.

Most werewolves were incredibly intuitive with their bodies. At least in that department, I could claim the same. While I didn't have a full-blooded werewolf's height or strength, I did inherit a natural inclination toward coordination.

I was just beginning to enjoy myself again when Tim's breath wafted against my neck for a second time. "You're really fucking sexy, you know that?"

I glared at him, trying not to let him interrupt my dancing. The dude was seriously getting on my nerves.

But then his hands curved around my hips to cup my ass.

I gasped. *Motherfucker.*

"I'd love nothing more than to feel your tight—"

Tim's hands were suddenly ripped off me. A wave of power slammed into my chest that was so strong my breath seized in my lungs.

"What the hell?" Tim exclaimed.

My mouth dropped when Tim landed two yards away sprawled across the dance floor.

Wyatt towered over him, rage strumming from my commander in waves.

Eyes widening, I gulped. I hastily reviewed the last few minutes on the dance floor. Had I done something? Said something I wasn't supposed to? Was I in trouble?

"I'm sorry, did I—"

"We need to leave," Wyatt cut in, his tone clipped.

Flustered, Eliza twirled around, as if searching for whatever rule we'd broken, while Charlotte pouted. But despite their surprise and irritation, my squad mates went to grab their things.

Wyatt stopped them. "It's only Private Meyers who needs to return to headquarters. You're welcome to stay and enjoy your evening."

Eliza cocked her head, her purple hair glinting off the flashing lights while Charlotte frowned. "But if Avery's in trouble, then surely—"

"It's regarding the Institute. It doesn't involve SF business."

My stomach dropped. "What?"

"We can still come back," Charlotte offered.

But I shook my head as worry strummed through me. "No, it's fine. Stay. Enjoy the night out. Really, it's okay," I added when my squad mates tried to protest. I shoved my Explorer's keys into Charlotte's hand. "Drive safely on your way back."

Her fingers curled around the key ring before she stuffed it into her dress's pocket. Even though we'd all been drinking, I wasn't worried about them driving back to headquarters drunk. Werewolves and fairies metabolized alcohol differently than humans. It would take more drinks than what Charlotte was downing to impair her driving.

I grabbed my things and followed Wyatt toward the main door.

Tim watched us, seething.

Outside on the sidewalk, the moon shone down on us. The air was still warm, a summer breeze flowing through the streets, as laughter, music, and conversation drifted in the air.

The downtown was alive, and the night was just getting started.

But my night had come to an abrupt halt.

"Sir, did I do something wrong?" I asked as Wyatt led me toward his vehicle at a clipped pace. "Is that why the Institute contacted you?"

Wyatt ran a hand over his face but didn't reply.

A sinking feeling formed in my stomach. This couldn't be good.

I mentally reviewed the handbook of rules the Institute and SF had sent me before my first day. I didn't recall anything I'd done that had broken protocol, but I must have done *something*.

"Major Jamison? If I've done something against SF protocol, I'm very sorry."

"You didn't do anything against protocol."

Confusion filled me, and with every step I took, my alcohol-laden brain cleared a little more. Come to think of it, why was Wyatt only telling me this now? If he'd come to the bar to retrieve me for ambassador business, why did he have a drink first? And why did he wait so long to approach me?

"Sir, what's going on?"

Wyatt ran a hand over his stubbly cheeks again, the power off him beginning to simmer.

I sucked in a breath, wondering if the humans we passed on the sidewalk could feel the volatility swimming beneath my commander's skin. It felt like molten lava was burning through me.

"I'll explain in the truck," Wyatt replied. He stopped at a black F-150 before opening the door for me.

Flustered, I climbed into the seat. No guy had ever opened the door for me before.

But before I could compose myself, Wyatt slammed my door shut and was on the other side slipping into his seat.

The engine roared to life before he deftly swung out of the parking spot and gunned it toward headquarters.

CHAPTER TWELVE
AVERY

My stomach twisted and turned as violently as the winding hills that Wyatt drove us through to reach headquarters. Evening was setting in, and a few stars peeked through the darkening sky like diamonds in an obsidian cave.

I tried to concentrate on those specks of light that had traveled millions of light years across the vast universe to reach us.

Instead, my head swam with vertigo.

Perhaps drinking so much hadn't been a good idea. Unlike most supernaturals, I didn't metabolize it any faster than humans.

I angled my body toward my commander. He looked tense, his hands gripping the wheel firmly. That edge of energy still clung to him, and my internal radar peeked at maximum capacity.

Wow, he's majorly peeved.

"Wyatt, what's going on?" I slapped a hand over my mouth when my unfiltered tipsy response didn't stay inside my head. "I mean, *sir*, what's going on? Why did the Institute call you about me?"

I blamed my drunken state for the fact that I'd once again addressed my superior incorrectly and so bluntly. Seriously, I was never going to get this right.

But Wyatt didn't chastise me. Instead he glanced my way in the dark cab. His green eyes glittered, his werewolf origins rimming them in gold. I knew enough about werewolves—I mean I *was* partly werewolf—to know that heightened emotions were the cause of glowing eyes.

As for what Wyatt's heightened emotion was, I didn't know.

"You're supposed to check in with the Institute this weekend." His attention returned to the road. His jaw worked rhythmically as he navigated the foothills.

I brought a hand to my forehead. It felt as if the car was spinning. "Supposed to check in with them? That's what you pulled me from the bar for?"

"Yes," he replied, his tone clipped.

"Is it urgent? Are they wanting me to contact them right now?" I couldn't imagine that anything was so pressing that I needed to wake somebody up. After all it couldn't be more than two or three in the morning in Geneva, but if Wyatt said I needed to contact them, then maybe something had happened.

"I suppose it's not urgent," he said gruffly. "You can wait until tomorrow to check in."

I shook my head in confusion. "So . . . why am I going back to headquarters?"

His teeth ground together, like rocks grating on concrete. "Perhaps I acted a bit hastily," he finally said.

I had no idea how to reply to that. He obviously thought my priorities were with the Institute, so I would want to call them right away, but to come all the way down to the bar to pass along that message?

That just didn't make sense.

However, I was drunk, so maybe it did make sense to sober people.

Not wanting to dwell on it further, I sat back in my seat. Most likely, I was missing something. With any luck, tomorrow it would become clear.

Wyatt steered around a sharp curve on the snaking road.

My stomach lurched. "Sir, would you mind slowing down?" I gripped my door handle in alarm.

A flash of concern crossed his features. "Are you not feeling well?"

"I think I drank too much."

He swore and immediately slowed the vehicle, and some of the dizziness abated. I sank lower in my seat and brought a hand to my head.

"Should I open a window for you? Do you need me to pull over?"

"I can open the window." I fumbled with the switch but managed to lower it down. Warm air swirled into the cab, but the speed of the vehicle made it feel slightly cooler. I tipped my head to the side and relished the soft breeze.

Wyatt didn't say anything further, but the steadily rolling energy off him let me know something deeper was going on with my commander. But I couldn't be bothered trying to figure it out. It was taking everything in my power not to barf up the half-dozen shots I'd downed.

The magical barrier to the SF headquarters appeared ahead. I kept my eyes closed when we crossed through the portal. The free-falling sensation made my stomach almost hurl, but I managed to keep my lips pressed firmly together until we emerged in the SF garage.

Most of the aircraft were gone. Only one sat dormant in the center, a tarp covering it. About fifty cars were parked on the perimeter, and only a handful of technicians worked, probably because of the late hour.

"Major Jamison, good evening." One of the technicians came

to my open window to address my commander. When he spotted me, his eyebrows rose.

"Hello," I managed.

He merely tipped his head politely at Wyatt before directing us to a parking spot.

As soon as Wyatt parked, I was unbuckling my seatbelt and opening my door. I hadn't managed to place a foot on the ground before Wyatt was at my side.

"You don't look well. Perhaps I should take you to the healing center."

My eyes widened in alarm. The last thing I wanted was a second trip to the healing center for the witches to see me in another embarrassing state. My weaknesses had already reared their ugly heads enough times during the past five days. I didn't need another mark chalked against me.

"No, I'm fine. I just drank too much and need to walk it off. And water, I should probably drink some water."

At least my words weren't slurred.

Small miracles.

However, the concern on Wyatt's face only grew. Before I could protest further, he was slipping an arm around my waist and guiding me toward the door.

The feel of his warm hand pressed against my side made me shiver, and his alluring pine and oak scent swam through my senses.

An entirely new feeling grew in my stomach. How long had I dreamed of Wyatt touching me this way? When I'd been in high school, it had consumed my thoughts.

My heels clicked as he led me toward the door. It wasn't lost on me that every male in the garage turned their head when I passed. When I'd left with Eliza and Charlotte, the same thing had happened. But now, as a lone woman in a miniskirt and crop top, I felt like a neon sign blazing for attention.

A soft growl erupted from Wyatt.

Every technician snapped their gaze away.

I frowned. It was the second time tonight Wyatt had shown displeasure at males showing me attention. Was that why he'd taken me from the bar?

Wyatt held onto me down the stairs and through the tunnel to the main buildings. After gliding up the elevator and out the doors, we were once again outside and heading toward the barracks.

The moon shone down on us, and with each step we took, I became increasingly aware that Wyatt still held me. I knew I should tell him I was fine, that I was perfectly capable of walking on my own, but then he would let go.

And for the life of me, I didn't want him to.

He was still as kind and attentive as I remembered him. He just laughed less.

"You're as kind now as you were back then."

"Back then?"

Oh shit. I said that out loud.

"Never mind." I had enough of my wits about me to cement my mouth closed. "Did the Institute say who I should ask for tomorrow when I call?"

Wyatt cleared his throat. "Um, no. I just believe you're supposed to check in."

Check in? That's all? I'd intended to do that on Monday, after my first week had completed, since I'd never been giving a specific timeframe on my check-in calls, but even *I* knew about those.

"So they didn't—"

"Here we are. I'll help you into your apartment."

We'd reached the barracks, and he opened the door for me. I felt somewhat like an invalid with how much he hovered, but I knew part of that was due to his alpha werewolf origins.

Wyatt's father, Walter Jamison, was the Alpha of the British Columbia werewolf pack. I knew Wyatt's eldest brother was in line to take over his father's alpha status once his father stepped down, but that didn't mean Wyatt was any less dominant.

And as alpha werewolves went, they were nothing if not attentive to females. I reminded myself of that as we trudged up the stairs, but the stairwell swam around me, and I swayed.

Wyatt tightened his hold on my waist, but I knew it didn't mean anything. He was simply following his instinct, which was to protect and attend.

It was just another thing that made my heart patter around him.

"This is me." I said when we reached my door. I fumbled in my purse for my keys, then remembered that I'd given them to Charlotte. "Shit. Char has my keys. I'm locked out."

Wyatt chuckled. "That's what these are for." He lifted my hand and placed my finger against the magical holograph.

The door clicked open.

Before I could register that Wyatt was touching more of me, he opened the door and flipped the lights on. I expected him to leave since I was safely home, but he accompanied me into my apartment and closed the door.

Okay . . .

I kicked my heels off, and for the briefest moment, Wyatt's gaze drifted to my legs before his chin shot up.

I stopped my fidgeting. "Um, thank you for seeing me home. I'll be sure to call the Institute tomorrow to check in."

We faced one another awkwardly, and for the first time in the years I'd known Wyatt Jamison, he looked unsure of himself. He shoved his hands into his pockets, then released one and threaded it through his hair. "How about I get that glass of water for you?"

He moved at werewolf speed into the kitchen, which meant it looked like he disappeared and then reappeared by the sink. Before I could take another breath, he was pressing a glass of cool water into my palm. Only a little bit sloshed over the rim from his abrupt stop.

"Oh, thank you." I brought the glass to my lips and drank greedily. My head had begun to clear a bit, but I was still far from sober, because I still couldn't understand why my commander hadn't left.

But, since he was still here, I should be a good host. At least, that was what my foggy brain felt was the right thing to do.

"Are you hungry or thirsty?" I asked. "I could bake something."

Wyatt grunted. "I'm usually hungry."

I breezed past him into the kitchen, the air fluttering against my bare midriff. A squeaking sound behind me let me know Wyatt had sat on one of the barstools. The middle one squeaked loudly every time someone sat on it.

"I've been wanting to bake all week. In fact, I've been wanting to try a new sponge cake recipe."

Wyatt's lips tugged up in a crooked smile.

My heart stopped. Gods, he was so sexy.

Swirling back around, in my ataxic state I went to the cupboard to grab supplies.

One of the first things I'd checked as we'd settled into our apartment, was what supplies the SF had stocked in our shelves.

I'd been delighted to find all of the essentials for baking. Flour, sugar, salt, baking powder and soda, cocoa, the list went on. And the fridge held milk, butter, and eggs.

I fumbled in the shelves and pulled out what I needed. Behind me, Wyatt watched.

If either of us thought that it was odd that an SF commander was overlooking his new recruit while she whirled around drunkenly in her kitchen in a miniskirt, neither of us commented.

I flashed him what I hoped was a confident smile. "This won't take long."

CHAPTER THIRTEEN
WYATT

What the fuck am I doing?

Avery stood at the counter, her hands flying over the ingredients as she expertly measured flour, salt, sugar, and other white powders I had no idea what one did with. For someone still intoxicated, her concentration on baking was truly admirable.

But that didn't explain what I was doing here.

In her apartment.

Seated at her kitchen.

With a hard-on rivalling the Empire State Building.

Thankfully, my hunched position hid it.

I draped my forearms over the counter and tried to act like my behavior was perfectly normal as Avery chatted nervously and baked.

Despite her carrying on a steady stream of conversation as though hanging out with her commander on a Saturday night in her apartment was to be expected, we both knew it wasn't.

As for why she hadn't kicked me out yet, I didn't know. Although, I imagined the alcohol could be partly thanked for that.

Still, the way I was behaving . . . it wasn't decent.

But it was as if I couldn't control myself.

The second I heard that she and her roommates had left the SF to venture downtown for a night out, against my better judgment, I'd checked the security footage.

And when I saw the replay of her, Eliza, and Charlotte waltzing through the garage to Avery's car, that primal need to claim Avery had again taken root. My wolf had whined, urging me on.

It didn't help that every male head had turned in the garage to admire Avery as she passed by. I couldn't blame them. She was gorgeous. With her dark hair spilling down her back, the off-the-shoulder top which highlighted her ample breasts, and the miniskirt that just begged for a man to run his hands up and under it . . .

Any male with a libido was probably having similar thoughts.

And the thought of *that* drove me fucking crazy.

So what did I do? Did I reprimand myself for invading her privacy by checking the security footage? Did I ignore my irrational desire to follow her while telling my wolf to get his balls under control? Did I remind myself of my debt to Marcus and how I *couldn't* risk getting fired?

Of course not.

Instead of joining my squad mates for our usual Saturday night basketball game, I'd headed straight for my truck and sped downtown as fast as I could to make sure that some asshole didn't take advantage of Avery.

When I'd reached the area, I'd scoped the streets out until I found her vehicle, then I'd tracked her scent to the bar they'd gone into. Basically, I'd acted like a typical irrational and obsessive wolf when chasing a female.

And on some level I'd been aware of that, so I'd meant to stop acting like a jealous werewolf. I'd truly intended to just sit quietly on the sidelines, watching and waiting. I hadn't planned to interfere, unless she truly needed my help, but seeing the reaction she was causing . . .

It had taken everything in me to control my wolf.

A group of guys had flocked around Eliza, Charlotte, and Avery. They'd been young, probably early twenties, and their dicks were just waiting to get free.

The scent of their lust had awoken revenge inside my wolf. He'd demanded that we tear out the throat of every male looking at Avery with lust in his eyes. That tall one, Tim she had called him, had *reeked* of arousal. And the few times he'd touched her . . .

I'd nearly gone apeshit.

It was only the years of discipline that I'd learned at the SF that had kept me from turning into a raging wolf, but when Tim had ground his hips against hers and then cupped her ass—

That I couldn't take.

Before I could stop myself, I'd ripped him off her and made up some story about the Institute needing to speak with her and that she needed to return to the SF with me.

She'd believed me.

Of course she had.

Why wouldn't she?

She had no reason to doubt me, but now I could add *liar* to my list of transgressions that had taken place in the week since her arrival.

I raked a hand through my hair as she poured batter into two cake pans. She'd pulled her hair back into a low ponytail, but several tendrils had released from the restraint and fallen in front of her ears. A smudge of flour marred her cheek, and that intoxicated glassiness still coated her eyes, but she was smiling.

She was happy, if a little tipsy, and that made my wolf and me growl in pleasure.

"Do you want to lick the spoon?" She held the spatula out to me.

"Sure, thanks." Our fingers brushed, and her breathing hitched before she released the utensil. Another scent rose over the sugary concoction laying in the pan, and it was a scent I could spend the rest of my life smelling—Avery's arousal.

I'd scented hints of it all week, although until tonight, I'd never been entirely sure if those musky aromas had been because of me or if she'd been turned on by some other guy in her new squad.

An immense feeling of satisfaction rolled through me. So it was me.

My wolf growled in approval. She may still be drunk, but her arousal was one hundred percent *mine*.

My cock hardened even more as I licked the spatula. The taste momentarily distracted me. Damn. It was good.

"This is really tasty."

Avery blushed, her cheeks turning the most attractive shade of pink. "Just wait until you taste it with the jam and cream." She twirled away and carried the pan to the oven. "This needs to bake for twenty-five minutes. I'll make the jam while it's cooking."

She bent over to place the pan in the oven. Heat rolled out from the appliance. My jaw tightened when a flash of her panties was revealed under her short skirt. The black lace made even more blood rush to my erection. What I wouldn't give to rip that flimsy material off her and bury my face between her thighs.

She straightened, and the peep show ended. I gave a silent thanks upward, since I felt like such a lowlife for not averting my attention when I should have, but I also cursed because I wanted nothing more than to continue enjoying the view.

I plowed a hand through my hair again. How the hell was I going to survive three more months of this?

CHAPTER FOURTEEN
AVERY

We only had one pint of berries in the fridge, but it was enough to make the jam. I mashed the raspberries, added the sugar, and then slid the mixture into a pan to boil. Once it was cooked, I set it aside to cool.

"Now for the buttercream." I offered my commander a tentative smile.

Wyatt still sat at the counter as the scent of the baking cake filled the kitchen. "Where did you learn how to bake?" he asked.

I shrugged and grabbed the butter. "I taught myself with the help of cookbooks. I moved a lot growing up, so when we arrived somewhere new, it took a while to make friends, so initially I always filled my time by baking."

His arms stayed crossed as he hunched over the counter. His wide frame looked massive in the small kitchen. "Have you made anything else this week?"

"Just a batch of almond scones the other night. Charlotte and Eliza have become my guinea pigs as I try out new recipes."

"I imagine they're not complaining."

"They haven't yet, but since it's only our first week together, that may change. Charlotte did make a comment about me trying to fatten her up."

Wyatt laughed, and that strange feeling swam through me again. He was still here, hanging out with me on a Saturday night while I made a sponge cake with raspberry jam and cream. It was all so . . . domestic. Something I would expect to do with my boyfriend, not my commander.

Fluttering began anew in my stomach as I struggled to make sense of it. I didn't know what was going on, but even if I still felt a bit intoxicated, it didn't stem my enjoyment of having Wyatt in my kitchen.

Just being near him felt good.

After I added the icing sugar and milk to the butter, I whipped it all together and held out a dollop of buttercream for Wyatt to taste. "Do you approve?"

Wyatt took the spoon and slipped it in his mouth. His lips wrapped around the spoon until he licked it clean. I wondered if that was how he'd suck on my breasts or clit if we ever—

I cleared my throat and twirled around. "I think the cake's almost done."

I bent down and opened the oven. Sure enough, the cakes were a lovely golden brown and pulling away from the pans' edges. I grabbed my hot mitts, then carefully extracted the cakes from the pans to let them cool on a rack.

Behind me, the energy off Wyatt swirled.

"Will I get to taste the final product?" he asked huskily.

Hearing his deep voice made my stomach tighten. It had been months since I'd been with a man, and while I knew I could have gone home with Nicholas the other night or with Tim tonight, I hadn't wanted that.

Only one male interested me now.

The same one that had haunted my dreams during my adolescent years.

"Of course." I gave him a wide smile. "That's why I made it." I checked the jam again. It was still warm, and the cakes were hot. "As long as you're happy to wait for everything to cool."

"I have time."

My heartbeat picked up for what felt like the millionth time. Now that my hands didn't have anything to do, I suddenly felt flustered.

"Are you thirsty?" I didn't wait for him to reply and instead went to the fridge. I rummaged around in the compartment, letting the cold air from the appliance cool my libido. As each second passed, it felt as if my head cleared a little more.

Yet, all that did was bring more questions to mind.

Wyatt Jamison was alone with me in my apartment. He'd whisked me away from the bar, telling me the Institute needed me, only to recant and say I could call them tomorrow. None of that made sense.

Man, I need a drink. And I needed one *badly*. Sober Avery and hot off-limits-commander Wyatt didn't mix.

"We bought a six-pack the other day. Do you want a beer?" I asked over my shoulder.

"Are you having one?"

"Most definitely."

He ran a hand through his hair, and another wave of power pushed off him. I wondered if he was even aware of it.

But one thing I knew for certain, he was feeling as charged as I was.

"Yeah, that sounds good," he finally said.

After he took his beer, I popped the top on mine and took a long swallow. I knew that I'd be hungover tomorrow, but at the moment, I didn't care.

I set my drink down, then crossed my arms on the counter and leaned forward.

Wyatt's gaze dipped for a moment before it snapped back up. I glanced down. My cleavage was on full display.

Warmth spread to my toes.

Wyatt just checked me out. Totally and completely checked me out.

WTF.

What was going on here?

Dating was against the rules between a commander and his subordinate. But the way he'd just looked at me, and the fact that he was here in my apartment after showing irritation *twice* tonight when males showed me attention, and the way he'd acted the other night while I'd been having dinner with Nicholas . . .

My eyes widened when the puzzle pieces clicked into place.

Of course.

My commander felt something for me, and I was pretty sure the SF wouldn't be okay with it.

Regardless, I had the ridiculous urge to grin like a Cheshire cat. Giddiness made my head swim even though the practical side of me knew Wyatt would be in trouble for pursuing this. But if there was one thing I knew, it was that a male wolf pursuing a female would not be dissuaded.

Rules or not.

"Do you like working for the SF?"

Wyatt took another drink from his beer, his gaze now firmly staying north of my chin. "I do. It's challenging at times, but I like teaching new recruits when we're not on assignment."

I nodded and took another drink. "You're good at it, teaching us, I mean. You push us when we need it, but back off when you know we're struggling too much."

He tilted his head. "Thank you. I try hard to be a good commander, so that's probably one of the nicest compliments I've ever gotten."

"Well, it's the truth."

His lips curved up. "Although I have to say that it's easy to do my job when I have a motivated and compliant group of recruits."

"Isn't every group you train like that?"

"Usually, but not always. Sometimes we mess up and accept people into the SF that aren't a good fit, but that usually becomes apparent within the first few months. Part of my job is weeding out those who aren't cut out for this work."

I scrunched my nose up. "That must be awkward."

He shrugged. "I suppose it could be, but I see it more as helping someone find a place that's better suited for them. It's best to know right away if something isn't for you than to spend years of your life at it only to realize you've wasted so much time when you could have been happier elsewhere."

"Yeah, you're right. I suppose if we only have one life, we might as well enjoy it."

His gaze darkened with lust. "Very true. I would love nothing more than to enjoy it."

My cheeks heated. I grabbed my drink and rounded the corner to join him on the stools, letting the alcohol swimming through my veins embolden me.

He straightened, his arm folding across his lap when I sat next to him.

His Adam's apple bobbed when our knees brushed as I arranged myself on the seat. With a start, I realized that my miniskirt didn't leave much to the imagination. It rode up my thighs, leaving ample skin exposed.

But instead of covering myself, I left it. Wyatt didn't seem in any hurry to leave, and my real-life fantasy was playing out before my eyes. Even if this was all a dream and I would wake up at any moment to find that Wyatt Jamison had never taken me home and spent the evening with me, I didn't care.

Right here, and right now, he was with me—truly with me—and I didn't want it to end. And I sure as hell wasn't going to change into my granny sweatpants to hide my legs. I bet money Charlotte would have approved.

I laughed inwardly as a golden glow rimmed Wyatt's irises.

The energy around him increased again, and electricity crackled between us. I was so tempted to place my hand on his thigh. He still kept an arm draped over his crotch, and a part of me wondered what it hid underneath.

"Tell me more about your life here," I said softly. I wanted to learn everything about him that I could. Everything that had happened to him in the last eight years.

He took a deep breath, his attention unwavering. "There's not much to tell. Unlike you, I haven't led a very interesting life. I left Ridgeback when I was eighteen and came here and have been here ever since."

"But you like it enough to stay, right? Do you plan to have a career here? To stay until you retire?"

"Maybe, but I don't know yet. There are enough wolves in the SF that I could stay indefinitely if I wanted to, but a part of me misses my pack. My brother, Lance—you may remember him—will be the next Alpha of the British Columbia pack when my dad steps down, but I know I'll always have a place there." He shook his head, then smiled fondly. "My mother would like me to come home, but I have to stay in the SF for a few more years because of a commitment I made. Besides, there's still so much I want to do."

"Like what?"

The light around his eyes brightened as he studied me. "I want to travel more. When we go on assignments, we can go anywhere in the world, but we're obviously not there to sightsee. So while my travels have broadened, they haven't been long. But it's been enough for me to see areas that I'd like to return to. Places I'd like to spend time in."

I perked up, my smile broadening. "What was your favorite place so far?"

His gaze dipped to my thighs again before he snapped it up. He took another long pull from his beer before shaking his head, as if trying to remember my question. "Um, I enjoyed

Thailand. We had an assignment in the south, near the beach in the jungle. It was beautiful and so different than what I grew up with. Monkeys jumped through the trees, spiders as big as my hand dangled from webs, giant rock cliffs soared from the ocean, and the food . . ." He gave a soft groan. "Damn, the food was *amazing*. I could eat there every day."

I laughed, then licked my lips. "Mmm, I love Thai food. It's one of my favorites."

Wyatt's gaze dipped to my mouth, his eyes darkening as I continued to nibble on my lip.

My breath quickened, and the urge to squirm grew so strong. When he looked at me like that . . .

His nostrils flared, and a part of me knew that my scent was giving away my arousal, but I couldn't help it.

"What about you?" he asked. "Tell me about your favorite place in the world."

"So many places to choose from," I said breathlessly, then took another swig of my drink. "Where do I begin . . ."

CHAPTER FIFTEEN
AVERY

Somehow, Wyatt and I ended up outside under the stars an hour later. The sponge cake layered in buttercream and raspberries sat between us. The remainder of the six-pack lay in the grass, and a blanket was spread out underneath our legs.

Thanks to the beer, I was still tipsy.

We'd wandered to one of the far training fields, near the woods, and away from the barracks and main building lights. A thousand stars shone above.

I settled back and clasped my hands over my stomach. "Do you know that whenever I look at the stars, I always think of Democritus."

Wyatt propped himself up on his elbow, looking down at me. In the dark night, I could barely make out his features, but his scent swam around me. "Democritus?" he said with amusement.

I slugged him playfully. "Yes, Democritus. He was an ancient Greek philosopher who, purely by using his mind, solved the mystery of how all things are created."

He cocked his head. "And you know this how?"

I laughed at his boyish grin. "When I was a kid, I lived in Greece for a year. During that time, my father took me to the ancient ruins in Athens, and that inspired me to learn more about Greek culture. Naturally, you can't study Greek culture without learning about the ancient philosophers."

"Naturally." He chuckled. "So tell me, what did Democritus discover by using only his mind?"

My lips parted in a smile since Wyatt seemed genuinely curious despite his amusement. "Democritus was the central figure in the atomic theory of the universe. In fact, he even created the term *atomon*, which we now call an atom. And by using only observation and common sense, Democritus hypothesized that everything in the universe was composed of tiny building blocks, or atoms, and those tiny atoms formed everything we see around us." I waved at the dark trees in the forest, the blanket beneath us, the stars in the sky. "He reasoned that all life and objects were created of atoms joined together, and when something died or burned, that those atoms broke apart only to reform into something new."

His eyebrows rose, his earlier lightheartedness evaporating. "Are you serious? He knew that everything was created from atoms before scientists did?"

"He did."

"But how is that possible?"

I shrugged. "He had a great mind. You could even argue that he was the very first scientist. I've always wondered what he would have contributed to the world if he'd lived in the modern age."

Wyatt's brow furrowed, and I couldn't help but wonder if he found this as mind blowing as I did. The first time I learned about Democritus's theory, I'd literally been speechless.

Wyatt scratched his chin, and his playful grin returned. "So seeing the stars reminds you of this ancient philosopher?"

"It does."

"You're gonna have to explain it, 'cause I'm not seeing the connection."

I laughed again. "Okay, so every time I look at the stars, I'm reminded of how small we all are. Seeing those tiny specks of light, millions and billions of light years away, makes me realize how truly vast the universe is, and how miniscule life is on earth. And naturally, the next line of thought is, *why*? Why are we here? Who are we? How did life start? How was the universe created?" I ducked my head when that glow formed around his irises again, and his amusement melted away. "Or maybe it's just me and everyone else sees the Big Dipper."

"No, it's . . ." He took a deep breath, his brow furrowing again. "You're right. That should be what people see when they look at the stars, all of the ancient questions of life that many of us forget on a daily basis."

I nodded and picked at a thread on the blanket. "I know it's easy to forget those questions. This week, all I've thought about is surviving and not face planting on a daily basis. I certainly haven't been questioning the meaning of life."

He chuckled, the warm sound making my insides sing. "Well, I can honestly say that you definitely have one of the most active and curious minds I've ever encountered. I can't remember the last time I contemplated the meaning of life on a Saturday night, but now, thanks to you, I don't know how I'll think of anything else every time I look at the night sky."

I scrunched my nose up. "Hopefully that's not a bad thing? Because, you know, all of this conversation could just be the beer talking. Alcohol always makes me contemplative."

"And here I thought it just made people fall over and have hangovers."

I laughed.

Wyatt cut another piece of cake for himself, then took a big bite. When he finished the piece, he lay back on the blanket.

I lay next to him but made sure to keep some distance

between us. More than anything, I wanted to feel the heat from his body, but he was my commander. Hooking up was against policy, even if nobody could see us out here.

The minutes passed, and the cool night air blew around us. "So what do you think the Institute will be like when you arrive?" Wyatt propped his head in his hand.

"To be honest, I'm not entirely sure. I've only visited the Institute with my parents and have never worked for them before, but I imagine . . ."

And just like that, we fell back into easy conversation.

The hours ticked by as Wyatt and I talked about our dreams and plans for the future. In all the time I'd known him in Ridgeback, we'd never connected as intimately as this, and my heart wondered what my future would have been like if we had.

Would we have kept in touch after my parents and I left for France? Perhaps texted one another as I drifted around the globe? Maybe we would have become true friends and seen each other for occasional trips as we explored our love of new places.

But that was something I'd never know, and those questions would only drive me crazy.

Back then, I'd been too shy to do anything other than watch Wyatt from afar, cherishing those moments he and I spoke like precious gems.

I'd always known there was something special about him, though. I'd felt it since the first moment I laid eyes on him in that ice cream shop.

What it was about him that called to me, I didn't entirely understand, but one thing I knew for certain—Wyatt had grown into the man I knew he would become.

Kind. Strong. Noble. Caring.

He could so easily capture my heart again.

If he hadn't already.

"Do you want another piece of cake?" I asked as I wrapped

the blanket around my legs. It was near two in the morning, and the six-pack was long gone.

Wyatt grinned devilishly. "Do you really need to ask?"

I laughed and gave him another slice.

He downed it in three bites. "Damn, woman. You really know how to cook."

"Maybe I'll fatten you up too."

He grinned. "You're more than welcome to try."

We both laughed again, then he set his plate down and fingered a lock of hair from my face, as though he wasn't even aware he was doing it.

I froze at his touch, and the laughter died between us.

I suddenly became aware that only inches separated us and we were truly alone out here. Nobody could see us. If each of us leaned forward, our lips would touch, and right now, I wanted to kiss him so badly. This was the Wyatt I remembered—the laughing, intoxicating, drop-dead gorgeous boy that had turned into a virile man.

Shallow breaths filled my chest. His lips looked so firm, and his pine and oak scent made my head spin.

The light around his irises grew, and his nostrils flared.

I crept forward more, my body moving on its own accord.

A low growl came from Wyatt as he did the same.

Before I could second-guess my actions, Wyatt moved the last inch and slanted his mouth over mine.

The feel of his firm lips made my breath hitch, but then instinct took over. I threaded my fingers through his hair, loving the feel of the silky strands, as he deepened the kiss.

The cool air breezed over my skin when he snaked his arm around my waist. He hauled me closer to his chest. Heat from his body enveloped mine, sending meteors of pleasure straight to my core.

I moaned, unable to help it.

A deep rumble vibrated in his chest, and his hand splayed across my lower back, pushing me flusher against him.

I felt every hard inch of him, the steel of his thighs, the ridge of his abdomen, the planks of his chest. Fuck, he felt *so* good.

"Avery," he whispered, his breathing ragged.

I kissed him back, dancing my tongue with his. He tasted like beer and man, and I couldn't get enough of him.

His kiss turned more urgent, and our lips molded together as we hungrily sought one another.

His leg drifted between mine, parting my thighs. The miniskirt rode up. Cool night wind brushed over my skin, making me shiver, but when his knee ground against my core, I gasped.

Liquid heat filled me, my sex already wet and willing for him. I moaned again, and he tore from my mouth only to press desperate kisses down my neck.

The feel of his mouth devouring my skin was heaven and hell wrapped into one. I wanted him even though hooking up could lead to repercussions.

But fuck it. I needed him. All of him. Inside me. On top of me. Around me. *Owning* me.

I wrapped my legs around his thigh when he rubbed against my core again. My thin panties didn't stand a chance against his onslaught. The friction made me gasp as lust shot through me.

"Fuck, you're responsive," he groaned.

"Wyatt," I whispered. "I need . . . I want—" But I couldn't continue. The sensations shooting through me ceased any coherent thoughts or words.

"I know what you need."

His hand slipped under my top, working its way up my stomach. When he reached my breast, he cupped it. My nipple ached, standing prominently for him to tweak.

Another moan slipped from my lips.

He growled and kneaded my flesh. "Fuck," he whispered. "I want to do everything to you."

"Yes," I panted. I arched against him more, straining for more, more, *more*.

He lifted my shirt, and then it disappeared. His shirt got whipped off, too, and his glorious naked chest was suddenly visible for me to admire.

"Damn, woman. You're gorgeous." Wyatt breathed heavily, his chest heaving as his gaze devoured my breasts. A strapless bra barely covered my nipples and left little to the imagination as the heavy weight of my boobs spilled over the top of the flimsy material.

Heady power filled me as Wyatt's erection pressed firmly against my abdomen.

He wanted me. *Really* wanted me.

He kissed me again, his hands going behind my back.

With a deft flick of his fingers, my bra came undone, my breasts freed. Another rumble filled his chest when he gazed at my peaks, my nipples taut in the night air.

His breath was so ragged now, his chest heaved. He bent his head and lifted one tit to his mouth. The second his hot mouth closed over my nipple, I bucked.

He growled in approval and swirled his tongue, licking and nipping.

"Wyatt," I breathed. Desire shot through me, as he continued to grind his knee against my core, my panties slipping over my slick folds.

I tangled my fingers even more through his hair, holding him at my breast and demanding that he continue.

He suckled and licked before moving to the other, all while his hands continually roamed up and down my back, kneading my flesh.

When my tits felt raw and aching, he released them to move up and kiss me again.

We kissed and licked relentlessly, tasting each other until both of us were panting. His knee continually rubbed me throughout it all, and I cried out again, but he swallowed the noise in his mouth.

I was about to come right there, half-dressed, while Wyatt knee-fucked me in the middle of a field.

As if sensing what was about to happen, he lowered his leg, but my sex was so swollen that I'd turned mindless, unable to stop a snarling protest.

He chuckled, then whispered, "I want to be tasting you the first time I make you come." He tilted my head to the side and kissed down my neck again. His tongue trailed along my skin creating goosebumps and a never-ending ache in my core.

When he reached my collarbone, he paused, his grip on me tightening. For a moment, he just stayed there until I felt the graze of sharp teeth on my tender skin.

But he abruptly pulled back, a harsh groan escaping him, before he continued his journey south. I didn't realize where he was heading until he kissed a trail down my abdomen and my skirt rode up and over my hips.

But when his hand curved around my thigh to tickle my clit, I nearly came undone.

A deep growl of pleasure rumbled from his chest as he tore my panties aside.

He slid a finger into me, my wet folds easily parting for his touch. He groaned. "Fuck, Avery," he whispered. "So wet. So sweet."

He brought my legs up, and his head disappeared between my thighs as he pulled his finger out and repositioned himself.

I whimpered, missing the feel of him, but when his tongue grazed that taut nub, my world exploded.

I moaned in ecstasy as he settled in to taste and suck. A throbbing need in me took root, and it wouldn't abate.

I needed more, more, *more*.

"Wyatt, please, *please*," I begged.

He groaned again, his licking increasing, and then his finger slipped back inside me. He added a second, and then a third digit, until I was stretched so full with him that I could no longer think.

His mouth latched onto my clit like a man intent on sucking me mindless while his fingers pounded into me, rubbing and sliding, hitting that deliciously deep spot inside me again and again.

He didn't let up as his tongue rubbed me harder and faster, lapping at me like a man dying of thirst.

The waves inside me kept building and building. I moaned continuously at the sheer strength of my impending orgasm that was climbing to a mountainous peak.

And when I finally came in an explosion of ecstasy, I screamed his name.

Wyatt's deep rumbles of satisfaction filled my ears as he continued to lick and torment me.

My orgasm went on and on, my moans filling the quiet air around us. He continued to lap and thrust, as I rode the never-ending waves from a climax that refused to end.

The night air continued to swirl around my bare flesh, and I shivered when I finally came down from my high. I couldn't think. Couldn't breathe. Couldn't understand how something that exquisite had just happened.

I'd never come like that in my life.

Wyatt slowly slipped his fingers out of me and then licked them clean one by one. His eyes glowed so brightly when he climbed over me, it looked like two candles lit his irises.

His dick was a prominent ridge against my thigh. I still panted, my mind numb, my skin on fire, as I lay a hand against his cheek, unable to find words.

A satisfied smirk lifted his lips, and a rush of his power rolled over me. He lowered his body, until his weight pressed comfortably on top of me, then kissed me tenderly and reverently on the lips.

"Wyatt," I managed to breathe.

"Yes, Little Flower?" he whispered.

I paused. "Little Flower?"

The side of his mouth kicked up, his expression sheepish. "It's how I thought of you in high school. As beautiful as the lilac flower your magical witch scent carries."

"No one's ever told me my witch magic smells like lilacs."

He growled. "Good. Then that means you've never dated another werewolf."

"No. I haven't." I shivered at the knowledge that he'd harbored a secret endearment for me all these years. Damn, I was falling *hard* again. "Wyatt, I need to touch you."

For a moment, he just looked at me, then he blurred to the side so I could move my hands.

"Yeah. Of course. Whatever you want. Fuck yes." His breath sucked in as my hands wandered south, and his jaw snapped closed when I dipped my hand into his pants and encircled his length.

My eyes widened at his width. "Whoa," I breathed. He was *huge*.

"Avery," he said hoarsely.

I stroked his length, marveling at his long, velvety steel. His breaths grew shallow, and I quickly undid his jeans and shimmied them down his hips.

He rolled onto his back, then I climbed on top of him. My boobs dangled in his face, and he growled and nipped at them.

I laughed, the sound playful, before I began to explore his chest. With each kiss, every bite, and every lustful slide of my tongue, the power around him grew and grew.

His body strained under my touch, his erection standing on end for all the world to see.

He groaned and clenched, his fingers threading through my

hair as I made the slow tortuous journey down his body, over each rippled muscle and sinewy plane, as a sense of power grew in me that I could make him so crazed with lust.

And when I wrapped my lips around his cock, his hips jolted, flying off the ground in an uncontrolled buck as a primal groan tore from his throat.

I slid his entire length into my mouth, loving the taste of him.

His breath stopped, his body rigid as I picked up my pace, sucking his cock up and down in rhythmic movements.

"Avery." His muscles tensed, his thighs turning to steel.

I increased my tempo as I turned into a siren intent on ensnaring this man with my touch.

He strained again, his fingers curling so tightly in my hair they fisted. And when I brought my hand to the base of his shaft, to encircle and rub him while I swallowed him whole, his roar of release blasted my ears.

His hips shot off the ground, his cock buried in my mouth, as his seed poured into the back of my throat. I swallowed and moaned while continuing to stroke him as his orgasm rocked his body.

It was only when his dick eventually started to soften that I released him from my lips.

He panted, his eyes closed, his grip in my hair loosening. I gazed down at him with a feeling of absolute power that I'd been able to bring Wyatt Jamison to his knees.

When he finally opened his eyes, he smiled at me lazily before hauling me up his chest. He rolled, pinning me beneath him before he kissed me deeply and slowly, his calloused hand cupping my jaw.

"Did you like that?" I asked tentatively when he released me from his kiss.

Wyatt scoffed, his eyes going wide. "Did I *like* that?" He

chuckled. "Like is an understatement. You made me see stars, woman."

My cheeks heated as a flush of satisfaction rolled through me. And it was only then, as I lay nearly naked in his arms, with him in a similar state, that I realized what we'd done.

We'd broken protocol.

We'd allowed our passion to supersede our judgment.

Consequences may arise, but in my mind, it had all been worth it. I'd wanted this for *so* long.

I cuddled into him, loving the feel of his hard body. He lazily stroked my back up and down, a low grumble of contentment filling his chest.

Minutes of blissful, sated silence passed between us. The air began to chill my back, not to mention, my boobs were still fully naked for the world to see, so I grabbed my top and pulled it back on. That got a glower and low growl from Wyatt.

I laughed, unable to help it, then settled back down beside him, leaning up on my elbow so I could ask him what we were going to do from here. We couldn't very well advertise our feelings for one another, but we *could* carry on a secret relationship until my training was done.

But then a distant shout rose in the distance. "Avery? Are you out here?" A door banged back by the barracks.

Wyatt's head snapped up, his eyes growing wide.

"Avery?" a woman yelled again.

Wyatt abruptly let me go and jerked his pants up before whipping his shirt over his head. "Shit," he whispered. "It's Charlotte."

Swishing footsteps sounded in the grass heading in our direction. "Avery?"

"I have to go." He gave me a quick kiss before standing. "She can't find us. I'm not supposed to—" His gaze turned regretful. "I'm sorry. I need to go."

I had just pocketed my bra when the air fluttered around me.

I blinked.

He was gone.

Jaw dropping, I surveyed the blanket and realized what it looked like. Wyatt was right.

It looked like we'd just fucked.

I quickly straightened the quilt before running my hands through my hair. The remaining cake still sat on the grass off to the side. I quickly chucked the beer bottles, Wyatt's plate and fork, and the scraps of my shredded underwear into a nearby bush. Thank the Gods we'd gone to the edge of the field near the trees, or I wouldn't have had anywhere to hide the evidence.

I muffled a laugh, all of this suddenly feeling funny. *Evidence.* As if we were teenagers terrified of being caught by our parents. But then I sobered, realizing our situation was actually graver than that. If Wyatt's boss found out what he'd done—hooked up with a subordinate—he would be in a lot of trouble.

Biting my lip, I made a mental note to retrieve everything tomorrow so I didn't leave our trash, aka evidence, in the woods.

A moment later, Charlotte's footsteps picked up when she spotted me. "There you are."

She dropped down on the blanket beside me, relief filling her features. "We haven't been able to get a hold of you since you left, and when you weren't in the apartment, Eliza and I assumed the worst and thought you got kicked out or something." She eyed the cake. "But instead you've been gorging on cake and enjoying the night sky, hmm?" She nudged me when I remained silent, her teasing mood evaporating. "Hey, are you okay? Is everything okay with the Institute?"

I mentally shook myself, feeling thankful that female were-wolves didn't have the olfactory powers that male wolves did. Otherwise, Charlotte would have scented *exactly* what had taken place out here. "No, I mean yes, everything's fine." I flashed a smile for good measure.

Charlotte eyed the cake again. "Any chance I can have a piece of that?"

"Oh, yeah. Of course." I fumbled with the dessert but managed to cut her a slice while my mind still reeled from the surreal night I'd had with Wyatt.

With flushed cheeks, I handed Charlotte a piece of the sponge cake. Sweet jam ran down the sides. She took one bite and moaned.

"Girl, you really know how to cook." She forked another large bite and added, "Screw calories. I'm finishing this entire piece and maybe another." She leaned back and continued to chew. "How long have you been out here?"

"Um, a few hours." I glanced around the field, searching for Wyatt, but he was nowhere to be found.

"Nice view," Charlotte commented when a small meteor blazed across the sky. "But what made you come out here?"

I settled back next to her, not knowing what else to do. "I needed some fresh air. Sometimes our apartment feels so small. I wanted to get out in the open." The lie slipped off my tongue so easily.

Charlotte snorted. "Oh, I get that. I feel like that every day."

"So how was the rest of your night?"

A grin stretched across her face as Charlotte began telling me all of the details after I'd left.

I tried to pay attention and managed to comment at the appropriate times, but my attention kept drifting to Wyatt.

I knew now without any doubt that he wanted me, but what we'd done . . .

It was against policy.

But then I reminded myself that Wyatt was a werewolf. And when a wolf wanted a woman, rules didn't apply—not even rules made by the Supernatural Forces.

A feeling of giddiness swam through me as Charlotte continued to chat. The boy I'd had a crush on during my teenage years, the one I thought would never give me a second glance, had just kissed me endlessly, gave me a mind-blowing orgasm, and had come in my mouth.

I fingered my lips. I could still taste him. My heart sang again because Wyatt liked me. *Really* liked me, and he wanted me with a hunger I hadn't felt from a man in, well, ever.

Around three or four in the morning, Charlotte and I finally stood to head back inside, but the entire walk back all I could think about were smoldering moss-green eyes, muscled shoulders, chiseled abs, and a mouth that I couldn't wait to taste again.

CHAPTER SIXTEEN

WYATT

I lay in bed, thinking about last night as the bright sun rose in the east. Light spilled into my room as scents of day and dew flowed in through my cracked window.

I still couldn't believe that last night had actually happened. Not only had I followed Avery to that bar downtown, but I'd taken her home, stayed with her in her apartment, then we'd wandered outside to lie under the stars before I'd kissed her, touched her, and nearly fucked her.

It had quite possibly been the most incredible eight hours of my life.

It had also been the most reckless and irresponsible.

An image of leaving her, haphazardly dressed in the field with the scent of sex in the air, flashed through my mind. *That* was how I'd ended last night with her, by running away like a sleazy douchebag.

What the fuck are you doing, Jamison?

I'd already pushed the boundaries of SF protocol. Following her. Spending time alone with her. Kissing her, touching her, finger fucking her . . .

Shit.

Just the memory made my cock ache, but *none* of my behavior was acceptable in the eyes of the Supernatural Forces. I was her commander. She was my subordinate. By that very definition, I was in a position of power over her. Because of that power play, the SF strictly forbade any relationships between those in varying rank.

Now if Avery were a permanent SF member who *wasn't* under my command, that was a different story . . .

But she wasn't.

Which only meant that I'd thoroughly messed up.

I tore a hand through my hair and banged my head against my pillow. My cock stayed rigid despite knowing I couldn't have her. I couldn't even blame alcohol on my behavior. Human beer was rarely enough to get me drunk. I'd been completely sober the entire time I'd been in Avery's company.

But she hadn't been.

And that only made my behavior worse.

"Fucking A." I grumbled and pushed the covers off me before swinging my legs over the side of my bed.

The movement made the air flutter, which disturbed the scent clinging to my shirt. I inhaled. Avery's natural lilac fragrance still permeated the fabric.

I brought my shirt collar to my nose and sniffed again. *Damn. She smells so good.*

My cock grew harder, pressing prominently against my boxers. I knew I should strip my clothes, shower, and get up for the day.

But I didn't want to.

Despite knowing *none* of this could go anywhere, I wanted to stay in bed clouded in her scent while fantasizing about her going down on me.

"Fuck it."

I leaned back and pushed my boxers down. An image of

Avery's thin waist, round hips, and bare breasts filled my mind. Gods, she was perfect.

I stroked my length while picturing Avery's mouth closing around my tip. Her tongue had been absolute magic. A shudder of lust shot through me. Jacking off wouldn't erase this tension inside me, but it might ease it.

Shit, I've got it bad.

Inside me, my wolf rumbled his contentment, then whined in eagerness that my thoughts about Avery were also aligning with his. He'd made it very clear on multiple occasions last night that he fully supported everything and anything that had to do with Avery Meyers, even if that meant breaking SF protocol and getting me fired.

He'd even wanted me to *claim* her. On our first date, if it could even be called a date.

A memory of my canines grazing her skin filled my mind. Fuck, but it had been hard to stop that instinct. I'd wanted to bite into her neck, and infuse my magic with hers, marking her forever as mine, which wasn't good, because my wolf didn't care about my promise to Marcus.

He didn't care about honor and code.

All he cared about was Avery.

But I couldn't think about what that meant.

So I pumped more, an orgasm already building. Just the thought of her did that to me. I sniffed my shirt again, my balls tightening, then stroked my cock faster.

I pictured her eyes, her laugh, the sultry curve of her lips.

Her legs, her soft tits, the roundness of her ass.

The sound of her voice, the fire in her eyes, and then her lust-filled look as she lay back with her legs spread open and wet, begging for me to slip my dick inside her as I leaned down to lick—

Oh fuck . . .

An orgasm exploded through my body, my seed shooting from me so hard that it splattered all over the sheets.

I breathed heavily, my chest heaving. My mind was so completely and totally consumed with Avery that everything else went blank.

For a moment, I couldn't move.

And that's not even the real thing.

I groaned in agony. I was like a horny teenager all over again. I grabbed a tissue to mop the mess up, shaking my head at what I was allowing myself to feel.

But my wolf didn't care. He whined again inside me. His eagerness only grew.

In high school, he'd also shown interest in Avery, but we'd both been young then—me an adolescent and him still a pup. Neither of us had truly understood our emotions as we worked together to co-exist.

But we'd both been infatuated with Avery, even then, although now our feelings weren't mere infatuation. Our mindsets were clear and any earlier youthful inexperience had faded.

Which only made this harder since we *both* wanted Avery.

"So this is how it is now?" I asked him as I cleaned the sheets. "I get fired from the SF for rutting with a new recruit? And then what? We follow her to Geneva to sit at home while she begins her new job? And what about Marcus? What about the promise I need to keep to him?"

But my wolf only whined again. According to him, following Avery to Geneva was the best idea I'd ever come up with.

I shook my head, irritated by his irrationality. While I knew Avery wanted me, that didn't mean she wanted to be *with* me. There was a big difference. I knew she'd sleep with me if the opportunity arose, but to be in an actual relationship?

I had no idea if she wanted that, and there was *no way* I was putting her in a position in which she needed to choose.

Because the only way a relationship between the two of us was even possible was if she never went to Geneva.

I had to stay here for at least two more years. Because of my promise, I couldn't leave.

Which meant Avery would have to give up her dream.

I growled.

Hell no.

That wasn't happening.

She'd worked too hard at school and wanted to join the Institute too desperately for me to mess it up by getting her tangled in a relationship that would damn any chance she had of being an ambassador.

My wolf whined, anxious over the veer my thoughts had taken.

He wasn't capable of speech, but our emotions and thought processes were so in-tune that I knew what he was trying to say.

Where there's a will, there's a way.

I laughed humorlessly at his cliché. "If only it were that easy, but it's not. Have you forgotten that I can't risk getting fired? I made a commitment. Does that mean nothing to you?"

He just snarled.

My tablet buzzed and its glow lit up the pocket in my cargo pants that I'd tossed to the side last night. I grabbed the waistband and pulled it out. My movements stopped.

A message waited on my tablet.

From my boss.

> Report to my office at 1000 today.

"Fuck." Abruptly, I started pacing, staring at Wes's order. "Fuck, fuck, fuck."

This wasn't good. It was Sunday. Wes didn't hold meetings in his office on Sundays unless it was serious, and considering I was the only one tagged on the message . . .

It was a private meeting.

I plunged a hand through my hair and glanced at the clock. It was already 9:30. I usually never slept this late, but considering I didn't go to bed until four in the morning, I wasn't surprised that I'd slept in.

I tore my shirt off and hurried to the shower to wash and shave. If I showed up at my superior's office with Avery's scent clinging to me . . .

"Shit!" I exclaimed before ripping the shower curtain open.

I ARRIVED at Wes's office within the main building at precisely ten. Damp hair brushed my ears, but the only scent that clung to me now was that of laundry detergent and aftershave.

After pressing my palm against the magical scanner by Wes's door, the familiar robotic voice stated, "Welcome, Wyatt Jamison. Please proceed."

The door clicked open, and I stepped inside.

Wes stood by the far wall, overlooking the Idaho foothills through the floor-to-ceiling windows. His office was huge, holding all of the magical holographic equipment that could be found in the main command center.

But today, none of those holographs lit up.

That didn't bode well. I'd been hoping this meeting was in regards to an upcoming assignment, but if that were the case, the magical tracking system would be running.

"Major Jamison," Wes said without turning toward me. "Have a seat."

While I'd never been one to fidget, the coolness of his tone immediately put me on edge. I did as he said, even though my wolf's hackles rose at the command. It was the hardest thing about being in the SF. As an alpha by birthright, it was instinctual to be the one commanding, not the one being commanded. But learning to submit had been good for me and my wolf.

It'd taught us discipline.

At least it had until Avery Meyers blew back into our lives.

Wes stayed at the window, his hands clasped behind his back. "I read the report yesterday about your new recruit's fall into the river. It was an oversight that shouldn't have happened."

Relief made my shoulders slump. So that was what this meeting was about. "Yes, sir, you're right. I take full—"

"And I also read the pilot's report that noted your territorial behavior regarding your other recruit, Avery Meyers."

I clamped my mouth shut.

Wes swung around, his face cold. "And then I heard other rumblings about you stalking her to a bar last night, only to return an hour later alone with her. So I checked the surveillance footage, and from what I can gather, the two of you went to her apartment, and you didn't report back to your own living barracks until eight hours later." He took an ominous step toward me and placed his hands flat on his desk. "Do you care to fill me in on what happened during those eight hours, Major Jamison?"

"Sir, I know it looks bad—"

"It doesn't just look bad, Major," he barked. "It looks like a fucking breach of protocol in which firing you is my only option!"

My breath stopped. *Shit.* I'd known this could happen, and now it was. *Fuck!* I took a deep breath as my wolf snarled inside me. *Okay, Jamison. Stay calm. Keep it together.*

I took another breath before replying evenly, "You're right, sir. It was a breach of protocol, and I'm sorry. I can also assure you it won't happen again."

"Did you sleep with her?"

"No."

"But you did other things?"

I grimaced as shame washed through me. "Yes."

Wes raised an eyebrow. "A week ago, I would have sworn on my life that nothing like this could happen with you in charge." Anger still simmered from him, but after a moment, he took a deep breath and sat down on his chair before sighing heavily. "Wyatt, what's going on? This is highly irregular for you."

I hung my head. I sat like that for a moment, trying to process what had changed in me since Avery arrived at headquarters. "Sir, I'm sorry. I didn't think this would happen, but I made a few bad judgment calls yesterday. It was wrong, and you have every right to fire me, and I would completely understand if you did." My stomach clenched at the thought. I couldn't be fired from the SF. *Couldn't.*

I waited for Wes to reply, but silence reigned.

Every muscle in my body tensed, anticipating the final blow that would seal my fate and be a one-way ticket out of the SF.

I'm sorry, Marcus. I'm so goddamned sorry.

But Wes said, "Major, you've been a loyal and trustworthy commander in this organization for seven years. I'd rather you explained to me what's going on."

My head snapped up.

Wes's brow furrowed while my wolf continued to pace and growl, but despite my wolf's irritation at where my thoughts were going, I knew it was the only way as gut-wrenching as that was.

My attraction to Avery had to stop. I *had* to keep my promise.

Pain exploded in my chest, rushing through me in fiery rivers. But it was the only way.

My mouth went dry. *You have to do this.*

Forcing the words out, I said, "It was a lapse in judgment, sir. It won't happen again."

Wes leveled his icy blue eyes on me. "I believe I asked you to explain."

"It's not really something I can explain, sir, because I don't fully understand it myself."

Wes cocked his head. "It's your wolf, isn't it?"

I leaned forward, placing my elbows on my knees. I might as well be honest. After this meeting, any relationship in the fore-seeable future with Avery wasn't happening. "Possibly. He's quite enamored with her."

"And are you as well? Or is this interest solely from your wolf?"

I worked my jaw but knew that I couldn't lie—not to Wes. "It's me as well, sir, but that doesn't mean I can't stop it."

Wes leaned back in his chair. "You say that, but if it's your wolf *and* you . . ." He sighed again. "Well, that certainly complicates things."

Since Wes was also a werewolf, he understood just how persuasive one's wolf could be. However, Wes was already mated and had been for the past seventy-five years. I didn't know if he remembered what it was like when he met his mate —the obsession, the infatuation, and the rage-inducing jealousy whenever another male glanced in her direction.

My eyes popped. *Holy shit. There's that word again. I'm now accepting that Avery could be my mate?* But I couldn't make her my mate. Not now.

What I promised Marcus would keep me in Idaho for the next two years, but after that, maybe then I could court her. Mate her. Claim her.

But even knowing that I could pursue her in the future didn't stop the regret that bit me hard. "Despite my wolf's and my interest, I won't let it progress, sir. You have my word."

Wes eyed me skeptically. "As much as I believe you intend to follow through with that, I'm not sure if you'll be able to, not if you *and* your wolf want her."

Think of Marcus. Think of Marcus. "Sir, I can and will do this."

Wes's eyebrows rose. "What makes you so sure of that?"

Because I owe Marcus my life. I cleared my throat and replied, "This wouldn't be the first time I've had to learn to control my urges and instincts. I've done it before, and I can do it again."

"But do you believe she's your mate? Your true mate?"

His loaded question had my jaw tightening. No, I couldn't think about that. I couldn't even allow myself to imagine Avery as my mate because if I did . . .

Even my promise to Marcus might not be enough to keep me here.

I took another deep breath before saying, "I don't know, sir. I'm not sure what it feels like to know that a woman is your mate since I've never been mated."

"So you don't have an innate need to protect her? You don't feel jealous every time another man captures her attention? You don't feel the urge to claim her?"

I imagined my canines elongating and biting into the smooth, pale skin on Avery's neck. My mouth watered at the thought, my wolf wagged his tail in excitement, and an intense feeling of satisfaction followed. *Mine.*

Shit. He was right. I'd come so close to claiming her last night.

"Major Jamison? I need you to answer those questions honestly."

My hands shook at the territorial reaction that *again* stole over me. My chest rose unsteadily as my breaths quickened. *No. That did not just happen. I can and will fight this.*

But I felt all of those things for Avery and more. But I couldn't tell Wes that I wanted to claim my new recruit. If I did, he would move her to a different commander's group. Having to reject my feelings for her was bad enough, but the thought of another man taking over her training, working with her every day, and being in charge of her safety . . .

My wolf snarled.

Yeah, that wasn't an option. I didn't know if I would be able to control myself if that happened. Then I would *definitely* be fired.

Meeting Wes's gaze again, I said, "Sir, I do feel things for her, I won't lie to you about that, but she's not my mate. I can control myself." I held eye contact. I didn't exactly lie. She wasn't my mate . . . yet.

But she could be.

I held my breath, wondering if he'd detect the white lie.

Wes stared at me for a long time, his eyes clear and steady. I knew I should dip my chin and show submission, but I didn't. I *wouldn't*.

I wasn't going to back down from this. Not if it meant someone else would be responsible for Avery's training and, ultimately, her safety. That wasn't something I would risk.

Wes finally broke eye contact and sighed. "All right, Major. I'll give you one more chance to prove that you can act as a respectful and responsible commander, but if I see any signs or hear any further rumblings about you or your wolf showing possessive behavior around Private Meyers, she'll be reassigned. Understood, Major?"

"Yes, sir." I stood and saluted him, but my hand still shook.

He dismissed me, and I headed into the hall.

Once outside, the mid-morning sun shone down on the surrounding fields. My shoulders slumped. More than anything I wanted to go to Avery's apartment, wake her up with a morning kiss, perhaps bring her breakfast in bed.

But that was a dream for a life I didn't lead.

I had responsibilities here. I had a promise to keep. And Avery had her entire life ahead of her. In a few short months, she would be off to Geneva.

And I would be here.

That ache formed in my chest again, and inside me, my wolf cried a long, lonely howl.

I thought again about last night. About the way Avery had

looked at me. About how she'd felt in my arms. I knew she had strong feelings for me.

But strong enough that she would give up her career?

Because that was the only way we could be together in the near future.

The thought was so tempting. I could ask her to.

Right now, I could go to her apartment and tell her what had happened. I could be one hundred percent honest and explain to her the situation I was in—I couldn't be with her now because of SF protocol. I needed to keep my job to fulfill a commitment, but in three months when her training was done, I could be with her then.

My stomach sank.

But what position did that put *her* in? What kind of pressure would that force on her?

I would be asking her to give up her *dream* job. She couldn't stay here with me and still work in Geneva.

Hell, she wouldn't even need to stay in the new recruit program because the only reason she was in it was to join the Supernatural Ambassador Institute in the first place.

Fuck, Wyatt. Why don't you just stomp on her dreams while you're at it?

I grumbled, but then had another thought. *What if we do long distance?*

I scowled. *For two years?* I knew I would wait that long. I would wait a lifetime for her if needed, but could she? That was asking a lot of her.

But as soon as my heart filled possessively at the thought of keeping her here and making her mine, so did the reality that I *couldn't* ask that of her.

What kind of relationship started in which you couldn't be together at all? Because of SF protocol, any romantic communication or interaction was forbidden for the next three months. I'd already fucked up last night. One more mistake, and I was out. So, what would we do, just stare at each other longingly for the next three months and never talk?

And then what would happen when her three months were up? She would be shipped off to Geneva with the stress of a new job only to Skype with me in her free time. Never mind the time difference. That would be a disaster.

What the hell kind of relationship was that? And what kind of expectation would that put on her?

I growled and wanted to slam my fist into a tree. I couldn't ask that of her. Only a selfish bastard would do that.

I hung my head. Timing. *Fucking timing.* If only I had met her again two years in the future and not now.

I couldn't be with her now, no matter how much I wanted it. But I *could* keep her safe. I could prepare her for anything that might come her way in her new job as an ambassador. And one day, in a couple of years, I could find her again, and then . . .

My wolf whined.

If the Gods were with me, and if she was willing, maybe then I could make her mine.

I shoved my hands into my pockets and began to plan as the sun blazed overhead. I knew that I couldn't personally conduct Avery's self-defense training—touching her would be torture. I damn well knew I wouldn't be able to control myself if that happened, and then Wes would be firing me in a heartbeat.

But I was still in charge of her training, therefore, I could pick the best candidate to fulfill that job. And I already knew who I would choose.

Dee wouldn't be happy about it since she had leave coming up for an extended vacation, but she owed me. She owed me almost as much as I owed Marcus.

I was calling in that chip.

I reached the barracks and scanned myself in. I trudged up the stairs as my thoughts whirled.

Because even knowing that Avery would ultimately still be

training under *me* didn't ring victorious.

As I stepped into my hallway, I waited to feel elation or a sense of accomplishment that I'd made the right choice. I thought for certain that I would have felt relief, if nothing else, that my job was still intact, that I could still fulfill my promise to Marcus, that I was still allowed to train Avery, and that I would be thoroughly preparing her for her job to come.

But all I felt was a deep aching pain in my chest.

It made me want to howl, to shed my skin until my wolf emerged, and to run until blood bled from our paws.

I closed my eyes, remembering Avery as she spoke animatedly about the stars, the sky, and her dreams for the future last night. Her image burned my mind—the curve of her lips, the glossiness of her hair, and the infectious nature of her laugh.

And the feel of her . . . Gods the *feel* of her. Her body fit perfectly with mine, as if she were made for me.

My breath rushed out as a bone-deep agony tore through my soul.

Because that was all I'd have of her for now—memories.

Last night had not only been the first night I'd spent with Avery Meyers, but it had also been the last—at least for the foreseeable future.

Nothing further could come of my attraction to her, not right now.

My wolf howled forlornly again. He knew I wasn't budging on this, but that was better than leaving her safety in the care of someone else, ruining her dream, and shattering the promise I'd made to Marcus and had vowed to keep.

As much as my heart *hurt* at the thought of her leaving my life in three months, I would do it for her, and I would do it for Marcus, which meant I had to teach Avery how to get out of any crisis situation that arose.

My blood chilled at the thought of her in danger.

I'd be damned if I failed at protecting her from that.

CHAPTER SEVENTEEN
AVERY

"What's got you so excited?" Charlotte asked as we ventured to the cafeteria on Monday morning. The dawn sun had just cleared the horizon, and only a handful of SF members walked the grounds.

"Who said I'm excited?" I asked innocently while trying to smother my cheesy smile.

Charlotte rolled her eyes. "Um, you've been in a good mood since yesterday morning despite your raging hangover, *and* you were the first out of bed this morning, *and* you haven't mentioned coffee once even though it's barely six."

I shrugged. "I woke up early and am eager to learn today. What's so wrong with that?"

Eliza and Charlotte shared a disbelieving look before Eliza said, "Avery, this is the first morning you've woken up without cursing the alarm. I have to agree. Something is quite amiss."

I rolled my eyes. "Can't a girl just be happy for a new day?"

Charlotte laughed. "If you were anyone but Avery Meyers that may be believable, but in the short time I've known you I'm certain of three things. One, you make the best chocolate truffles I've ever tasted. Two, you may have shit for magic but you

155

don't give up when the going gets rough. And three, you hate mornings. Like *hate* them. In fact, I've never met anyone quite so angry at the sun for rising each day."

"Well, it can be quite bright and annoying. Surely, I'm not the only one who feels that from time to time."

Eliza smiled, her pointy teeth sparkling white. "Do you know that in the summers in my village, the sun only sets for four hours? Something tells me it's not a place you would enjoy inhabiting."

"But the winters are probably fantastic, eh?" I joked. "Only sunshine for a few hours total then?"

Eliza laughed, the sound like tinkling bells. "That is also true."

"Meyers, you're weird." Charlotte shook her head. "Who doesn't like the sun? I could bask in it every day."

"Um, vampires don't like the sun, and I have nothing against the sun. I just don't like how it rises so early."

She shoved me playfully, and we all laughed.

A few minutes later, we reached the cafeteria and headed inside to meet our squad. Today marked the first day of group training. I had no idea what that meant exactly, but if it meant training under Wyatt, I was all for it.

My stomach flipped at just the thought of our commander. All day yesterday, I'd reveled in one truth—Wyatt Jamison had feelings for me. *Real* feelings. That had to be the reason behind his behavior. It was the only thing that explained his actions.

Since my mother was half werewolf, I'd spent a decent amount of time amongst her pack and other werewolf packs while I was growing up. And there were two things that all male werewolves had in common. One, when they were interested in a female, they showed possessive and territorial behavior around her. Any other male who showed the female attention got an immediate reaction from the territorial male. I smiled, thinking of Wyatt's pulsing anger when I'd had dinner with

Nicholas, how he'd thrown Tim across the dance floor when the frat boy touched me, and how he'd snarled at the technicians in the garage.

Two, if the werewolf male wanted the female badly enough, he would be willing to break rules and social norms to be with her. Last night, Wyatt had created time to be alone with me and had kissed me, touched me, and given me the most mind-blowing orgasm of my life.

Even voicing feelings for me was against SF protocol—and I would know, since I'd reread the handbook following my dinner with Nicholas—but what Wyatt had done, had not only broken the rules, it'd stomped on them, burned them, and given them the middle finger.

You couldn't get more rule-breaking than what we'd done Saturday night. In other words, Wyatt Jamison *wanted* me.

I knew now that when Wyatt whisked me back to headquarters, claiming Institute matters, he'd been lying.

I'd called the Institute yesterday, and they'd sounded surprised at my apologies. Yes, they'd expected me to check in, but no, it hadn't been urgent. I could do my weekly check-ins at my leisure.

I smiled smugly. Wyatt's behavior on Saturday was only explained by his werewolf origins—wolves that wanted a female acted as he had.

Wyatt was interested in me.

Plain and simple.

And knowing that, made me feel freakin' fantastic. I wasn't even mad at him for lying to me about the Institute.

I inhaled the scent of doughy waffles and sizzling bacon as we stepped into the cafeteria.

"There are the guys," Charlotte said, nodding ahead.

Chris, Zaden, Bo, and Nick had arrived through the cafeteria's south door. My breath caught when I looked over their shoulders.

But Wyatt was nowhere to be seen.

Sighing, I picked up my tray and got in line. We all meandered through the serving area, but every time I heard a male speak, laugh, or cough, I looked over my shoulder eagerly.

But each time it wasn't Wyatt.

"That's weird that Major Jamison isn't here yet," Charlotte said when we all sat down at a long table. The din was picking up as more and more SF members filled the cafeteria. "He ate breakfast with us each morning last week."

"I was thinking the same thing." I drizzled syrup distractedly over my waffles, continually eyeing the doors.

"Hi, ladies." Zaden's grin split his face when he pulled out the chair across from us. His skin looked particularly pale this morning next to his dark-green shirt. "You gorgeous girls are a pleasant sight for sore eyes. It was a long and lonely weekend without you. I hear you all went out and didn't invite me." He pouted.

"He's just peeved 'cause Nick and I went out for drinks on Saturday night and didn't bring him along," Chris said, taking the seat across from Eliza.

Charlotte snorted. "And here I thought he was coming on to us again. My mom warned me that vampires were always horny."

Eliza laughed. "My mother said the same thing."

Zaden brought a hand to his chest, as if wounded. "I feel so labeled."

"But it's true, right?" Bo said, sitting beside me. The mid-level sorcerer had also chosen waffles, except instead of syrup, he smothered his in peanut butter.

Zaden grinned again. "Well, I mean if any of these women *want* to fuck, I'd be all for it."

I rolled my eyes, for once looking away from the doors. "So charming."

"Just wanted to make sure the offer's clear." He winked at me.

I took another bite of my waffles and tried to pay attention as my squad mates continued to banter, but my gaze stayed focused on the cafeteria entry points. *Where was he?*

Before I could take another bite, the corner door opened. A tall woman stepped inside, her black hair pulled back into a severe bun. Her complexion was a dark brown, and she looked like she could bench press more than most men.

And then Wyatt appeared right behind her.

I nearly dropped my fork, but I managed to catch it at the last moment.

"Whoa," Nick said. "Careful there, Meyers." He blotted at the syrup droplets that had flown from my utensil onto his shirt.

"Sorry," I mumbled just as Wyatt approached our table with the tall woman following him.

He stopped when he reached us, nodding in greeting. "New recruits, good morning."

The woman didn't say anything.

Everyone mumbled, "Morning, sir," as I did my best to do the same.

I looked at him expectantly, willing him to show me a flash of *something* that indicated his heart was beating as fast as mine.

But Wyatt's jaw was set, his gaze staying over our heads.

"Finish eating, then join us outside." Wyatt glanced at his watch. "Ten minutes."

With that, he turned on his heel. He and the tall woman left the cafeteria as quickly as they'd come.

I frowned and picked up my fork again, but then I figured his snub was to be expected since technically dating one another was against the rules.

I still didn't know how we'd continue seeing each other, but I figured we would work something out.

Smiling, I dug into my food.

CHAPTER EIGHTEEN
WYATT

Ten minutes later, all of my recruits were standing on the training field. The air whipped around us, and Avery's long mahogany-colored ponytail slapped against her face. The angle of the wind sent her lilac scent careening in my direction.

I ground my teeth together. The inevitable had arrived.

I'd scented her excitement in the cafeteria. More than anything, I'd wanted to pull her aside, wrap her in my arms, and seal her mouth with a kiss. My wolf had whined eagerly, urging me to follow my desires, while sending me more images of our teeth elongating and biting into Avery's neck.

But I couldn't do that.

Not now.

Not for at least two years.

Fucking hell. Despite knowing that, my attraction to her was still growing.

And seeing her face and her reaction to me when I'd approached their table . . . I could tell this wasn't a simple crush for her either.

We were made to be together.

I was as sure of that as I was the sky was blue.

Which only made this harder.

I tried to mentally shake myself from those thoughts as my recruits all looked to me and waited for my orders. Dee stood beside me on the sideline. It was another sunny day, but gray clouds hovered near the western horizon. Rain looked to be in the forecast.

Only ten feet separated Avery and me. Her gaze kept darting my way, raking over my frame. I wore my usual cargo pants and T-shirt. So did she.

My cock twitched when I took in the curve of her neck, the swell of her breasts, and the flare of her hips. Damn.

Damn. Damn. Damn.

I shouldn't be noticing things like that.

A scent of desire coated in lilacs floated toward me. My lips parted. Avery was feeling as charged as I was.

But as I had in the cafeteria, I continued to ignore her.

Avery's smile faltered, and Chris gave her a side-eye, a knowing smirk curving his lips. He'd scented her desire too.

My wolf snarled, and an image of me lunging at the young wolf and snapping his neck filled my mind. My heartbeat picked up, and I had to physically stop myself from reacting.

Inside, I turned a deadly growl on my wolf. *Attack my new recruit? You want me to* attack *a new recruit because he scented Avery's desire?*

My wolf's only response was a snarl.

Yes. Yes, he did.

I plowed a hand through my hair. This was madness. My wolf was legit going insane because I wouldn't claim our mate.

Major Armund needed to take her away. She couldn't take her away fast enough, because I couldn't think with Avery around, and I sure as hell couldn't do my job.

Dee gave me an expectant nudge as I continued to stand

there, and I wondered how long I'd been complacent while an inner battle waged within me.

Snapping myself out of it, I stood straighter and shouted, "New recruits, this is Major Armund." I waved to her. "She'll be joining us daily from now on."

Dee scanned all of them, not missing a thing. She had sharp eyes that reminded me of a hawk, and as one of the leading self-defense instructors at the SF, I valued and respected her authority.

She placed her hands on her hips and nodded at my recruits. When her attention shifted to Avery, she gave a small smile.

"Major Armund is our most skilled self-defense instructor. After warm-ups this morning, she'll be leaving with Private Meyers to do one-on-one training."

Avery's lips parted, and disappointment splayed across her face. I tried not to be affected by that, but a stone settled in my stomach.

I yanked out my stopwatch. "We'll start with running again today. On my mark."

All of my recruits began to run, and Avery picked up a jog. The path was clearly marked in the field as everyone set their pace.

My jaw stayed tight as I watched all of them. Unlike last week, Eliza didn't hover near the back of the group with Avery. She'd obviously fully acclimated to earth as she picked up an easy sprint. She quickly gained ground, running alongside Nick, which left Avery on her own, alone to bring up the rear.

My wolf rumbled. He didn't like seeing Avery left behind.

Avery's face clouded when she finally finished her first lap. She craned her head, taking in the rest of her squad already on the opposite side of the track, some ready to lap her a second time.

"Figures," she muttered under her breath.

The comment drifted to me on the wind. From the looks of

it, her mood was suddenly matching the growing gray clouds in the west. I didn't know if that was because I still hadn't acknowledged her or if it was because she was coming up last again—or both.

Dee and I watched as my new recruits ran for twenty minutes, doing lap after lap as the wind steadily picked up. Everyone encouraged or greeted Avery when they ran past her, but unlike last week when she didn't seem to mind being the slowest in the group, with each lap her expression grew more frustrated and resigned.

I hated seeing that dejection in her. I could practically taste it.

I crossed my arms, my stance rigid. It took everything in me not to go to her. I wanted to comfort her and reassure her that she was perfect as she was. Just because she was lesser magically didn't mean she was *less*.

But I couldn't do that. Not here and not now.

"Everyone drop and give me a hundred," I said after they finished the twenty minutes. I softened my tone when I turned to Avery. "Private Meyers, you may do twenty."

Her teammates all fell to the ground, immediately in the push-up position as they began doing the morning drill.

Avery was the last to begin, her cheeks bright red. She slowly pushed up and down.

Her gaze darted to Bo. Among the men, he was the weakest, but he was still moving twice as fast as Avery.

Then she looked at Eliza. Unlike last week, the fairy was pushing up and down quickly, breezing through this exercise.

I gritted my teeth. It was so obvious that Avery was comparing herself to others.

Major Armund seemed to reach the same conclusion. She gave me a knowing look. Already she was learning how she needed to train Avery.

Avery's confidence was low.

That needed to change.

When my recruits finished with the push-ups, I had them all spread out and begin sit-ups. After that, it was jumping jacks followed by lunges.

Avery was gasping for air by the time drills finished, even though she was doing less than everyone else. A flush now filled her neck, and her humiliation was so strong I could scent it.

My jaw locked as I fought my instincts tooth and nail to protect her. I wanted to tell her that she would get stronger and faster. That training took time.

But I also knew that singling her out would only add to her embarrassment, so I kept my mouth clamped shut and only addressed her when drills ended.

"Private Meyers, may I have a word with you?" I looked over her head, fearful my eyes would give away the emotional war raging inside me. So I concentrated on the clouds gathering in the west. They'd moved steadily closer.

Sweat slid past Avery's ears as she struggled to slow her breathing. She also kept a hand on her side, probably feeling a stitch, but she stood straight and replied, "Of course, sir."

I stepped away from the group and Avery followed me to an area near the trees. We weren't far from the others, but it was enough that non-werewolves and vamps couldn't hear us.

When I finally faced her, a small hesitant smile curved her mouth. My lips thinned. When she looked at me like that, I wanted to say to hell with everything.

But I couldn't.

Her hesitant smile grew. "It's so nice to talk at last—"

"Major Armund is going to be training you today." I cut her off, more harshly than I intended, but I *had* to keep my wits about me and having her so close was pushing me to the breaking point. I kept my gaze over her head, refusing to make eye contact. If I did, I would drown in her eyes.

From my peripheral vision, I saw her smile falter, but I kept my expression distant and cold. If my control snapped now, it would be the end of me.

Think of Marcus. Think of Marcus.

"I'm sorry, what?" Avery finally managed.

My stomach tightened at the hurt in her voice. *Stay professional. What would you say if another recruit addressed you like that?*

My nostrils flared. "Do you care to try that question again, *Private?*"

Her eyes widened, and another flush stained her cheeks. "Sorry, *sir*. I don't understand—"

"I've called Major Armund in to do one-on-one training with you. From now on, you'll do drills in the morning each day with your squad, but then you'll spend the rest of the day training with her. She's incredibly talented at teaching self-defense. I've asked her to work privately with you so that we may ready you for the Institute. Your training officially begins now."

Confusion clouded her face. "Of course, sir. So I won't be partaking in the group training at all . . . sir?"

"No, you won't do any of the group training. For the rest of your time here, your training will be tailored to fit you exclusively. As an ambassador student, your training requirements are vastly different than what we expect of SF members."

The scent of humiliation flared from her.

Shit. I didn't mean that as anything other than a practical declaration, but she'd taken it completely the wrong way. I wasn't singling her out because she was inferior. I was singling her out because it scared the crap out of me to know that she could someday be in danger, and the only hope she had at saving herself depended on how well *I* trained her.

But she didn't know that.

She just saw that she was the weakest.

Her shoulders sagged, and my wolf snarled at me so viciously, I feared he would erupt from my chest.

Swallowing down his fury, I forced myself to stand still, staying as cold and unyielding as a glacier. But I couldn't calm the raging power that vibrated within my limbs. My alpha magic flowed so hotly against my skin, it felt like magma, yet I kept it contained even though my muscles strained against the onslaught.

"I understand, sir," she eventually said, eyes down.

The silence stretched between us.

My fingers curled into my palms. I was so close to losing it. *So* close.

Remember your promise. Remember Marcus.

I closed my eyes and took a deep, shuddering breath. Keeping my voice rigid, I said, "Report back with your group at 0600 tomorrow morning. Good day, Private Meyers."

And with that, I strode off.

CHAPTER NINETEEN
AVERY

"Oww," I moaned when I landed on my back for what felt like the fiftieth time. Seriously, this freakin' *hurt*. Nobody had told me that learning self-defense would be so degrading and painful.

"Up. Try it again," Major Armund said from ten feet away.

We were in an indoor training room, and once again, she'd managed to flatten me with one hit. The woman hadn't even broken a sweat since we left my squad mates a few hours ago, yet I felt so sticky and bruised that I didn't know how I was going to survive another day without going to the healing center for a potion.

"Meyers, up," she repeated sternly.

I sat up gingerly, my butt so sore it felt numb. I looped my arms around my knees, struggling to catch my breath. "Do most new recruits do this badly, ma'am?"

"Most, but not all." A twinkle lit her eyes when she sauntered over. She held out her hand and pulled me to my feet.

"Now, again. Feet wide, knees bent, arms up. Since you don't have spells to assist you, you need to use your physical attributes."

I did as she said but gingerly. Even moving my legs hurt. "But if I'm ever in a crisis situation, ma'am, I'll most likely be trying to escape from supernaturals that *do* have magic."

"True, but they still have vulnerabilities even if their magic's strong. And you may feel weak, but your magic is useful, especially in this circumstance. You'll be able to immediately gauge how strong they are, which means you'll know what you're up against. That could prove lifesaving."

"Not if I can't get away from them."

"Also true, but that's why you're training with me." She flashed me a smile then brought her hands up. "Okay, enough talking. Widen your stance. A wide stance gives you stability. Remember, you won't be able to overpower anyone. The point is to incapacitate long enough to get away, which means you need to go for pressure points and vulnerable areas. To review, you're aiming for here, here, or here." She moved her hand to her eyes, the base of her throat, then the nerve in the midline of her thigh.

I had to say, when it came to working and getting down to business, Major Armund didn't mess around. Already, I'd learned about areas on a supernatural's body that were perfect for attack. Well, at least the areas on witches, sorcerers, female werewolves, sirens, psychics, and half-demons. Well . . . most half-demons.

We hadn't gotten into fairy, male werewolves, or vampire anatomy yet. She said that since they were the most powerful supernatural creatures, she would train me to deal with them later.

Considering how badly I was doing on the less powerful species training, I figured it would be *much* later.

"All right, try again." Without warning, she came at me. I dodged left just in time or I would have been knocked flat on my back again.

"Good!" she said encouragingly and came at me a second time.

I feinted right at the last moment.

She grinned. "You managed to avoid being pinned twice now, which means you're still free." She mock punched me, but I jumped back, swallowing my wince and how much that abrupt movement hurt. "You're forgetting what your ultimate goal is. Remember, the threat is *real*, which means you need to escape. So what should you be doing now?"

"Distance," I said, then locked my jaw and took another huge step backward as my nerves flared in pain. "I need to put as much distance between my attacker and me as possible."

"Yes, and then?"

"Exit. I need to find my exit points promptly and get away from the threat."

"Precisely." She smiled, obviously pleased that I was turning out to be an apt pupil.

I smirked humorlessly. I may be magically weak, but I could memorize and prioritize like the best of them. After all, I hadn't been accepted into the Institute for my looks. My straight-A grades and ability to remember details had been the real contributing factors.

Which meant I now needed to ace this training.

"All right, again," she said.

MY BODY WAS SO sore by the time we finished that afternoon, I wanted to cry. But for the first time since starting my three-month training stint at the SF, I was actually feeling more confident that I could survive a crisis situation in my upcoming job.

"How'd it go?" Charlotte asked that evening, as she kicked off her boots and plopped down on the living room couch.

I lounged across from her in the armchair. "My body is

screaming at me, but it went well. Major Armund is a really good teacher."

"That's probably why Major Jamison called her in," Eliza replied. A smudge of dirt marred her cheek, and twigs stuck in her purple hair from some drill they'd done requiring tree climbing. "Chris knows her. I guess she's one of the most accomplished female fighters the SF has ever had."

Wincing, I sat up straighter. "Really? What else did Chris say about her?"

"Not much, just that she's a full-blooded werewolf and is from the Idaho pack. He was a kid when she left their pack to come here, so he doesn't know her well."

"Well, she really knows her stuff." With a groan, I stood from the chair and headed for the kitchen, walking gingerly.

I was *definitely* going to need a healing potion before bed tonight. At least when I'd shown up at the healing center before heading back here, I didn't feel too awkward. Rosalie had readily greeted me, and Cora had handed a vial over without even asking what I needed.

Charlotte flipped on the TV, and the supernatural news blared in the background. A story popped up about a coven of witches being captured in Germany. The SF believed they'd been behind several apothecary burglaries in which rare herbs were stolen.

"What should we do for dinner?" Charlotte called from the couch. "Make something or go to the cafeteria?"

I pulled out baking supplies from the cupboard. My legs hurt even standing, but baking would take my mind off things. I still hadn't talked to Wyatt since his cool responses this morning.

"I'm going to make a batch of cookies. Do you want me to make dinner while the cookies are baking?"

"Um, yeah," Charlotte replied. "If your cooking's half as good as your baking, I'm nominating you to cook every night."

Eliza stayed by the counter. "I also agree. The human food

you cook is vastly superior to the cafeteria food. Do you want some help?"

I eyed her smudged cheek and the twigs in her hair. "It's okay. You can go clean up if you want. I got this."

"I wouldn't mind a shower," Eliza admitted, smiling as she let her magic loose, a glow humming along her skin. The dirt on her cheek vanished as a swell of her magic flowed toward me. "Even though I can use magic to cleanse myself, I've grown quite fond of the showers here. My village doesn't believe in the modern ways, preferring the ancient ways of self-induced cleansing."

With that, she twirled around and headed to the bathroom. I was left gripping the counter as her magic dispersed.

One thing I'd come to learn about Eliza? She was much more magical than I'd originally given her credit for. Now that she'd acclimated to the lesser magical environment on earth and was no longer suffering from fae lands withdrawal, her immense power was impossible to miss.

Thinking of Eliza's brief sickness, and our dual plunge into the river, reminded me of my commander. I eyed my baking ingredients, an idea forming.

After seeing how much he enjoyed the sponge cake on Saturday, I figured he'd welcome a batch of homemade cookies, and there was a recipe I'd been working on that I'd almost perfected.

Smiling, I began mixing ingredients. I could bring him a plate of cookies and talk to him privately—truly privately—without anyone around to see or hear us. Then we could figure out how we were going to keep seeing each other.

That fluttering began in my stomach again as I mixed the wet ingredients. Even though Wyatt had been aloof and cool today, I knew I hadn't imagined his behavior on Saturday. I may have been drunk, but I wasn't *that* drunk.

Which ultimately led me to believe that his detached

demeanor this morning was due solely to our audience and not his feelings.

Some of my uneasiness evaporated as I cracked the eggs and whisked them in a separate bowl. If I showed up at Wyatt's doorstep with a plate of warm cookies, alone in his building with nobody to see us . . .

A memory of our passionate encounter stole my breath as my smile turned into a grin.

It was near eight in the evening by the time I made my getaway. Since I didn't want my teammates knowing about my interest in our commander, I had to wait until Eliza and Charlotte were occupied.

At last the opportunity arose when Eliza escaped to her room to conjure a magical connection to the fae lands. She wanted to speak with a friend from her village, which meant she would be busy for at least an hour. And Charlotte finally vanished in the bathroom to shower, which left me alone in the kitchen.

I snatched the plate of cookies I'd set aside and made my way out of our apartment to the commander's quarters at the end of the living barracks.

The evening was warm, the scent of rain still lingering. Small puddles collected on the sidewalk, still present from the afternoon rain shower, but it wasn't until I reached Wyatt's building that I realized I had two problems.

One, I had no way of getting in, and two, I didn't know which apartment was Wyatt's.

Crap.

Biting my lip, I stared at the locked door, wondering what I was going to do when the door swung open and a fairy emerged.

"Hello." He was tall with bright orange hair and a dagger strapped to his waist.

"Good evening, sir." He was about to turn away, so I asked, "Sir, would you be able to tell me which apartment belongs to Major Jamison?"

"You're looking for Wyatt's apartment?"

"That's right."

He looked me up and down. "And you are?"

"Private Avery Meyers. I'm one of his new recruits."

"Place your hand here." He nodded toward the glowing scanner by the door.

I did as he said, and magic enveloped my skin. "Welcome, Avery Meyers," the robotic voice stated. "Access denied."

I gave the fairy a quizzical look.

"Just needed to confirm your identity. We don't get many new recruits wanting to access the commanders' barracks." He placed his hand on the scanner, the robotic voice welcoming him back, and the door clicked open. He held the door open for me. "Wyatt's on the top floor, two doors down on the left. Have a good evening."

"Thanks." I breathed a sigh of relief as I stood in the doorway. "Would you like a cookie for your trouble?"

He raised an eyebrow. "What kind of cookie?"

"Toasted pecan with dark chocolate." I fished a cookie out from under the plastic wrap and handed it to him.

He took a bite and was about to turn away when his eyes widened. "Bless the Queen, where did you get these?"

"I made them."

He took another bite, his eyes closing as he chewed the soft cookie. Two bites later, it was gone. He dusted his hands off as a swell of magic cleansed the butter from his fingers. "That was quite possibly the best cookie I've ever consumed."

I grinned. "Thank you, sir. It's my own recipe. Would you like another?"

He readily held out his hand, so I dropped a second cookie onto his palm. "Much obliged." He gave me a small bow. "And if you're ever inclined, feel free to drop off a plate of those lovely delicious biscuits at my door. First floor, first door on the right."

After the fairy commander left, I took the elevator to the top floor. As soon as I stepped out, butterflies began flapping in my stomach. While this had seemed like a good idea back at my apartment, now I wasn't so sure. Was I being too forward? Too presumptuous?

But then I remembered what I knew of male werewolves.

Nope.

Wyatt liked me.

Plastering a smile on my face, I stopped in front of his door and knocked. Footsteps sounded on the other side before the door swept open.

CHAPTER TWENTY

WYATT

My breath caught in my throat as the scent of lilacs pummeled me. My wolf whined eagerly. Avery stood at the threshold, wearing an unsure smile while she held a plate of cookies.

I tightened the towel around my waist. I'd just showered and had hurried to answer the door, assuming it was another commander—not Avery Meyers.

Her eyes widened, and her nostrils flared, before her gaze traveled up and down my stomach and chest.

My muscles tightened automatically under her heated stare.

And then I remembered that nothing could come of this. I let my eyelids grow heavy, dipping to conceal my pleasure at seeing her again, but I would be lying to myself if I said I didn't like the effect my naked chest was having on her.

I felt like puffing up like a peacock. Immature, but true.

Avery finally stopped ogling and lifted her face to mine. "Hi . . . I, uh, made you cookies." She held the plate out. "You know, to fatten you up," she said playfully.

I made sure to keep my look veiled and my expression neutral. "Oh, right. You didn't need to do that."

When I made no move to grab the plate, her hold faltered, and she brought the cookies back to her chest. "I'm sorry. I thought you'd like them, but—"

"No, it's okay," I said coolly. *Dammit.* As much as it thrilled me to see her, the sooner I got this done with, the better. "It's a nice gesture, and I appreciate it, but I can't accept them."

"You can't?"

"No, I . . ." I ran a hand through my wet hair, the other hand still holding the towel. "Shit, this is awkward."

Her face fell, and she took a step back as my heart beat so hard I was certain she could hear it.

I gritted my teeth and prepared myself for what I had to do. We needed a clean break, which meant I needed to reject my mate. Fuck, I *hated* this. But in a couple of years, after my promise was kept and I could leave the SF, I could pursue her and beg for her forgiveness.

But now wasn't an option. I couldn't ask her to give up her future and career to sit here waiting around for me.

My wolf snarled.

Yeah, I know buddy, but fucking timing. I can't control that.

I lifted my gaze above her head, unable to witness the impact my words would have on her, which was cowardly and I knew it, but if I saw it . . .

I didn't know if I could continue, and I *had* to. I owed Marcus that much.

Keeping my eyes up, I bit out, "I'm sorry, Avery, for misleading you on Saturday. I mistakenly thought the Institute needed to contact you more urgently than was needed."

"Oh, okay." Her breathing picked up. "For what it's worth, I already knew that, but I thought you got me from the bar because you . . . you know, *like* me, and then when you kissed me, I thought for sure—"

"I shouldn't have done that. It was against protocol and an unfortunate choice on my part. You have my apologies." She swayed, but I kept talking, forcing myself to get it all out. "I'm sorry I gave you the wrong impression."

"Wrong impression?" she parroted.

I clenched my jaw, and a swell of power rose from me of its own accord. "My behavior was inappropriate and of poor judgment. It won't happen again."

She stood there, looking dazed. "But we practically slept together, and the things you said, and the way you acted at the bar, and you're a male werewolf—" She shook her head as confusion fogged her expression. "I thought males werewolves didn't act that way unless it meant something. Not unless they were complete manipulative assholes who were playing a female, and you're not like that."

I still couldn't make eye contact. She wasn't wrong. Male werewolves didn't act that possessive unless it meant something, well, unless they were total dicks and playing a woman like she said.

But I didn't reply. If I did, my true feelings would come pouring out.

She frowned. "Unless what we shared wasn't real for you . . ."

I let her process my rejection as much as it killed me to see the hurt growing on her face. The floor shifted beneath me, and I wanted to sink through it. My wolf snarled, enraged at what I was doing.

But what choice did I have?

Being with her now wasn't an option.

I forced myself to think of Marcus. I pictured his bloody face when the last breath left his chest, and managed to keep my face cold and expressionless. I owed him this. I owed him my *life*.

Avery took a step back, her heart hammering so hard it sounded like thunder in my ears.

"I'm sorry," she finally said. "I thought what we did was the beginning of . . ." Embarrassment stained her cheeks red as tears pricked her eyes. She rapidly blinked, but the tears stayed.

My heart sank. *Oh, Little Flower, it* was *the start of something.* I started to cave because seeing her so dejected . . .

I couldn't do this.

My foot lifted, my body moving forward. I wanted to reach for her, to pull her into my arms and to say to hell with everything, but then Marcus's bloody face filled my mind.

I jerked to a stop.

Avery's throat worked a swallow, her tear-filled eyes watching me, but when I just stood there, a sad resigned acceptance filled her eyes.

She abruptly turned and fled down the hall.

My breath rushed out of me as I stared at the empty threshold. My chest heaved, my heart racing so fast it slammed against my ribs. I gripped the door handle tightly, my knees nearly buckling beneath me.

Oh fuck. What did I just do?

I closed my eyes.

It's not too late to go after her. My wolf whined in agreement.

I pictured myself catching up with her, twirling her around, and begging her for her forgiveness. I could come clean about how I really felt.

But then I would be fired from the SF.

No, stay strong. Don't cave!

I couldn't think about what I just did. It would *kill* me to think that way.

I had to live with this. For two more years, I'd have to live without her. For now, things between us were done. I'd made the right choice—the *responsible* choice.

But I just stood there, the door still open while water droplets fell from my hair onto my shoulders.

Because none of this *felt* right.

Agony clenched my gut, making me want to rage.

Yet, I'd made the best choice. *Right?*

Eventually, I closed the door and leaned my head against it. Blood pounded in my ears, and despair ripped apart my soul.

Even though I'd made the responsible choice, that didn't stop how I'd made her feel.

You're a real asshole, Jamison. As much as you don't want to admit it, there was nothing right about treating her that way.

Gods, the look on her face.

The confusion.

The disbelief.

And then the sudden acceptance and embarrassment.

It had all been written in her expression, as plain as day, and she'd so quickly accepted it—her self-esteem and confidence that low that she didn't believe I'd actually wanted her.

She'd thought I'd cared for her, and I cared *so* much, more than she could ever know.

She'd thought on Saturday we'd shared something special, and we had. It would no doubt haunt me for years to come.

Yet I'd just made her feel that it was all in her head. That it wasn't mutual. And that I didn't want her in return.

I'd *gaslighted* her, even though that wasn't how I'd meant for it to go. Not at all.

"Fuck, Jamison. Fuck. *Fuck!* How are you ever going to repair this? What if she never forgives you?"

My wolf snarled inside me, furious at what I'd chosen. His magic swelled, hairs appearing on the back of my hands.

He wanted *out*.

I pushed him down, but that didn't stop my self-disgust.

My chest heaved as images of Avery flooded my mind. The flush of her cheeks when she'd seen me in my towel. The way she'd held out a plate of cookies to me.

It was obvious she'd made them from scratch, had made them for *me*, and I hadn't even accepted them.

I'd shoved that gift right back in her face.

I banged my head on the door. "I need to get out of here."

I grabbed a pair of shorts and tossed them on before flying barefoot from my apartment.

I was in the entryway on the main floor, about to head out the door, when the scent of cookies filled my nose. I whirled around, my heart pounding. *Avery?*

But all that remained was her plate of cookies, discarded by Bavar's door—the fairy commander of Squad Three, Charlotte's future squad leader.

Avery had obviously set them down in haste. Two had slipped from the plate, resting upside down on the floor, crumbs scattered on the carpet.

I bent down and grabbed a cookie from underneath the plastic wrap. The buttery, soft morsel smelled like heaven. I took a bite, my eyes closing when a burst of flavors coated my tongue.

My chewing slowed, and I dropped the cookie. It landed like the other two, upside down while spewing crumbs everywhere.

Even though it was probably the best cookie I'd ever had, I couldn't eat any more. I couldn't think about the fact that she'd made them for me, and I'd . . .

A snarl ripped from my throat as magic swelled inside me, the hot power erupting from my wolf as he strained to run free.

I barreled through the front door and welcomed the night.

I shifted mid-run on my way to the woods, my shorts shredding and falling behind me. I let my wolf take over, embracing his pain and rage.

I deserved it.

I deserved nothing less than his anger for me.

But it wasn't just *his* pain I felt, it was mine, too, only it was too torturous to bear.

My mind closed off as my wolf took over. All that filled us now was the scent of rain, the damp earth thundering beneath our paws, and the night sky that shone above.

I gave into his instincts—his need to run, escape, and forget what I'd done.

A howl ripped from our throat, the sound achingly alone, as remorse consumed us.

Even though there was no running from this, we ran and ran, trying desperately to outrun the heartache that burned our soul—my wolf and I as one, as the miles escaped beneath us.

CHAPTER TWENTY-ONE
AVERY

I hurried back to my apartment, my arms wrapped around my chest as I desperately wished for the earth to open up and swallow me whole.

Wyatt had just rejected me—fully and completely rejected me.

How could I have been so stupid? How could I have actually believed that he cared for me?

I'm such an idiot!

I bit my lip and rethought the details of Saturday night. Obviously, I'd embellished things. I scoffed. Or perhaps the truth was that I'd fabricated everything.

I scrunched my eyes together as mortification flowed hotly through my veins.

I will never be able to look him in the eye again.

My mind transported back to high school, when I'd secretly crushed on him as every other girl in our school tried to catch his attention too.

Shame filled me as I came to see Saturday night in an entirely new light.

Nothing had changed.

Absolutely nothing.

I would never be good enough for Wyatt, worthy of him, someone who he would consider an equal.

He had once been the unattainable golden boy of his pack, only now his status had risen so much higher since he was also a respected and high-standing commander in the SF.

And who was I? A barely magical ambassador recruit who would have never qualified to be admitted into the SF as permanent staff. I probably wouldn't even qualify for their cleaning team, so why did I think one of their strongest members would want me in return?

Embarrassment flamed my cheeks as every insecurity I'd ever felt came roaring back.

In the distance, a long, forlorn howl rose, carrying to me on the wind.

A shiver wracked my body that had nothing to do with the wolf out there. All I could think about was how I'd made an absolute fool of myself. How wanting so badly to be with Wyatt had made me see things that weren't there.

What have I done?

I DIDN'T LOOK at my commander the next day. I couldn't. I was still so humiliated by everything, so I kept my head down, did my drills, then escaped with Major Armund to continue my self-defense training.

Major Armund pushed me hard, mercilessly.

And I welcomed it.

I welcomed the pain, the sear of my muscles as they strained against her attacks and the heave of my chest as I struggled to breathe.

All of it kept me from thinking about Wyatt, about my

embarrassment, about my shortcomings, about knowing that I would *never* be good enough for him.

But by my second week of training with Major Armund, my humiliation floated away and anger took its place because Wyatt now treated me as if nothing had ever passed between us.

But it had. The more I thought about it, the more I realized I hadn't imagined anything.

For fucks sake, the man had *fingered* me, we'd gone down on each other, he'd called me *Little Flower*—using some fake term of endearment to trick me—and then he acted like it'd all been a dream. In my *head*.

Damn him.

He'd played me. Totally and completely played me. It hadn't been in my head. He'd used me and then acted like I was the crazy one to think he liked me.

I never would have thought he was the kind of guy to do that, but if he actually cared for me, he wouldn't have acted like that Saturday night never happened, even if it was against the rules.

And now that some time had passed, I knew I hadn't imagined a few things. It wasn't normal for a commander to throw other men off a new recruit in a fit of rage, or to whisk that new recruit from a bar and then hang out in her apartment before escaping to the outdoors to eat cake while gazing at the stars. And it *definitely* wasn't normal for a commander to kiss a new recruit and get naked with her.

The only explanation for his behavior was that he'd found me attractive and had acted on it, but he didn't like me enough to actually pursue a relationship with me. In other words, he'd used me, and *that* made me question if I ever knew Wyatt at all.

Because the Wyatt I remembered from high school never would have acted that way with a woman and then pushed her away.

I punched again at the bag Major Armund held, taking all of my aggression out on it.

"Good!" she said with a grin. "Again."

I punched harder, my hurt and embarrassment exploding through my movements, not even caring when my wrist ached and my stomach muscles burned.

Because at the end of the day, Wyatt hadn't acknowledged that he'd made a mistake. He hadn't been honest about his feelings.

No.

He'd thrown me under the bus, pretended it was all on *me*, then said it could never happen again and sent me on my way.

Fuck him! I slammed my fist into the bag again.

It was only after thirty minutes of relentless punching, as sweat poured from my forehead like rain down a windowpane, that Major Armund finally stopped me.

"Okay, Meyers. That's enough for today." She handed me a towel.

I grabbed it and bent over. My chest shuddered as I struggled to catch my breath, so I rested my hands on my knees as my muscles quivered.

Major Armund cocked her hip and placed a hand on it, then quirked an eyebrow. "Are you gonna tell me what's going on, Private?"

I straightened, wiping at the sweat on my face. "Ma'am?"

She sighed. "The kind of rage you've been showing lately isn't from training. Something personal's going on. Do you care to enlighten me?"

I pressed my lips together. I couldn't tell her. No way.

Even though a part of me screamed to confide in someone, I couldn't tell Major Armund anything. Part of being a good ambassador was learning to control your emotions and not giving into your impulses, yet I'd done both during the past week of training. Besides, Major Armund was Wyatt's friend. If

I told her, she might tell him, and I'd already been humiliated enough for a lifetime.

"No, ma'am. I'm fine."

Her arched eyebrow rose higher. "So that's how you're gonna play this? That you're fine when you're clearly not?"

I nodded curtly. If I really needed to talk to someone, I would call someone outside of the SF. I couldn't confide in anyone here, not even Eliza or Charlotte, but I could tell my mom. She would understand since she and my dad were both ambassadors.

From them, I'd learned how crucial it was to maintain social niceties. Growing up, if things got rough, my mom and dad would lean on each other and confide in one another when work became too stressful to manage on their own. Their intensely close relationship sometimes made my heart ache. They loved each other *so* much, and I wondered at times if I would ever experience that.

But one thing I'd learned year after year from them was that they never aired work stressors with others. Diplomatic alliances could be precarious, and they had to be protected at all costs. Confiding in girlfriends or my trainer was a luxury I didn't have. A good ambassador would never do that.

My shoulders slumped. I wiped more sweat from my brow and forced a smile. "I just want to get better, ma'am. Since I can't rely on magic, I need to become physically stronger. It's frustrating at times. That's all."

She relaxed her stance. "Speaking of magic, I've been thinking. We should try to develop your magic more." She held up her hand when I started to protest. "I know, I know. You've never been magically strong, but you've also never had intense magical training. I spoke with Reese, one of our sorcerers, about you last night. He's willing to dedicate a few hours to training you. And if you show any aptitude, he'll continue, and if you don't . . ." She shrugged. "At least we tried."

"Do you really think I could improve, ma'am?"

She smiled crookedly. "Only one way to find out."

My palms were sweating the next day. Major Armund said we'd be starting with Reese today when my training began after drills.

"Drop and give me a hundred," Wyatt called from the front of my squad. "Privates Larson, Lane, and Morris give me two hundred. Private Meyers, twenty."

I gritted my teeth and began doing push-ups. "I can do more, sir." I pushed up and down mechanically. My muscles burned, but I was growing stronger. After a few weeks of this, I'd improved.

Wyatt's feet appeared in my peripheral vision. He'd moved like a werewolf—completely silently—but now that he stood right over me, I felt his energy.

It strummed toward me in steady waves, rising higher. "You may do more if you wish, Private Meyers," he said quietly.

I pumped up and down harder and faster, putting everything I had into showing him that I wasn't going to let the SF or him break me. He took a step back, but I felt him continue to watch, his energy as sharp and acute as a tracking hex.

"Up!" Wyatt called a minute later. "Jump lunges then knee tucks." His expression remained stoic, but several times his gaze drifted my way.

My heart beat erratically from the exercise, and lactic acid burned so strongly in my muscles that I feared I would collapse, but I forced myself to keep moving.

Charlotte grinned at my side, her speed increasing with every jump.

Chris and Zaden were no different. The vamp and wolf now trained side by side, the earlier angst they had with each other not as apparent. I didn't know what Wyatt was doing with their training, but I knew he made them work together a lot.

When we finally finished drills, I was gasping for breath while my thigh muscles burned in agony. I managed to stay upright but barely.

"Private Meyers," Wyatt said from the side. "You may join Major Armund now."

I nodded curtly, still too out of breath to speak. After waving goodbye to my squad mates, I headed toward the training center, but Wyatt's call stopped me.

"Private Meyers?" He'd left the group, silently approaching me from behind. When I tilted my chin up, he said haltingly, "How is your training going?"

"Fine, sir."

He gave a nod, his green eyes a stormy torrent. "Do you feel you're improving then? That you'll be able to handle a crisis situation at the Institute should one arise?"

I tried not to be affected by the deep ache in his voice. It made me think that he actually cared about what happened to me, but then I remembered he was simply doing his job. "I do, sir. I mean, not yet, but I feel after my time is finished here that I'll be better off."

"And Major Armund isn't pushing you too hard?"

"No more than you, sir."

His lips quirked up in a sad smile. "I'm glad to hear it. Carry on."

I nodded stiffly and began walking toward the training center again, yet with each step I took, I still felt Wyatt's energy. It rolled into my back in warm waves, and a shiver ran down my spine.

Despite recovering from the earlier drills, my heart pattered again for an entirely new reason, and I wanted to stab myself for it.

Yet, when I reached the door, I couldn't help it. I glanced over my shoulder.

The rest of my squad was already in the midst of a new training exercise, yet Wyatt's attention was focused on me.

But the second he caught my curious glance, he turned his back, his body once again a wall of rigid stone as he walked away.

CHAPTER TWENTY-TWO
WYATT

I excused my new recruits for lunch, then headed to the training center. I told myself that I was only going to check in on Avery's progress. She was already in her third week at the SF, and as her squad commander, it was my duty to ensure she was progressing adequately.

I snorted inwardly. *That's right. It's duty that calls you.* It wasn't because I simply wanted to see her, even if it was from afar. No, it was strictly professional.

Just keep telling yourself that, Jamison.

I silently opened the training room door, and the pungent scent of old rubber, dry sweat, and metallic magic from the wards greeted me. But underneath it all was that floral aroma I had begun associating with longing, lust, and unrequited wanting—Avery's signature lilac scent.

Fuck, Little Flower, I miss you.

I crept to the wall in the shadowed entry, as silent as a stalking wolf. Nobody detected me, not even Dee who was used to working with other werewolves.

"Try again," Reese, one of our sorcerers, said. He positioned himself behind Avery and lifted her arms, helping her swish her fingers in a precise pattern through the air. "And your cadence on the second word is off. *Leminee*, the last syllable is lower."

"*Avartus contorum leminee*," Avery repeated, the *ee* sound on the last word longer. A slight spark shot from her fingertip, but it quickly fizzled out.

"Better. That's better." Reese waved his hands and repeated the incantation. A blast of sparks shot from his hand before turning into a glowing blue ball. He wove the ball through the air, the energy from it crackling. Another second passed, then his hands shot out and the ball exploded into the wall. The wards around the room vibrated, effectively stopping it, and a shower of sparks rained. "That's the potential strength this particular binding spell has."

I stayed where I was, hidden in the shadows, lurking like some crazy lovestruck stalker. But I couldn't help it. That was exactly what I was, and I *had* to see her.

Avery frowned. "I'm sorry, sir. I've never been skilled at spells and incantations."

Reese smiled, his expression encouraging. "Don't apologize. Let's try again, except this time I want you to close your eyes. Feel for your magic inside your chest and pull it to your fingers."

I crossed my arms, my back rigid as I watched him work with her. A snarl wanted to erupt from my chest. Reese was touching Avery, even if it was only her wrists.

It didn't help that Reese was a nice guy, a highly trained sorcerer, and was good with recruits. A lot of his students adored him.

He was also incredibly talented and was called in to assist with sorcerers who showed advanced aptitude. Ultimately, he would be in charge of Nick's training.

But as for why Major Armund had called him in to work with Avery . . .

That was unusual, and I thought since Avery was a witch

that wouldn't have happened. Normally, sorcerers and witches taught their own, so if anything, a witch should have been in charge of Avery's magical training.

But whatever Reese was doing, it seemed to be working.

My chest tightened with pride when another spark shot from Avery's fingers. There were at least three blue sparks that time, and they lasted longer before extinguishing.

A grin split across her face, and she turned shining eyes up to Reese. "That worked better!"

He dipped his head, a scent of satisfaction erupting from him.

Despite feeling so damned proud of her that I wanted to grin, my nostrils flared, and my wolf growled. Reese's satisfaction was obviously because Avery had done better, but it didn't stop the hot flow of jealousy that scorched my skin.

Only two weeks ago, Avery had smiled at *me* like that. Her eyes had shone with hope and laughter as the undercurrents of desire had filled her lilac scent.

Has it already been two weeks since that night under the stars?

It felt like a lifetime.

Agitation oozed from my wolf at the addition of a male trainer to Avery's schedule. I knew I would be having a private conversation with Major Armund about what she was up to. Never in our discussions had she divulged bringing a sorcerer in to assist.

And it didn't help that Reese was young and single, but at least as another SF superior he also wasn't allowed to date Avery.

Still . . . it didn't stop my jealousy. *I* wanted to be the one touching Avery, yet Reese was the lucky bastard who got that job.

I gritted my teeth and finally pushed away from the wall. I exited the training room as silently as I'd entered it. Anger and regret strummed through me as I strode through the halls.

I pictured Marcus again, and thought of Avery learning her new job unencumbered by a wolf lusting after her half a world away—a wolf she couldn't even properly be with.

I needed those reminders right now of why I'd turned my back on her, because every time I walked away from her, it still felt so wrong.

I WAITED for Major Armund outside of her barracks later that evening. Twilight had set in, bringing with it chirping crickets and the scent of night.

"Major Armund, may I have a word?" I asked when she approached the brick building.

"Sure, Jamison. What's up?" She placed her hands on her hips, her stance casual on the sidewalk. A light breeze whistled through the trees, rustling the boxwood hedges near the barracks.

"I happened to walk by the training room earlier today and noticed that Reese was working with Avery." I paused, wondering how to word my question without sounding like a jealous wolf. "To be honest, I was a bit surprised. I didn't realize you planned to pull him in."

She shrugged. "I didn't initially, but Avery's not easy to train. Physically, she's not much stronger than a human, so the only chance she has of effectively dealing with a crisis situation against a powerful supernatural is if her magic improves. She needs *something* to use other than her wits, and she'll never pass her final test unless she has some magic, and we both know if she doesn't pass that test, she can't continue on to the Institute."

My jaw worked. Dee was right. Without any magic whatso-ever, Avery would have a hard time passing her final test.

But more than that, she needed magic to defend herself. Just the thought of another supernatural trying to harm her, pin her, or hurt her, made my blood turn to ice.

I frowned. "And you think Reese is the answer? Wouldn't a witch be a more appropriate teacher given Avery is a woman?"

Dee cocked her head, her expression thoughtful. "Initially, I thought so, too, but then I looked more into her background. She attended magical school during her childhood, and some of those schools were quite prestigious, yet she never showed any aptitude for witch spells or incantations, despite sufficient training. I know that's not unusual for a half-breed witch whose magic comes from a sorcerer father, but her father is also a rare breed of sorcerer. Like Avery, his abilities lie in detecting other's magic, so I thought why not have a sorcerer give her training a go. Their spells are slightly different. Maybe her magic will respond to it even though that's rare. If I can just get her to master one defensive spell and one offensive spell, she'll be much better off."

My earlier conviction that I'd done the right thing by asking Major Armund to train Avery came roaring back. I never would have thought to give sorcerer magic a try with Avery. But I kept picturing Reese touching her.

Dee frowned. "Everything okay, Wyatt?"

I raked a hand through my hair. *Damn*. I was losing it again, and Dee had obviously just picked up on that.

"Yeah. Of course." I reminded myself that Avery's training was my priority, even if that meant other men touching her during training—as long as those touches stayed respectful and professional.

Because if they didn't . . .

I growled, but then cut it short, my eyes widening that I'd allowed the sound to escape.

But Dee's attention had shifted to something on her tablet. She sighed and held up a picture of a few of our squad mates on a beach in the Caribbean. "Damn, and to think that's where I could have been right now."

I dipped my head. "I'm sorry. I didn't mean to stop your trip, but I do appreciate you training Avery."

She chuckled and slipped her tablet back into her pocket. "Just as long as we're even after this."

"Of course. I won't ask for a favor like this again."

"Good." She loosened her stance, looking toward the door. "Well, if there's nothing else?"

"No, have a good evening, Major."

She nodded curtly before disappearing into the barracks.

I let out a deep sigh. It was sheer luck that Dee hadn't noticed my second territorial reaction to Avery. If that message hadn't come through from our friends . . .

I seethed. I couldn't keep up this charade much longer. Dee was too good at analyzing people and too apt at reading between the lines. Sooner or later, she would see that I couldn't help myself where Avery was concerned.

It was only a matter of time before she found my intense interest in Avery's training peculiar. Because even though I was required to train Avery, I *wasn't* required to watch over every second of her progression.

"Shit," I whispered. I needed to back off. I could check on her once a week while she trained with Armund, but that was it. More check-ins than that and I was bound to do something foolish.

I straightened when a group of SF members strolled by on the sidewalk. Their conversation floated toward me. "Did you guys hear about that comet that's going to pass over the fae lands? It hasn't happened in two thousand years. Should be a pretty wicked sighting."

"When's it going to happen?" another asked.

"In earth time, two months from now."

I concentrated on their conversation, trying to distract myself with it. I'd heard, too, about the comet barreling toward the fae lands' solar system.

But my hope of using their conversation as a distraction backfired. The comet only reminded me of that night with Avery. The night she'd baked me a cake, we'd lain under the stars, and had touched and kissed with such intense passion that it still haunted my dreams.

My heart throbbed with the need to claim her. I'd wanted so desperately to claim her that night. I *still* felt that way. Weeks away from her had only made the urge grow, not lessen.

My wolf whined within. He again wanted out, to run, to forget the torment I was forcing on him. Each day at morning drills while we merely existed in Avery's presence, he'd grown more demanding and irritated when I refused to submit to his desires.

But I couldn't.

Avery wasn't ours. Not yet.

She *wasn't* our mate even if we wanted her to be.

And we both needed to remember that.

But a run for my wolf? That I could oblige.

"I can probably use one myself," I said to him. I headed toward the woods, my pulse quickening as magic shimmered over my skin. The heat built inside me as my wolf urged the shift.

I stripped out of my clothes, setting them behind a tree to retrieve later. Standing upright, I let the shift take hold. Heady magic pulsed over my body, heating my skin, and then my wolf emerged in an explosion of magic.

The release eased the throb of longing squeezing my chest as my mind faded to the background and my wolf's took over.

But his mind still ached for Avery, too, and his desire to be with her bordered on obsession.

We can't, I said to him.

He whined again, knowing I wouldn't allow it.

But we can run.

He took off, the call of the woods and the pull of the moon the only things keeping us from howling in pain at the loss of Avery Meyers.

CHAPTER TWENTY-THREE
AVERY

Days turned into weeks. Then weeks turned into months. Before I knew it, my three-month stint at the SF was almost up, and I was only two weeks away from my final test.

My mornings with Wyatt and the rest of my squad were routine and short now. I only saw Wyatt for an hour each day. I hardly ever saw Bo, Chris, Zaden, or Nick, and I only saw Eliza and Charlotte in the evenings in our apartment.

And as each week had passed, I'd questioned more and more why I ever thought Wyatt was interested in me. Because even though Wyatt was professional, he was also aloof, and I swear he only looked at me when he had to. And why wouldn't he? I wasn't one of them—I would never be an elite SF member—and he'd effectively wiped his hands of me.

I figured my lack of skills and my blunder at the start of my training explained his disinterest. And our hookup was also probably why he'd pawned me off on Major Armund, so I wouldn't get the wrong idea. Either that or he'd realized I was too difficult to train so he couldn't be bothered.

But that dismissal had only made me work harder, determined to show him that while I may not be strong, I wasn't completely useless.

Each day, Major Armund pushed me relentlessly. I worked with Reese, too. He became a constant shadow, and slowly, my magic improved.

I would never be what one would call *magically inclined*, but I was stronger than I'd ever been. I managed to master one defensive shield spell by the end of my second month and was progressing toward mastering an offensive binding spell. With any luck, I would have both mastered before my final test.

It was the best I'd ever done.

To say I was proud would be an understatement. I'd never mastered any spells in school while growing up. When all of the other students were a dozen spells ahead of me, each year I was placed in the back of the class with the other less magically inclined to study spellcraft since the practical aspects of it weren't possible.

However, that studying had now come in handy since I'd long ago memorized the spells Reese retaught me, but with his tutelage, I was now also *practicing* them.

"We're going to have you try out your spells on one of the more advanced species today," Major Armund said in the training room.

October had arrived, bringing with it cooler temps. Even though the sorcerers' wards kept the outdoor temperature controlled around headquarters, it was still chilly for training, so we mostly worked indoors now.

"I've called in someone from another squad to work with you this morning," she continued. "I've also told him not to go easy on you."

"Oh?" My curiosity piqued. I'd finished drills a few hours ago and thought we'd be breaking for lunch soon. Apparently not. "Does that mean he's a werewolf, vamp, or fairy?" So far, I'd only practiced with Major Armund, Reese, and a handful of low-magic individuals that she called in at random—witches, sorcerers, half-demons, psychics, and one siren.

She gave me a cheeky smile. "That's for you to figure out."

The door opened in the corner, and a tall man strolled in. My eyes bulged when I recognized the bright orange hair and devilish smile, but the memory of how we'd met made my stomach clench.

"Private Meyers, this is Major Bavar Fieldstone, Squad Three's commander." Major Armund waved the introductions.

"The cookie baker. We've already met." Major Fieldstone dipped into a bow. "Tell me, will I be awarded with another plate of sweets if I best you today?"

"Um, sure. I mean no, because you won't beat me . . . sir." I stumbled over my words. Shock still rippled through me that I'd be battling the fairy—apparently the commander to Squad Three, Charlotte's future squad no less—that I'd met the night I brought a plate of cookies to Wyatt. The night Wyatt had rejected me. It was like pouring salt on an open wound that refused to close.

Not that Major Armund knew that.

"Are there any rules in this sparring?" Major Fieldstone asked Armund.

She shook her head. "Try and take her down. No rules. No honor. She needs to learn what it's like to fight a full-blooded supernatural who's intent on harming her."

Shit. I swallowed the trepidation in my throat. Major Armund was getting serious, which wasn't surprising since my final test was coming up in a few weeks. During that test, I would be assessed on my skills, and it was possible I'd be battling a full-blooded fairy.

I knew my only chance of getting out of a spar with them in one piece was to move quickly and not get caught in hand-to-hand combat. I would never be able to beat a full-blooded male fairy if that happened, but a female in hand-to-hand? Maybe, only because of everything that Major Armund had taught me, but still unlikely.

Major Fieldstone stepped onto the large mat in the center of the room, and I readied myself at the other side. The training rooms often reminded me of gymnasiums in human schools, the difference being that spells and blasts from the magically induced weapons couldn't pierce the warded walls.

And neither could my body flying into them.

I gulped. "You're not going to break any of my bones are you, sir?" I laughed uneasily.

He only grinned. "We have a healing center for a reason, and I believe I was told to take you down."

"But if you want cookies . . ." I tried for a lighter tone since a predatory gleam had filled his eyes.

Major Armund and Reese stood on the sidelines, arms crossed while they wore astute expressions, yet Reese's tapping fingers on his bicep gave away his true feelings. He looked almost as nervous as I felt.

But glancing at him was a mistake. Out of nowhere, Major Fieldstone came at me, his arm locking around my waist and taking me to the mat in a heartbeat. The wind knocked out of me, and for a moment, panic filled me.

I gasped, or tried to, but my lungs wouldn't work.

The commander hovered above me, his skin glowing and his teeth wickedly sharp.

But a moment of concern flashed across his expression when he took in my wide eyes. He probably hadn't realized that I had next to no defenses against him.

But my trainer wasn't nearly as sympathetic. "Up, Meyers," Major Armund said. "Remember what we've been teaching you."

Reese brought a fingertip to his mouth and bit into a nail.

Bavar helped me to my feet, an apology spilling from his lips. "Perhaps I shouldn't be quite so rough."

I gasped, then gulped in a breath when my diaphragm finally kicked in. I shook my head, my nerves fried, but Major Armund was right. I needed this. "No, don't, sir. I need to learn what to expect if I ever find myself in a situation like this."

He dipped his head. "If you wish."

"Again," Major Armund barked. "Remember your spells, Meyers."

Right. As soon as Major Fieldstone was on his side of the mat, I whispered one of my spells under my breath. *"Glosius neforium peesi lumi—"*

He charged.

I hurried the last of it. *"Luminity strogo!"*

The fairy stopped in his tracks, the spell momentarily binding him. I didn't waste any time. I knew I only had seconds before my hold on him dissolved.

I sprinted toward the exit. Elation filled me as it neared.

The door was only two feet away when an arm clamped around my waist. I was about to start kicking, using the combat maneuvers Major Armund had taught me to get out of situations like this, when the door opened.

Wyatt stepped into the room, and when he took in our position, his composure went from relaxed to enraged in a split second.

A snarl tore from his mouth just as Major Fieldstone threw me over his shoulder. I spiraled toward the mat.

I would have hit it, too. I expected to, and I was already curling into a ball to soften my fall and allow me to roll onto my feet again, when a pair of arms caught me and stopped the blow.

Before I could react, Wyatt set me down and was on top of the fairy. He grabbed Major Fieldstone by the shoulders and swung him onto the mat. Major Fieldstone groaned when he hit it, landing flat on his back, but Wyatt was already on top of him.

"What the hell are you doing, Bavar?" Wyatt lifted the fairy by the lapels of his shirt before smacking him back on the mat again. "Are you trying to kill her?"

"Wyatt!" Major Armund yelled. "Get off of him!"

Energy crackled in the air as Reese stepped forward. The sorcerer wove his hands, a spell blasting from his fingertips. It hit Wyatt and seized him.

My commander clenched his teeth and glowered at Reese. Another second passed, then sparks showered around Wyatt when he broke through the sorcerer's binding spell.

Leaving Major Fieldstone on the floor, Wyatt stood up and glared at my trainers. "What the hell is going on here?"

Major Armund rolled her eyes. "We're training her. Remember?"

"Since when is throwing an ambassador recruit across a room considered training? She's not SF. We've *never* trained them like that before. She could break a bone!"

"I know she's not SF, but you asked me to train her for worst-case scenarios, so I am. And she's not a delicate flower, Jamison."

My breath caught as I stood there mutely. *Flower.* It was so close to that term of endearment Wyatt had called me. I clenched my teeth together. *No. I wouldn't* remember that.

Major Armund continued cutting into Wyatt. "I've taught her how to land when she's thrown. She was already maneuvering into the right position when you interfered." She stepped forward, her eyes shooting daggers. "And remember, as an ambassador, it's possible she'll one day be near an assassination attempt or kidnapping. Knowing what it's like to be fully attacked will only help her. The more she knows, the better."

Wyatt paled as I stood immobile on the center of the mat, my eyes burning. My commander slammed a hand through his hair, his face still visibly blanched, but he held out his hand to help Bavar up.

"Fine," Wyatt said stiffly. "Continue."

Rising energy pulsed off him, and Major Armund studied him, a curious glint in her eyes. However, when Wyatt's alpha magic reached me, any thoughts over my commander's peculiar behavior vanished. I shuddered and tried desperately not to react to his power, but my shoulders folded, and my knees weakened.

I seethed. He was so damned powerful, and no matter how hard I tried, I would always cower under his magic.

Damn him.

Gritting my teeth, I waited for it to pass. When it finally did, I took a deep breath and faced Major Fieldstone again.

"Shall we have a second attempt, Private Meyers?" He winked, which alleviated some of my anger toward Wyatt.

My commander moved to the sidelines to stand by Major Armund and Reese. Wyatt's expression was now schooled into blank professionalism, but power still radiated off him in waves.

I tried not to react to his presence, but this was the first time he'd entered the training room, and it was throwing me off. It was just another thing I could be mad at him about.

"When you're ready," Major Armund said.

Not even a second passed before the fairy leapt into the air. I managed to dodge and roll at the last second. If I hadn't, he would have landed on me.

But as soon as I was on my feet again, he was there, reaching for me. His hand wrapped around my arm. I dipped and turned, falling back on the maneuvers Major Armund had been relentlessly drumming into me for months.

His grasp tightened, but my uppercut to his sternum made him grunt. It was enough of a surprise that his fingers loosened, allowing me to twist away.

I was already running toward the door, my binding spell halfway out of my mouth when he pounced on my back.

I shrieked and fell. My chin hit the floor, pain cracking through my jaw. Wyatt pushed away from the wall as Major

Fieldstone pinned me from behind so I was flat on the ground. I tried to wiggle free, but all he did was straddle me and sit on me. I swear the fucker was laughing.

Sure enough, a chuckle escaped him. He flipped me onto my back, still holding me down by the wrists. But as soon as I started to mutter my spell, he clamped a hand over my mouth and leaned down, his crystal eyes filled with mirth.

"Now, now, none of that." He grinned, still straddling me, and it felt as if a truck had parked on my hips. I couldn't move. At all.

Major Armund sighed, and my shoulders slumped in defeat. But it wasn't until I stopped struggling that I realized how intimate our position was. Wyatt growled, the pulsing power off him rising.

However, Bavar swung his leg off me and jumped to a stand, the movement so fluid and graceful that envy stole my breath. I may be coordinated and getting stronger, but hell's bells, I would *never* be able to pull off a move like that.

"Have my actions put my cookies in jeopardy?" the fairy asked as he held out his hand to me.

I grasped it, letting him pull me to my feet. Out of the corner of my eye, Wyatt's heavy stare weighed down on us, but at least he'd retreated to the wall again. "I suppose not, but I may withhold the chocolate chips. They're the best part."

Major Fieldstone laughed, the sound as rich as molasses and as deep as a bass drum.

A shimmer of power strummed toward us. When I faced my trainers again—about to ask what I should have done differently to avoid that pin—all coherent thought left me when I saw my commander.

Wyatt was seething at Major Fieldstone, his jaw clenched so tight it was a miracle his teeth didn't crack.

Major Armund crossed her arms and gave Wyatt a curious look. "Let's do that again. Same maneuver, only this time . . ."

I tried to concentrate on what she was telling me, but it was near impossible to focus with Wyatt hovering on the sidelines.

But I memorized her advice as best I could, and Major Fieldstone and I squared off again.

Thirty minutes passed of more sparring, me fighting, him pinning me, and eventually me conceding defeat. He was nice about it, though, always helping me to my feet at the end and offering encouragement—and maybe a comment or two about his future cookies.

I expected my commander to leave after the first ten minutes or so, but it was like his feet had glued to the floor. Despite the energy pulsing off him—that all of us were ignoring—he didn't excuse himself.

"You're getting better." Major Armund cocked her head thoughtfully. "But we still have a lot of work to do before your final test. I'm confident you'll pass it since ambassador recruit requirements are lower than SF standards, but I'm still not convinced that you'll be able to safely extract yourself from the more powerful species. That's what we'll be focusing on for the rest of your time here."

I breathed heavily as sweat beaded on my forehead. "Of course, ma'am."

"Thank you for your time today, Major Fieldstone." She dipped her head toward the fairy.

"Much obliged." He bowed, then whispered to me, "Don't forget those lovely biscuits you promised."

"I would never, sir," I replied, momentarily forgetting that he was my superior as I smiled sweetly, if a bit sarcastically. "Plain biscuits with too much salt and no chocolate. Coming right up."

He laughed again, a rich bellow that made goosebumps rise on my arms.

I headed toward my water bottle, figuring we were done for the morning when Major Armund said, "Jamison, since you're here, will you have a go? She's never faced a male werewolf before. It will be good for her to learn what to expect and will help me plan the last few weeks of her training."

My feet stilled in their tracks. *Fight my commander? Now?*

I swallowed, my stomach clenching, but Wyatt shook his head. "I don't think that's a good idea. She's not ready."

Major Armund raised an eyebrow. "She only has a few weeks left. There's no time to wait. Besides, she'll never be ready if we don't push her."

Wyatt's brow furrowed, his expression darkening. "Pushing her to fight—"

"I'm sorry, Jamison, who's in charge of her training right now? You? Or me?"

His jaw clamped shut as Major Armund pointed at the mat. "One more round, Meyers. I know you're tired, but since Jamison is here, I want to take advantage of that. You'll be hard pressed to find a stronger werewolf. Better to get an idea of what it can be like so you're not surprised if the situation ever arises."

CHAPTER TWENTY-FOUR
AVERY

oly shit, she's really going to make me do this. Major Fieldstone wished me good luck before he exited the training room. That left me with Major Armund and Reese on the sidelines, while Wyatt prowled the perimeter.

Reese's anxiety pulsed toward me, but this was just training, right? My commander wouldn't actually hurt me. Right?

Oh please, let that be right!

"No going easy on her, Wyatt." Major Armund's dark eyes flashed his way, her meaning clear.

I gulped. Okaaaay. Maybe he *would* hurt me.

Wyatt's nostrils flared before he stepped onto the mat. Energy undulated from him, hitting me again and again. Already, I was having a hard time standing upright, and the man hadn't even done anything yet. How the hell was I supposed to battle a supernatural like him?

I'm dead if this ever happens in real life.

And I knew I would be. While my training was proving more useful than I'd ever dreamed of, I also knew my limits. If a rogue alpha werewolf ever set his sights on me, I was a goner— end of story.

"When you're ready." Major Armund crossed her arms.

I took a deep breath. Seriously, the woman was a bit of a sadist. I knew she had my best interests at heart, but two full-blooded, uber-powerful supernaturals in one morning?

That was just mean.

I bent my knees, not knowing what to expect from Wyatt, as his alpha power continued to barrel into me. I gritted my teeth and whispered my spell under my breath. Surprisingly, he didn't pounce.

"Jamison . . ." Armund said in a warning tone.

My spell hit him, making him go rigid.

I turned to sprint toward the door, but I hadn't even gone two feet before he landed on the ground right in front of me, catapulting over my head as if he were hopping a crack on the sidewalk.

My eyes bulged. He'd moved that fast in his *human* form and had broken through my spell in milliseconds.

I backpedaled, but it was no use. Wyatt wrapped his arms around me and hauled me to his chest. He spun me around, and my back was pressed against his hard abs as his arms locked around my waist.

Ignoring the quiver that began in my stomach, I immediately started to kick, going for the arch of his foot and kneecap, but he shifted his weight, deflecting my blows each time as if he were coddling a toddler having a tantrum.

I tried every defensive maneuver Major Armund had taught me to break out of his hold, but each time I tried something new, Wyatt seemed to anticipate it, effectively halting my efforts.

No wonder the fucker was a high-ranking SF member. He knew every move in the book.

"Dammit," I muttered, and finally gave up. My chest heaved, and my muscles were screaming in agony at the never-ending onslaught of torture from this morning's training session. "You can let me go. I can't break your hold."

Without a word, Wyatt released me. The feel of him vanished, and damn me for missing it. I laughed humorlessly to myself. My trainer may be a sadist, but evidently I was a masochist, because Wyatt had treated me like garbage, yet I still wanted him touching me.

Seriously, Avery. That's just sad.

Anger scorched through me that I was still attracted to him after his soul-lashing rejection, but I squashed it down as far as it would go, and when I faced him again, my expression was carefully blank.

Energy strummed from him as we stared at each other, his eyes like emerald sparks, until Major Armund's command jolted me out of my immobility.

"Again!"

Wyatt growled. "You said one time, and she lost!"

I flinched. Was it really so horrible to spar with me that he couldn't stand doing it? But I immediately stitched up the hole that tore into my heart. I would *not* let him affect me.

Thankfully, Wyatt didn't seem to notice my momentary relapse in feelings. His attention was focused on my trainer who either didn't care or chose to ignore Wyatt's reluctance.

She took an assertive step forward. "I said *again*. I'll decide when we're done for the morning. Avery needs this, and it's helping me too. It lets me see where her weaknesses are so I'll be able to train her better. I don't have much time left. She needs this, Wyatt, and so do I."

Well shit. I grumbled. *How do you argue with that?*

I eyed my commander, wondering if he would even try to.

With a snarl, Wyatt stalked back to the other side of the mat.

Apparently not.

I took a deep breath and tried not to let humiliation flood me. My commander obviously didn't want to be here, but Major

Armund was right. I did need this, but surely Wyatt wasn't the only alpha werewolf in the SF.

"Maybe there's another werewolf I could spar against, ma'am?" I offered. "If Major Jamison would prefer not to?"

Wyatt spun around. "What? No."

"But you seem—"

"I said no!"

I jolted at his harsh tone, my embarrassment turning to confusion, and then to anger again. He seemed grumpy that he'd been roped into this, yet when I offered an alternative he refused.

Fucking typical. Act one way but say something else. Why did I ever think he was a noble person to be admired?

Grumbling beneath my breath, I retreated to my side of the mat. "Fine. Whatever."

"What was that, Private Meyers?" Major Armund asked.

I forced a tight smile. "Nothing."

"And Jamison, what about you?"

He just tipped his chin higher.

Major Armund scowled at us, letting us know that she didn't approve of our attitudes.

I checked myself, even though it was hard. I was letting Wyatt get under my skin again, and hadn't I learned better? And what would the Institute think of their newest member not being able to control herself around a werewolf? They wouldn't approve.

Remember your ambassador training, Avery.

Smoothing my expression and suppressing my emotions, I dipped my head respectfully. "I'm sorry, ma'am. It won't happen again."

Her scowl lessened. "Thank you. Now, again. This time, try the maneuver we practiced last week. Okay?"

"Yes, ma'am." I figured she was being purposefully vague so my commander couldn't anticipate that move.

"Major Jamison?" she said.

Wyatt glared at her before turning his attention back to me. Strong energy still pulsed from him in never-ending waves. Annoyance at his dominance flared in me, but I forced myself to let it go.

The Institute was right about one thing. Training at the SF definitely had its merits. Because if I could survive three months with Wyatt Jamison and not kill him, surely I could survive anything the Institute threw at me.

Gritting my teeth, I held my ground and whispered my spell again, but I wasn't even halfway through it before he was standing in front of me and knocking me to the ground.

I shrieked and windmilled my arms—my mind and body blanking at his unseen attack—but before I could land flat on my back, Wyatt was breaking my fall and lowering me to the mat.

My breath rushed out of me, surprise stealing my voice. One second I'd been standing, casting a spell, and the next I was flat on my floor with my commander hovering over me.

The only positive aspect of my predicament was that his body wasn't directly touching mine. He maintained the plank position, so all of his weight fell onto his forearms and the balls of his feet, yet his scent still flooded me, and only inches separated us.

I stared up at him, my heart suddenly beating two hundred times a minute. Moss-green irises stared back at me, their bottomless depths pulling me in like a siren's call ensnaring an unsuspecting sailor at sea.

Why? Why did my body betray me like this? *Why* did I still find him attractive even though he'd made it clear we would never be anything?

His nostrils flared. Something flickered in his eyes, then his face tightened and he sprang up, the air rustling around me from his abrupt movement.

"She's not ready for this," he growled. Anger radiated in his tone as he addressed Major Armund and Reese. "I was on top of her before she'd said two words of her spell."

"I know." Reese let out a heavy sigh. "Her spells work when she uses them, but against someone such as . . ." He gestured toward Wyatt. "She doesn't have many defenses."

"What she needs is a bodyguard twenty-four seven if the Institute's going to put her life in danger," Wyatt snapped.

My jaw dropped, and I scrambled to my feet. "A bodyguard? Are you kidding me? No ambassador travels with a bodyguard, even if they have low magic. That's not going to happen."

Wyatt rounded on me. "So, then what? You walk into a new position, in unstable territory, only to be put in jeopardy? Are you telling me *that's* okay?"

"Well, no, but the chances of me ever being in that situation are very small. Most positions are in territories that are peaceful, and yes, I know there's a chance I'll be assigned to an area of the world that's experiencing unrest, but that's what *words* are for, sir."

"Words?" Wyatt huffed. "Do you really think a discussion is going to stop a rogue werewolf or an ancient vampire? They won't listen. What you need is either a bodyguard or better magic, because this isn't cutting it!"

His chest heaved as anger strummed from him in powerful waves, but instead of arguing further, I took a step back.

I tried not to let his stinging accusations hurt me, but he was right.

I was weak.

Even though I'd been training my butt off, I would never be strong. And the truth was, no matter how hard I worked, I would never stand a chance against someone like him.

I forced my chin up, hoping he wouldn't see the pain needling my heart. "You're right, sir. I'm not strong. I never have been, but this is how I was made. I can't change it, and ambassadors don't get bodyguards. The Institute doesn't have funding for that, so what I have when I leave here is all I'll have to fall back on. I'm sorry that disappoints you."

To my utter mortification, tears welled in my eyes. Blinking rapidly, I turned to Major Armund. "If it's all right with you, ma'am, I would like to break for lunch now."

She gave a brisk nod, then turned her glare back on my commander.

I hurried from the room as quickly as I could without making it look like I was running away, but that was exactly what I was doing.

Because even though I was trying so hard to keep my emotions in check and not let Wyatt affect me—it hurt. It hurt so *damned* much that Wyatt pointed out my shortcomings time and time again.

The bottom line?

I would never be good enough for him.

CHAPTER TWENTY-FIVE

WYATT

The door closed behind Avery as she exited the room, her retreating lilac scent drifting toward me.

"Well, I can see why you want me training her," Major Armund said tartly. "If that's how you treat your new recruits, it's amazing any of them graduate."

I hung my head, shame washing through me. I'd fucked up. *Majorly* fucked up. I hadn't meant to tear into Avery like that, but it scared me to the depths of my soul to think of someone hurting her.

I couldn't bear the thought of it, and every instinct inside me demanded that I protect her and keep her safe.

Yet I couldn't.

Once she left here, she would be on her own, and there wasn't a damned thing I could do about it.

"I'm sorry. You're right."

Reese looked between the two of us, then checked his watch. "I gotta do a few things before this afternoon. See you guys later?"

We both nodded.

After the sorcerer left the training room, the silence

descended around Dee and me. I knew I should leave, get lunch, then get ready for another afternoon with my recruits, but I didn't move.

My insides were churning.

Major Armund cocked her head, her brow furrowing. "This isn't like you, Jamison. Want to fill me in?" She waited, watching me, and from the sharp gleam in her eye—

Shit. She knows. I groaned. *Of course she knows.* Alpha power had been raging from me ever since I stepped in here.

I locked my jaw, knowing if word got back to Wes that I was acting strange again that I would be out of the SF by the evening.

"Wyatt, come on." She put her hands on her hips. "How long have we had each other's backs?"

I sighed heavily and ran my hands roughly over my face. My wolf growled inside me. He'd been in constant agitation ever since we opened the door to see Major Fieldstone manhandling Avery. It didn't help that I'd had to watch him touch her, even *straddle* her.

Then I'd been forced to spar with her. I'd had to physically exert my dominant side to go along with it, since my wolf's instinct was to protect her. Even though it was training, it still went against every fiber of our soul.

"Is it that obvious?" I asked.

She sighed, her expression softening, well as much as Dee softened. "To me, yeah. You've got territorial wolf written all over you. I grew up in a pack, remember?"

Shit, shit, shit. "Does Reese suspect too?"

"I don't know. I don't think so, but he will if you're not more careful. It's not normal for a commander to be so aggressive when other men spar with his recruits." She leaned against the wall, her arms falling to cross casually behind her. "Is it as bad as I think?"

I took a deep breath. "Yeah."

She gazed at me knowingly. Nothing else needed to be said. She *knew.*

"Wes can't know," I said. "I'll get kicked out."

"He won't hear anything from me."

I gave her a small smile. "Thanks."

She just nodded, then reached down to grab the empty water bottles on the floor. I knew if I wanted to talk more, she would listen, but she didn't need to deal with my crap. She'd done enough by training Avery for so long.

I said goodbye and headed out. The concrete halls surrounded me as I made my way to the exterior doors.

Images of how I'd attacked Bavar for simply sparring with Avery swamped my thoughts. Disgust rolled through me that once again I was behaving in a way that contradicted the code all commanders vowed to uphold in the SF.

He was my friend, yet I'd *attacked* him.

Outside, the midday sun shone down. But it did little to warm my mood.

One thing I knew for certain, in less than two weeks, Avery would be leaving the SF, and not only was I hopelessly in love with her, but I couldn't have her, and she still wasn't ready to face a potentially life-threatening situation.

Everything was a mess, and I had nobody to blame but myself.

CHAPTER TWENTY-SIX
AVERY

Even though I promised Major Fieldstone cookies, he was getting cake. I laughed humorlessly as I mixed the ingredients in a bowl on the kitchen counter. *Let him eat cake.* As if I were Marie Antoinette.

The cliché was fitting, considering I was making a cake with yeast. Before the mid-1800s it was how all cakes were made, since baking powder and baking soda didn't exist. It meant I needed to manually work the dough, though not too much, otherwise I would lose the air. I had to watch it closely as well. Too much warmth and it would rise too quickly, yet too cool and it wouldn't rise enough.

Despite the extra effort, this cake was exactly what I needed right now. It required concentration, which made it the perfect distraction after my disastrous training with Wyatt this morning.

The doughy scent of yeast wafted around me as my commander's grassy-colored eyes filled my mind. I pictured the way he'd hovered above me in the plank position, anger and anxiety pulsing off of him in intermittent waves. I'd been right beneath him, flat on my back, and all I could think about was how close he'd been.

Stupid woman. I knew berating myself wouldn't help, but it seemed fitting given my reaction. Hadn't I learned that Wyatt Jamison would bring me nothing but heartbreak?

Ugh. The next few weeks couldn't pass quickly enough.

The timer dinged, forcing my attention back to the task at hand, yet anger with myself still lingered.

"Why did I ever allow myself to have feelings for him?" I whispered quietly, before slipping the cake into the oven.

I yelped when I accidentally touched the scorching oven rack, a burn singeing the side of my palm. I slammed the oven door closed and proceeded to the sink, holding my hand under the nozzle's cool spray.

The front door opened behind me, and a chipper voice rang through the apartment.

"Hello to you, Avery!" Eliza called cheerfully.

Charlotte walked in behind her and kicked off her heavy boots. Dirt flaked on the mat like brown snowflakes. She sniffed. "Are you cooking again? Whatcha making this time?"

I turned the water off and inspected my burn. "A cake, but it's for Major Fieldstone since I promised I'd make him something if he bested me at sparring this morning." I grumbled. "Obviously, he had no problems doing that."

"You sparred with my future commander?" Charlotte's eyes bugged out as Eliza's eyes widened.

"Are you speaking of Major *Bavar* Fieldstone?" Eliza gaped.

I winced when an angry red welt lifted on my hand. "Yeah, Charlotte's future commander. Do you know him, Eliza?"

"Oh yes, everyone does. He's from the royal line. The king is his uncle."

My jaw dropped, and my hand fell, all concern for my burn fading. "Seriously? He's a royal fae?"

"Indeed he is."

Excited energy danced around Charlotte. "Pretty wicked, eh?"

My thoughts raced as I tried to remember every interaction I'd had with the fairy. Chances were that at some point in the future I would be interacting with Bavar in my ambassador role since most political problems in the fae lands required involving the royals.

I shook my head, embarrassment flooding me that I hadn't realized his heritage. I hadn't even known I'd been wrestling with a fairy who was damned near immortal. Well, not immortal. He would die eventually, but unlike normal fairies who lived to around two hundred years of age—sometimes three hundred if they were lucky—the royal fae often lived a millennium. Some said they could even live several thousands of years if luck was on their side.

"Well, that explains his cockiness." I sighed to myself.

Eliza plopped down on the couch and switched on the TV. The news flashed to life. An image of planets aligning in space filled the screen.

Eliza squealed. "Oh, I am most excited about the comet!"

I peered at the screen. "Those look like planets, not a comet."

"I know, I know. They are discussing what is going to happen next month because they probably already conversed about what is occurring tonight. Did you not know? The Safrinite comet is appearing tonight!"

"Is that supposed to mean something?" Charlotte asked blandly.

Eliza gave her a pointed look. "Don't you keep up on fairy celestial events?"

"Um, no," she replied nonchalantly and plopped down on the armchair.

Eliza sighed in exasperation. "You should, because this event is something even you would enjoy." She settled herself more on the couch, excitement making her skin glow subtly. "The Safrinite comet only comes every two thousand years and it's coming only weeks before my realm's solar system alignment." She looked at Charlotte expectantly, clearly waiting for a reaction, but Charlotte merely arched an eyebrow.

"Again, what does that mean?" she asked, her tone bored.

"It's nearly unheard of to have *two* celestial events this rare occur in such quick succession."

Charlotte snickered. "So the astronomy geeks are geeking out tonight in the fae lands? And that's supposed to be exciting?"

Eliza smacked her forehead. "No. It means the entire fae lands is celebrating. My planet's magic comes from our astronomical and celestial events. We all celebrate their occurrences, even more so when they're this rare."

Charlotte's eyes widened, understanding finally dawning. "Which means wicked-crazy parties in the fae lands will be happening tonight."

"Yes, parties everywhere."

Charlotte jumped up from her chair. "Well, why didn't you just say that in the first place?"

Eliza rolled her eyes. "I thought it would be obvious."

"Does that mean we're going to the fae lands tonight?" I asked.

Eliza beamed again. "That is what I had planned on doing. Would you two care to join me?"

I poured the batter into the pans, my mood lifting at the thought of a fun night out. "Sure, I'm game."

"I'm always up for a party." Charlotte grabbed a beer from the fridge and cracked the top. She then gave Eliza a quizzical look. "Does a comet really recharge your planet with magic? I mean, isn't it just little specks of light in the sky or whatever?"

"Not this one." Eliza put an arm over the back of the couch so she could face us. "It will pass within a hundred thousand miles of our planet and will appear larger than the moon here."

"No shit?" Charlotte took a swig of her beer. "Okay, you're

right. That does sound kinda cool, even to someone who's not an astronomy geek."

Eliza's expression turned hopeful. "So you'll both really go?"

"Definitely." I eyed the timer on the oven. "As long as you're okay with waiting for this cake to finish so I can drop it off?"

"We can wait. The comet won't be visible until midnight." Eliza clapped her hands. "How exciting! Between the Safrinite comet and impending alignment, the magic will be alive tonight and will feel . . ." She sighed. "It shall be something. Our magic shall be rejuvenated. There shall be much celebrating in the fae lands tonight and during the coming weeks in the build-up to the alignment."

Charlotte grinned. "Partying and heightened magic. Sounds like the start to a good month."

My mood lifted more as I thought about fairies dancing around their villages and the capital hosting festive parties over the weeks to come. Weekends in the fae lands seemed like the best way to enjoy my final weeks at the SF.

And while it wasn't the first celestial event I'd heard of in the fae lands, this was the most unique I'd ever come across—especially since it refueled their realm's magic.

Considering the fae lands' planet resided in a parallel universe, it was the norm for their solar system to have events entirely separate from earth's. I still remembered when I was little, and my parents had explained it to me. According to fairy historians, there were many parallel universes, each as big and vast as our own, and it was only luck that our universe and the fae lands' universe bent at an odd angle that allowed them to touch, permitting realm crossings.

Still, those realm crossings weren't for everyone. The fae lands resided in a universe more magical than ours, which was why humans couldn't access it, but supernaturals could.

At least I've got enough magic to realm transfer.

I made a sour face, remembering Wyatt's comments this

morning about how magically weak I was. Apparently, I wasn't the only one who'd been taken aback by it. Since Major Armund let me out early today after doing her best to bolster my self-esteem all afternoon, I knew my memory hadn't over-exaggerated Wyatt's sharp tongue and soul-lashing comments.

Ugh.

"When will that cake be done?" Charlotte asked. "Do I have time to dress up?"

I arched an eyebrow. "We're dressing up for a comet?"

"Not a comet." She smiled mischievously. "For the hot fairies who are gonna be out watching it. If it's anything like their other celebrations, you'll want to be dressed up too. If we're lucky, we'll be going home with some hotties tonight."

I shook my head and laughed. If there was one thing I'd come to love about Charlotte, it was that she embraced her sexuality and didn't have any shame flaunting it.

Maybe it was time I took a page from her book.

CHAPTER TWENTY-SEVEN
AVERY

The nearest fae lands' portal waited at the supernatural marketplace in downtown Boise, so after I left the cake for Bavar in front of his apartment door, the three of us left in my Explorer.

We were all dressed up, but none of us wore heels. The fae lands may be more magical, but they didn't have the technological advances of earth. In other words, if enchanted carpets or *domals*—fae animals that were similar to horses but more intelligent—weren't around to ride, walking was the only option.

"I'm so immensely happy to be sharing tonight with you both," Eliza said as she skipped along the sidewalk.

I clicked my key fob, making sure my Explorer was locked, before slipping my keys into my purse. "If the comet is as big as you say it is, it should be worth the trip."

"Oh yes, I hear it's to be most impressive." Eliza beamed.

"When was the last time you were in the fae lands?" I asked Charlotte.

She shrugged. "A few months ago? I can't remember, but it's been a while."

We ducked into the alleyway between a mom-and-pop hardware store and a bakery. At the end of the alley, the portal to the supernatural marketplace waited. We would have to hop through it to enter the marketplace, then we could find the fae lands' portal.

The barrier glowed red, and I sucked in a breath before stepping through it. The sensation of falling, popping, and being pulled apart made me want to squeal, but it was over quickly.

A second later, I stood at the entrance to the marketplace with Eliza and Charlotte at my side.

A buzz of activity filled the air. Vendor stalls lined the cobblestone walkway as peddlers sold their wares. Rich, vibrant carpets hung from one stall. Enchanted clothing, trinkets, and magical bobs filled another. Scents of roasted meats, spicy stews, and fragrant potions filled the air. And a hum of conversation rose around us as supernaturals shopped. I loved the marketplace, but we didn't have time to wander it tonight.

"This way." Eliza tugged me.

Farther down the side street near the supernatural marketplace's entrance lay other portals. Supernaturals popped in and out of them, arriving from different countries from all over the world. There were many supernatural marketplaces around the globe, however, the one here in Boise was the largest and most popular. And since the portals made country hopping easy, it was common to hear a variety of accents.

"Holy shit, there's a line," Charlotte exclaimed when we reached the end of the lane.

Two dozen supernaturals waited in front of us, the line moving steadily forward as everyone jumped through the glowing green portal to the fae lands.

Eliza squealed. "It's gonna be hoppin' in my realm tonight!"

Charlotte and I laughed.

Our time finally arrived to transfer, and we jumped through the portal together. It spat us out in a field just outside of the fae lands' capital. The nighttime sky loomed above us. During the day, the sky was pale green with white and pastel-colored clouds, but at night it was a sea of black with luminous stars, three moons, distant planets, and a strip of the cloudy galaxy. It was even more beautiful than earth's night sky.

Around us, a city of supernaturals had camped out on the field, stretching out on blankets or hovering on enchanted carpets that floated inches from the grassy field, which bloomed with an abundance of foreign, fragrant, and brightly-colored wildflowers. Everyone left a wide berth around the portal, giving those jumping through ample room to maneuver.

"Sounds like the parties are getting started." Charlotte rubbed her hands as we all stepped away from the portal to prevent being knocked over by more supernaturals jumping through.

Music carried from the capital into the field along with the sound of distant laughter. The capital, which rested on a natural rising mound that rose like a mountain about a quarter mile from the portal, glowed with lit bonfires, fiery torches, and magical lanterns. The stone buildings and thatched-roofed houses were all illuminated.

At the top of the mountain, the castle shone most splendidly of all. Its jutting spires and stone walls soared toward the heavens, each peak alight with crackling sparklers that reminded me of fireworks in the midst of exploding.

"Do you know of any parties we can crash once the comet's passed?" I asked Eliza.

"My friend informed me about one in the Huntsman Quarter. It's supposed to have the best music and dancing tonight." Eliza smoothed her skirt.

"Then that's where we'll go after the comet passes." Charlotte looked around. "Now, where should we sit?"

"It looks pretty crowded around here," I replied. "Most of the families seem to be sticking close to the capital. Should we leave the open spots for them and walk farther out?"

Eliza nodded. "Yes, we should."

On the golden walkway that led from the capital's looming gates, a steady progression of fairies walked with their knapsacks while tugging children in their wakes. Most of them squeezed into open patches in the field, probably wanting to stay close to the capital so their children wouldn't have to walk too far.

Considering that thousands of supernaturals were already camped out, we would have to travel a fair distance if we wanted to have enough space to stretch our legs.

"Good thing we didn't wear heels," Eliza quipped.

"But my boots still look hot." Charlotte bent her knee, admiring her tan thigh-high boots with platform wedges. The wicked-looking boots were a true statement next to her denim booty shorts and fluffy cashmere sweater. They also showed off how toned she was, and even though they were still kinda heels, Charlotte insisted they were mostly comfortable to walk in.

Eliza and I had opted for more practical clothes, much to Charlotte's disappointment. I wore flats, black leggings, and a long, trendy V-neck sweater which hung to mid-thigh. It was still cute but warm, while Eliza wore traditional fae attire—an ankle-length fluffy skirt the same color as her hair, and a metallic-silver top with slashes of hot pink.

We hopped onto the walkway and strolled away from the capital. The glowing fires from the parties grew dimmer behind us.

About a quarter mile down the walkway, Charlotte pointed to an open patch of grass. "How about there?"

We'd walked far enough that there were plenty of spots to choose from, but supernaturals still lingered everywhere. A steady hum of conversation and laughter drifted through the air, reminding me of crowded events in big cities back on earth.

My thoughts drifted to Wyatt, to the fact that if he and I had actually started a relationship, I could have attended this with him. Instead, in a few weeks, most likely I would never see him again.

A punch of melancholy, then annoyance, flared through me. *It's in the past and done with, Avery. Time to officially move on.*

"Good call on bringing the blanket." Charlotte nudged Eliza.

"Why thank you." Eliza spread out the purple and green checkered wool. "Please make yourself comfortable, ladies."

I firmly shook off thoughts of Wyatt and the inevitable pang of longing and anger all rolled into one messy ball.

We laid down and propped our hands behind our heads. Above, a million stars shone so brightly that I was transfixed.

"This sky is amazing," I whispered.

"It really puts earth's to shame, does it not?" Eliza replied.

Charlotte snorted. "I'm more interested in those three over there." She waved toward three fairies that had grabbed a spot near us. One had a Mohawk and a heavy brow. A strong push of magic pulsed from him, bringing with it a feeling of dread. A tingle of unease slithered down my spine, spiking my internal radar.

"Um, I don't think they're fairies, Char," I whispered.

She propped up on her elbows and cocked an eyebrow at me. "No? What do you mean?"

"I'm pretty sure they're demons, masking themselves as fairies. They're probably looking for an easy lay."

Charlotte's breath sucked in. "No shit?" She waggled her eyebrows. "Hmm, I wonder what a full-blooded demon's like in bed."

I laughed and swatted her arm. "Pretty good from what I hear, but that's only if you don't piss them off. Then, the outcome isn't so pretty."

Eliza settled more on the blanket. "Stay away from demons and vampires is what my mother always told me."

Charlotte eyed the trio again. Mohawk demon winked in her direction.

Charlotte grinned wickedly. "Too bad I've never been good at following any mother's advice."

I opened my mouth to second Eliza's warning, when a deep voice carried through the wind. I stiffened, all worries about demons evaporating.

"There's a spot. Does this work?" I heard Wyatt say.

I pressed my lips together, my senses suddenly on high alert, when Wyatt and a group of his friends strolled by on the walkway. But instead of continuing on, they stopped and parked themselves upwind, across the golden walkway from us. They couldn't be more than thirty feet away.

Seriously? I groaned. The Gods were obviously against me.

Another familiar voice carried from Wyatt's group. "Looks about perfect."

I caught the silhouette of Major Bavar Fieldstone before he spread himself out on the grass, the wildflowers crushing beneath him. They hadn't bothered with a blanket.

Two other large males accompanied Wyatt and Bavar. I could only surmise they were werewolves given their builds and pulsing power. It was times like this that I wished my magical ability was something else. Being surrounded by a field of supernaturals made my internal radar remain constantly on high alert since magical energy came from everywhere.

Unexpectedly, the wind changed direction, and Wyatt stiffened. He turned slowly around, his nostrils flaring and his movements deliberate.

When he spotted the three of us, Charlotte lifted her arm, waving before she said respectfully, "Good evening, commander."

It never ceased to amaze me that Charlotte could go from being crude and on the hunt for a good lay, to humble and respectful a moment later. But I supposed that was why she'd been chosen for a numbered SF squad. At the end of the day, she knew her boundaries, and stayed within them when protocol called for it.

Wyatt dipped his head, but his jaw tightened. "Privates." He turned back to his friends. "Maybe we should move—"

"Is that Private Meyers?" Bavar said sitting up. When he spotted me, he grinned. "T'was a lovely cake you left for me. It's already half gone. I may have to best you again in sparring if this is how I'll be rewarded."

A low growl came from Wyatt, but he abruptly swallowed it and plowed a hand through his hair.

My pulse jumped, but I managed to reply, "I'm glad you enjoyed it, sir."

"You should try her eclairs, sir," Charlotte called to him. "She made ones with pecans and maple glaze last week. I about died and went to heaven."

"You don't say." Bavar stood, dusting himself off before addressing his group, nodding toward the three of us. "Shall we join them? Might as well. Seems silly to be having a conversation so far away from one another."

The two other wolves stood, but Wyatt looked at his watch. "It might be best to stay put. It's almost midnight."

Bavar cocked his head. "Almost midnight? It's over an hour away."

Before Wyatt could reply, Major Fieldstone ambled toward us, then dropped down on the ground to my left and gave me a cheeky grin. "Please tell me I'll be awarded with more of your sweets this week. I believe I may even be desperate enough to pay for them."

I snorted, unable to help myself. Even though Major Fieldstone was my superior, he wasn't my commanding officer, and I was leaving the SF soon. Come that time, he could actually be someone I called a friend, not a superior.

I arched an eyebrow, my expression gravely serious. "How much are you offering, sir?"

Bavar's eyes widened, then he laughed, his entire chest shaking with mirth. "How much are you requesting?"

Another growl erupted from my commander before he stalked to our side of the walkway, then lay on the grass. A loud huff came from Wyatt when he stretched out and placed his hands behind his head. At least six feet of distance separated us, but I still bristled.

He'd made it abundantly clear that he didn't want to be anywhere near me, but that didn't mean he needed to spoil the evening for everyone else.

The two wolves that accompanied them lay in between Bavar and Wyatt but extended their hands toward us, introducing themselves. One was a werewolf from Wyatt's pack in British Columbia. I vaguely remembered him from high school, since he was someone Wyatt had hung out with a lot. The other was from the Idaho pack, not someone I'd met, and was friends with Wyatt outside of the SF.

Charlotte perked right up at the addition of two new, hot, and single males to our mix. I gave silent thanks. Hopefully that meant she wouldn't be going home with any demons tonight.

I sneaked a peek at Mohawk dude, but he'd already set his sights on someone else, a drop-dead gorgeous siren from the looks of it.

Poor lady. Hopefully she knew what she was getting into.

As for Eliza, she'd fallen into an awkward, star-struck conversation with Bavar. It was only then I remembered that in the fae lands, Bavar was royalty. That probably explained my friend's halted sentences and mooning.

But unlike my friends, I couldn't relax. I told myself I was being ridiculous. I argued internally that it was stupid for my heart to be racing and my pulse to be quickening, because hadn't I learned, time and time again, that Wyatt Jamison was *not* the man I'd thought he was, and in a couple of weeks I would never see him again?

Yeah.

If only it were that easy.

THE HOUR PASSED QUICKLY, if somewhat awkwardly. Between Bavar's sarcastic quips, the two new wolves' blatant interest in Charlotte, and Wyatt's stony silence, it made for an interesting if nerve-racking night.

"It's almost time!" Eliza said when a magical firework exploded from the capital. The number '5' blazed brightly in the sky, erupting in a shower of golden sparks before it dispersed in the atmosphere.

I hadn't realized the capital would be counting down the minutes, but I had to admit, their intermittent fireworks helped us keep track of when the comet was coming and only heightened the anticipation buzzing through the field.

"It's strange, though, isn't it?" I said to Eliza, as we all lay back and waited for the final minutes to pass before the comet arrived. "On earth, comets can be seen for weeks as they travel closer to our planet. Is it always like this in the fae lands? I mean, why can't we see it now? Surely it's close enough that we should be able to."

Eliza shook her head. "Not with this one. The reason this is such a big event is because this comet's traveling through a portion of our solar system known as the Dark Night. It's an area in our realm that's cloaked in magic and makes all light appear dark. You're right that the comet is already close, but we can't see it until it passes through the Dark Night."

I shook my head, trying to process that. It only reminded me that the universe I grew up in and the universe the fae lands resided in were vastly different. Even trying to comprehend how things functioned here would take years of study. Physics on earth was not the same as physics in this universe.

"Two minutes," Eliza whispered and nudged me when another glowing firework erupted.

Meanwhile, Charlotte was already making out with one of the wolves. He'd moved to lie at the edge of our group, and my roommate had made quick work of securing her stud for the night.

"What do you think it will look like?" Major Fieldstone asked me quietly.

I shrugged. "I don't know. A big ball of light maybe?"

He settled more on the grass, not seeming to mind the stalks that crunched underneath him. "Legend says that it's the most dazzling purple color you'll ever see. That its beauty is enough to blind those who are lucky enough to see it."

I chuckled. "I'm not sure being blinded is lucky . . . sir."

He laughed, the sound deep and rich just as a hush fell over the crowd. A golden '1' erupted in the sky.

The countdown had officially begun.

I stared at the stars, wide-eyed, my breath shallow. Magic from Wyatt continued to pulse toward me, but I ignored it. I'd felt power surges from him all evening, but I wasn't about to let him ruin my fun.

"Less than ten seconds now," Bavar whispered. "Ten, nine, eight . . ." He continued the countdown.

With each second that brought us closer to the comet's reveal, my skin tingled. Goosebumps sprouted on my arms as a new sense of magic permeated the air. My breath quickened even more as I gazed above, searching for the phenomenon that nobody had seen in thousands of years.

"Three . . . two . . . one!"

Out of nowhere, an explosion of fiery purple light shot through the sky. Gasps, yelps, and squeals of glee broke out across the field. The comet blazed in a gigantic sphere with a shining tail erupting in a shower of fuchsia and cobalt sparks. It was larger than the fae lands' moons, the orbiting planets, and the sun.

Applause and cheers burst all around.

The energy in the field grew, the feeling of electricity pulsing along my skin. A deep sense of power vibrated from *everywhere*, and my internal radar shot through the roof at the feel of the comet's magic.

My hair stood on end.

My heart thumped erratically.

The rejuvenation was *immense*.

I clapped in delight, joining everyone in their excitement of the comet's rebirth.

But then the magic shifted, moving inward.

My clapping slowed. Something swelled and cracked in my soul, pushing and beating inside me.

I gasped, not realizing the comet's magic affected individuals too.

I didn't know if I should laugh or smile, but then my lips turned down as what felt like a slumbering beast opened up in my chest.

My breaths came faster as magic rippled along my skin, down my arms, and around my toes. My heart pounded as the power inside me rose. It grew taller and higher, wider and stronger.

"What the hell?" I whispered. The comet continued to zoom across the sky, growing brighter and brighter with every second, until the field looked like twilight.

The cheers and applause continued, but all I could do was gasp shallowly as energy manifested and erupted within me.

"Do you feel that?" I asked Eliza, grabbing her hand and squeezing tightly. "Is it happening to you too?"

She only gave me a brief quizzical look before returning her attention to the sky, her grin never faltering.

Heat began to pound through my limbs.

Blood, filled with crackling energy, rushed through my veins.

Something twisted and squeezed my organs, infusing them with awesome power.

"What's happening?" I whispered just as the comet reached its peak, blazing bright and centered in the middle of the sky.

And when it reached the apex, the celestial event at its climax, a cataclysmic explosion rocked my core.

I screamed.

Stars.

Light.

Power.

A rush of energy so strong burst through me that I jolted as if electrocuted. It felt as though I was ripped apart and then sewn back together. Died and then reborn.

The comet's magic raged through my soul, crushing the weak magic in my chest and encapsulating it in a simmering shell.

Then, it *exploded*.

I screamed when a surge of purple-tinted light shot from my body. Immense magic as bright as glittering orchids bathed the field around me.

Wails from supernaturals followed.

The magic. It was *pummeling* them.

I tried to stop it. I tried to pull it back in, but my ears rang. My lungs felt about to explode. Blood whooshed through my temples. And I had no control. *Everything* was out of my control.

No. No. NO. What the hell's happening?

I gasped, trying to hold onto my centered yet weak magic that had always resided in my core. But the comet's magic had grasped it, snared it, *owned* it. Power so strong that it surged through me vibrated amongst my organs, gobbling my cells like Lucifer himself commanded my soul.

I cried out and collapsed back.

I couldn't breathe.

Couldn't think.

The power was too great—too *tremendous*.

And I couldn't control it.

Everyone around me cowered, running and diving to avoid the cataclysmic reaction that was shattering my soul.

Blood thundered in my ears as my heart beat so hard I thought it would burst. "Help me," I wailed pitifully.

But nobody could help.

The magic was too great.

Purple glittery waves continued to pour from me, barreling into everyone in their path.

My vision dimmed as the colossal power was more than I could bear.

I rolled on the ground, crying out when the magic shot through my limbs.

Then everything went black.

CHAPTER TWENTY-EIGHT

WYATT

I grimaced and called upon my alpha magic to shield myself. Power still fired from Avery's pores, shooting out of her and making me shudder.

Bavar had taken control of the crowd. Most had vacated the immediate area, but some still stood at a barely safe distance while watching the bizarre display.

The only positive aspect was that the purple magic didn't actually hurt people if it hit them, but *damn*, it packed a punch. It was enough for me to see stars.

Despite that, I refused to leave her side. "Avery! Avery, open your eyes!" I held her in my arms, her body limp and unresponsive. Steady waves of purple magic shimmered from her skin, knocking into me, making my teeth grit. *What the hell is going on?*

"We need to get her back to headquarters, to the healing center. Now!" I snapped.

Eliza, who stood twenty feet away, nodded wide-eyed, while Charlotte gaped.

I snarled, my pulse racing. "Who has a portal key?"

I cradled Avery's body to my chest. Warmth pulsed from her,

along with the molten simmering magic. The strange purple light coming from her was so strong. I gritted my teeth again, ignoring the pain the light evoked.

Both Eliza and Charlotte took another step back when a purple wave hit them. Eliza nearly collapsed.

"Anyone?" I shouted. "Who has a portal key?"

"I do." Bavar jogged toward me from the back of the crowd. He'd just relocated a family with four small children. The fairy reached into his pocket and extracted a key.

"Thank you. I'll get you a new one." Everyone knew how precious portal keys were.

Bavar nodded. "I'll be right behind you. Wes will undoubtedly want a full report about this."

I didn't stick around to see what the others were planning to do, not even my wolf friends who I'd invited to join me for the festivities and parties in the capital after the comet.

All of my focus shifted to Avery, who still lay unconscious. I grasped the key and whispered the magical words to activate it, *"Open key, for though I ask, I need a door for this new task."*

I imagined where I wanted to go and the world swirled around me. The SF headquarters appeared, the healing center only feet away. The magic dispersed, the portal key I'd been holding disappearing into dust.

I owed Bavar big time.

I dashed inside the healing center, the assault of healing magic swamping the air. But any hope I'd clung to that transferring to a different realm would stop whatever had happened to Avery vanished.

Even traveling to earth hadn't abated whatever fae lands' magic had been activated inside her.

I nearly stumbled up the stairs when another thought overtook me.

Maybe magic *hadn't* been activated. Maybe somebody had cast a spell on her or conjured a hex. For all I knew, in twenty-four hours, whatever the purple light was could mean Avery wouldn't be breathing.

An aching chasm opened inside me. *No.*

I snarled and sprinted faster up the stairs. I knew my eyes were glowing. My wolf was so close, straining to make the shift. He wanted Avery cared for *now.*

I reached the healing center ward and barreled through the doors, knocking them off their hinges.

A startled witch yelped, but I didn't stop until I stood in front of her. She looked young and must have been new because I didn't recognize her.

"Where's Farrah?" I demanded.

The young witch stuttered and pushed to a stand, her chair swiveling away behind her. "I . . . she's not on tonight. What's wrong? Is she hurt?" Her eyebrows pinched together when she studied the purple magic pulsing off Avery. She took a big step back, her eyes rolling back in her head, when a wave hit her, but she didn't collapse.

I growled again, hairs spearing through the back of my hands. "Get Farrah!"

"Ye—" She cleared her throat, fear rising from her scent, but at least she hadn't passed out. "Yes, sir." Her hand wobbled when she reached for her tablet.

Another witch appeared in the hallway, coming from an open doorway. She took one look at me and Avery and pointed to a room. "Bring her in here."

I blurred into the patient room, unable to control myself. I knew I needed to lay Avery on the bed, but I couldn't let her go.

The witch eyed me warily. "Major, I can't help her if you don't put her down."

It was only then I realized I was growling. Fuck. *I'm a mess.*

I set Avery down, loathing to release her, but knowing I had to.

The witch immediately began assessing her, swirling her

hands over Avery who still lay unconscious, like death had already claimed her. The healing witch winced when a plume of purple magic hit her.

She gripped the edge of the bed, her knuckles white, until she steadied herself. "What happened?"

"We were in the fae lands, watching the comet, and then . . ." I took a deep breath. My heart raced. "She started asking her squad mates if they felt it. I didn't know what she meant. She probably didn't even know I was listening. And then this look of panic came over her, she flew back, and then this pulsing purple magic started shimmering from her skin. She fell unconscious shortly after that."

"It happened during the comet?" The witch, who I now recognized as Cora, eyed me shrewdly.

"Yes."

The door burst open, and Farrah—the healing center's lead witch—bustled in. "What is it? I was told it's an emergency."

"It's Avery Meyers, the ambassador recruit," Cora replied.

Farrah took one look at Avery and stopped in her tracks. The purple magic continued to shimmer and pulse from her. It rose in undulating waves, like steam rising from a kettle and drifting in a breeze. "When and how did this happen?"

Cora recounted the story I'd just told.

"And your assessment?" Farrah asked, already coming to Avery's side and waving her hands over her.

"She's stable, but I don't recognize this magic. It's powerful, though. Very powerful."

"Is it a spell? Or a hex?"

"I'm not sure."

Farrah winced when a wave burst from Avery's skin and hit the witch full on. She gasped and stepped back before righting herself. After a moment, she returned to Avery's side.

"You're right about the powerful part." Farrah gave me a

pointed look. "Please wait outside. Cora, call Douglas. I need his help."

"Yes, ma'am." Cora bobbed her head and pulled out her tablet.

The new witch, the one who I'd scared the socks off when I entered the ward, approached me warily from the hallway. "Please follow me, Major."

My hackles rose at being removed from the room in which Avery still lay unconscious, but I also knew they couldn't work with me prowling around them.

Once in the hall, the young witch asked haltingly, "Do you know her next of kin or emergency contacts?"

My heart dropped.

"We should notify them of her condition, just in case."

Just in case.

It felt as if the earth tilted off its axis.

I took a step back, my brain refusing to function. No. This couldn't be happening. Avery couldn't be seriously ill. *I won't let that happen, dammit!*

I took a menacing step toward the door, but the young witch stepped in my path. "Please, Major. We need your help to help her."

She looked at me imploringly, and I knew that she'd sensed my wolf growing even more agitated, yet she was giving me a job to do, and right now, I desperately needed something to do.

"Of course. I'll access her files and notify her emergency contacts."

"Thank you."

The door at the end of the hall opened, and Douglas, one of the SF's head sorcerers strode in. The young witch pointed to Avery's room, and Douglas headed inside.

I backed up against the wall, my entire body shaking. With a shattering breath, I pulled out my phone. I'd left my tablet in my apartment, not thinking I would need it on a night off, but I kept all of my new recruits' information on my personal device as well. Now, I thanked the Gods I'd done that.

Although the fact that I was needing to access those files . . .

No. She will be fine!

I couldn't contemplate a world in which Avery Meyers didn't exist.

CHAPTER TWENTY-NINE
WYATT

The only emergency contacts listed for Avery were Bryce and Danielle Meyers—her parents. They were also impossible to get a hold of.

"Hi, you've reached Danielle Meyers, I'm not—" I hung up again. It was the fourth time I'd gotten her mother's voicemail in the past three hours.

I placed my head in my hands. I'd been waiting at the end of the healing center's hallway since the witches had booted me out of Avery's room.

I knew I could go home. My apartment was only a five-minute walk from here, but I didn't want to be gone if something happened.

Charlotte and Eliza had shown up, too, cutting their time in the fae lands short and wanting to stay as well. But I'd sent them back to their apartment, telling them that Avery would be okay but she was spending the night in the healing center.

All I could do was hope that was true.

Despite being forced to look calm for the sake of my new recruits, internally, my mind raced, and my only "job" to do while I waited was proving futile.

Avery's parents were currently living in India, which meant it was afternoon there. It was possible they were working, which explained why neither was answering their phone. And there wasn't much more I could do now except wait.

I hung my head. I'd already left three messages on both of their cells, hoping they would call, yet dreading when they did. Because how did I tell them that their daughter had suffered an unknown magical event? Or possibly been hexed? Worse, how could I tell them that it had happened under my watch? I was her commander. She was my ambassador recruit. What happened to her during her time here essentially fell on my shoulders.

"How are you holding up?" Bavar's question cut through my thoughts like a blade. He sat down on the chair beside me, the vinyl squeaking in protest, then handed me a cup of coffee.

It was near four in the morning, so I took it and gulped a drink of the bitter brew, hoping the caffeine would help keep me sharp. "It's not me I'm worried about."

He eyed the closed door to Avery's room. "Wes wants to talk to you."

"I know."

"I can keep watch if you want to meet with him."

I drained the rest of the cup and tossed it in the trash. A growl rumbled my chest.

Bavar eyed me warily. "I'll keep watch. You can go. I won't let anyone hurt her."

I suppressed another growl, knowing he was only trying to help. I had a feeling the fairy knew how I felt about Avery, but that was a conversation for another day.

I stood and gave him a sharp look. "You promise you'll let me know immediately when someone comes out of that room and lets us know what the hell's going on?"

"On the Queen's honor, you have my word."

I tried for a lighter tone, knowing my friend didn't deserve my agitated aggression. "That's saying something, considering she's your aunt."

Bavar gave a mock bow. "Exactly. You have nothing to fear." He grew serious again. "It's okay, Wyatt. I shall alert you immediately, friend. Go."

My instincts told me to stay, but I also knew I wasn't of rational mind right now, so I stalked down the hallway.

My wolf whined, anxiety lacing his tone. Avery's scent clung to her room's doorway. Inside, I detected murmuring voices, but one of the witches must have cast a cloaking spell around the room since I couldn't make out actual words.

My heart thumped when I sprinted down the stairs and out the door.

Earth's nighttime sky shone above and reminded me of the night Avery and I'd shared under the stars. How long ago that now felt.

When I reached the main building, I scanned myself in. The halls were quiet, only nighttime staff on duty, yet Wes's light was on in his office when I reached the top floor.

He sat at his desk, the holographs alight around him. A six-foot-tall globe shimmered in the middle of the room, highlighting various SF members' locations throughout the world.

"How is she?" Wes asked. Despite being pulled from bed at one in the morning, he looked alert.

"I don't know. They haven't given me an update."

Wes paced near his windows. "I've been in touch with my fae informants. To the best of their knowledge, Avery was the only one who suffered from whatever magical malady that comet created. *If* it was caused by the comet."

I tried to voice that it was good news no one else had been affected, but I couldn't. Anger rose in my gut that Avery had been the only one singled out. Not that I wished her condition on anyone else, but dammit, why did she have to be the one?

"I was also told that you used a portal key and have been

quite protective of her since she returned." He stopped pacing to face me, his face impassive.

"She's under my command, sir. It's my job to protect her."

"I'm aware of that, yet once you brought her to the healing center, your responsibilities regarding her well-being stopped. And I understand it's normal for a commander to stay with an injured recruit, but I've also heard of your territorial responses."

I clenched my jaw. Considering this was our second serious conversation about my behavior, I knew where this was going, except this time I didn't care. If it meant I would be fired from my job for staying by her side, even if Avery hated me now after how I'd treated her, so be it. I wouldn't leave her. I would win her back, groveling if I had to. I would do whatever was needed to make things right with her.

But the one regret I would have to live with? Marcus. I'd let him down.

I'm so sorry, brother.

Wes sighed. "I'm on your side, Major, even though you may not believe it. If Avery survives this, I'm tasking you with her safety and uncovering answers to explain what happened to her."

I cocked my head. "Sir?"

"Wyatt," Wes said with a deep sigh. "I believe Avery may be your mate. You might not have known it, but I've been monitoring your behavior. While you haven't broken protocol since our last conversation, your feelings for her are obvious. I'm a wolf. I know the signs, and I think it's time that you consider the fact that you and your wolf have chosen her as your mate and what that will mean for your future. You don't need to worry. Your job here is secure. Your admirable control has proven you're worthy of maintaining your position."

My mouth went dry. I couldn't reply. Wes knew that Avery was my mate. And she was. I felt it in the depths of my bones, only I'd been trying to fight it, thinking it was best to wait until

I pursued her. I'd wanted what was best for her, believing her dream was what mattered most.

But I'd been a fool.

She'd had feelings for me. I'd seen them that night she showed up at my doorstep with the plate of cookies, but I'd rejected her, distanced myself, and treated her appallingly—all in the hope that I wouldn't shackle her to a long-distance relationship that proved too stressful and difficult.

Wes studied me, no doubt scenting the depth of my remorse.

"I've been amazed at your control over the past few months," he said quietly. "A lesser wolf wouldn't have been able to resist the pull of his mate, yet you did what you felt was right for her, even though it sacrificed your happiness in the process." He came around the front of his desk. "But if you let her leave without telling her how you truly feel, it will destroy you."

I hung my head, and my chest swelled. The thought of Avery leaving my life . . .

My wolf howled.

But I'd been willing to do that for her. I would do anything to ensure Avery's happiness.

I shook my head. "Her dream is becoming an ambassador, sir. It's not being tethered to me."

Wes put his hands in his pockets. "She won't have the chance to be an ambassador if we don't figure out what happened to her."

My head whipped up, my heartbeat turning erratic. "But the healers, they'll save her. They'll fix her—"

"I don't know if they can, Wyatt."

"No! She can't die—"

Wes raised his hands. "She's still alive, but I've been in this business long enough to know that what happened to her in the fae lands won't be fixed tonight. Therefore, if she survives, we'll need answers to explain what happened to her. If not, whatever event created her sickness could have lingering effects or come back in the future to harm her. At this point, we don't know, that's the problem, but in my experience, events like these rarely have an easy explanation or solution. That's why I need someone to delve deeper into this. Besides, if this happened to Avery, it could happen to someone else. Our ultimate responsibility at the SF is to keep all supernaturals safe, and unknown magic or hexes cannot be tolerated."

He stepped closer until we stood eye to eye. "I've sent messages to Masters Mallory and Alarus, the gargoyle scholars here at our SF library, asking them to look into the Safrinite comet the second they wake up in the morning. And I've already sent a petition to the supernatural courts, asking for access to the Bulgarian libraries. Assuming, they eventually give us clearance, I've been in touch with Nicholas Fitzpatrick, our gargoyle scholar representative, as you'll be working with him as he guides you through the intricacies of Bulgaria's libraries."

"Nicholas Fitzpatrick? The vampire?"

"Yes. If we're granted access, you'll need to be civil to him even though I know you don't care for him given your history."

My hands curled into fists, and I took a deep breath, trying to dispel my anger about the vamp. "What about the libraries in the fae lands? Have you sent word to those?"

"Not yet, those may require you to visit them directly."

I gave a curt nod. "And what's to become of my other recruits while I search the fae lands' libraries?"

"Bavar will take them under his wing and will complete their training. It shouldn't be hard. They have less than two weeks left. So, starting now, I'm giving you a three-month leave from the SF to uncover what happened in the fae lands tonight. Do you believe you're up to the task?"

I imagined Avery lying on the ground unconscious as unknown magic spilled from her. My wolf snarled. He and I were in agreeance on this. We would give our life to protect her, and if uncovering what had happened to her guaranteed that, I would travel to the ends of the earth or the fae lands to find it.

"I'm up for it, but I can't leave until she wakes up. I need to know that she's okay."

"Of course. In that case—" A buzz emitted from Wes's tablet just as a call rang on my phone. Wes pulled his tablet from his pocket while I extracted my mobile.

Bavar was calling me, and Douglas—the sorcerer currently attending to Avery—was messaging Wes.

Dread filled my stomach as Wes tapped a button on his tablet. Before I could answer Bavar's call, a miniature holographic image of Douglas rose from Wes's tablet.

"Sir, you need to come down here," Douglas said urgently.

Hearing his demand made terror flood my lungs. "What happened? How's Avery?" I demanded as I silenced the call from Bavar.

Douglas startled, his holographic image turning toward me, as if he hadn't realized I was there. "She's alive, Major Jamison, but I don't know for how long." Douglas shook his head. "What we've found . . . I've never seen anything like it."

The sorcerer turned his attention back to Wes. "Hurry. You need to see this."

BOOK TWO
SUPERNATURAL INSTITUTE

Avery

The job I've dreamed of at the Supernatural Ambassador Institute awaits me...if I can stay alive long enough to claim it.

An unknown darkness is slithering through my veins, poisoning me with its deadly venom. Still, I'm determined to fight. To survive.

I can see Wyatt's desperation to help, probably out of guilt for rejecting me as his mate, but I can't risk trusting him again. Now, more than ever, I have to be strong.

Wyatt

I refuse to let Avery die, even if her withering glances threaten to burn me to ash. I tried to fight fate, but now I'm at its mercy.

Still, I'll do whatever it takes to protect my mate. Teeth bared, I will battle my way back to her side, even if she resists me every chance she gets.

But little does either of us know, a prophecy is in the works, and Avery is the catalyst to it all.

Will she allow me to stand at her side and face what's to come? Or will her isolated cries haunt me forever in the silvery moonlight?

ABOUT THE AUTHOR

Krista Street loves writing in multiple genres: fantasy, sci-fi, romance, and dystopian. Her books are cross-genre and often feature complex characters, plenty of supernatural twists, and romance in every story. She loves writing about coming-of-age characters who fight to find their place in this world while also finding their one true mate.

Krista Street is a Minnesota native but has lived throughout the U.S. and in another country or two. She loves to travel, read, and spend time in the great outdoors. When not writing, Krista is either chasing her children, spending time with her husband and friends, sipping a cup of tea, or enjoying the hidden gems of beauty that Minnesota has to offer.

THANK YOU

Thank you for reading *Fated by Starlight*, book one in the *Supernatural Institute* series.

If you enjoy Krista Street's writing, make sure you visit her website to learn about her new release text alerts, newsletter, and other series.

www.kristastreet.com

Links to all of her social media sites are available on every page.

Last, if you enjoyed reading *Fated by Starlight*, please consider logging onto the retailer you purchased this book from to post a review. Authors rely heavily on readers reviewing their work. Even one sentence helps a lot. Thank you so much if you do!